WICKED AND RUTHLESS

WICKED LOVERS: SOLDIERS FOR HIRE

SHAYLA BLACK

WICKED AND RUTHLESS

WICKED SOLDIERS FOR HIRE LOVERS

NASH & HAISLEY DUET PART 1

SHAYLA BLACK
SUSPENSEFUL. SPICY. ADDICTIVE.

WICKED AND RUTHLESS
Wicked Lovers: Soldiers for Hire
Written by Shayla Black

This is an original work of fiction, crafted exclusively by Shayla Black.

Copyright 2024 Shelley Bradley LLC

Cover Design by: Rachel Connolly
Edited by: G. G. Royale
Proofread by: Fedora Chen

ISBN: 978-1-958075-50-0

The characters and events portrayed in this book are fictional. Any similarity to real persons, living or dead, is purely coincidental and not intended by the author. All rights reserved. No part of this book may be reproduced in any form by an electronic or mechanical means—except for brief quotations embedded in critical articles or reviews—without express written permission.

eBooks are not transferable. They cannot be sold, shared, or given away, as it is illegal and an infringement on the copyright of this work.

All rights reserved.

ABOUT WICKED AND RUTHLESS

She knows love is a fairy tale...until her ruthless operative ex steals her heart.

Haisley Rowe has always believed that happily-ever-afters are pretty lies. But after a scorching, year-long fling with a rugged operative, she committed the ultimate sin: falling for a man who will never love her back. Carrying her secret, she left town. Two years later she's back, and a fateful run-in proves he alone still ignites her—body and soul.

Nash Scott disavowed marriage and babies...until Haisley blazed into his life, all fiery red hair and saucy sexiness, awakening his insatiable desire and becoming his deepest obsession. Now that she's returned, he'll do whatever it takes to make her his for good.

When he tackles a twisted abduction case, he discovers Haisley is embroiled, too. In a high-stakes world of vast power and unthinkable danger, they will have to repair each other's hearts and their shattered trust before it's too late. But as darker forces zero in, shocking secrets will be uncovered and threaten to tear them apart forever...

Wicked and Ruthless is part of the Wicked Lovers: Soldiers for Hire romantic suspense series. Stories in this series are told in a duet of two full-length novels. Each duet can be read as a standalone. Happily ever after guaranteed. Enjoy!

PROLOGUE

Christmas Eve
Lafayette, Louisiana

Festive carols filled the crowded mall as Kaylee Wright hurried beside her mom, dodging last-minute shoppers loaded down with bags and boxes, and headed to the food court. The scent of cinnamon, sugar, and waffle cones wafted through the air, giving a definite holiday vibe to the hurried bustle around her. Despite the frantic energy, she couldn't fight her swell of excitement.

It was Christmas Eve, and the mall was decked out in all its holiday splendor—towering trees dripping with lights and ornaments, lush evergreen garlands wrapped around the railings. Even the potted poinsettias seemed to glow a little brighter. Kaylee scanned the packed food court, finding a table that a pair of senior citizens with their grand-toddler in tow were vacating.

"Look." She pointed to the table, then tugged on her mom's hand.

"I'll grab it if you'll stand in line for hot chocolate."

"Deal. But I really need to go to the bathroom first."

"Go. I'll hold the table and rest my sore feet," her mom said. "Here's some money so you can grab the cocoa when you come back."

As Kaylee pocketed the bills, she grinned. "I'm glad we came today. It's crowded, but it's festive."

"And I've loved being here with you, sweetie." Her mom set their packages on the table and sank into her chair with a groan of relief.

They'd been on their feet for hours now, but they still had a few last-minute gifts to grab, especially one for her boyfriend. She'd finally earned enough money to buy him the Blu-ray movie box set he really wanted.

And on Christmas night, they'd arranged to spend a few hours alone. She planned to give him her virginity. She was nervous, but she was ready.

"Me, too." She smiled at her mom. "This has been super fun. I'm sure this will be the best Christmas ever. Be right back."

"I'll be here, trying to convince my feet that we can still shop more."

Laughing, Kaylee clutched her purse tightly as she picked her way between the tightly packed tables, flashing shoppers apologetic smiles as she squeezed past. Inside, the bathroom was crowded, and she had to wait. The janitor came in just behind her and put a closed sign across the door before rolling his mop near the door and patiently waiting for the place to clear out.

After she emptied her bladder and washed her hands, she reapplied her lip gloss, full of giddy thoughts about tomorrow. She exited, flashing the janitor a polite smile as he entered behind her, rolling his mop in the sudsy water, and closed the door.

In the little hallway that led from the restrooms to the bustling food court, the lights suddenly flickered, then died, leaving her in shadow. She frowned when she realized she was alone. Where was everyone? There had been at least a dozen people here five minutes ago.

A cold chill zipped down her spine as she dashed for the opening. She could see her mother sitting at the table, staring at her phone. Thank god she was almost out of here. This creepy hallway was giving her the willies.

Before she made it to the light, a thick arm like an iron bar clamped around her from behind.

Kaylee tried to shriek, but a rough hand clapped over her mouth, muffling her cries. Her purse tumbled from her grasp and fell open, sending her phone clattering across the floor. Violently, she was hauled back into the shadows. She thrashed wildly, terror clawing at her insides as the unmistakable barrel of a gun dug into her ribs.

Oh, god. Was this really happening?

"Don't make a sound, pretty girl," a gruff voice hissed in her ear, hot breath washing over her face. "I'd hate to have to blow your brains out on Christmas Eve. Not that you won't wish you were dead soon enough."

When she tried to scream again, the iron grip across her chest constricted, cutting off her airflow. She fought against the paralyzing panic, but black spots swam in her vision as something smashed against the back of her skull, a searing wave of pain and nausea cresting over her.

Kaylee's world tilted violently, shrinking until all she could make out were the muffled sounds of jingling bells and bright laughter from the food court—so achingly close yet utterly out of reach as her reality contracted into darkness.

She was vaguely aware of his thick-soled boots crushing the screen of her cell phone into shards of glass and plastic. Then everything went dark as her assailant hauled Kaylee out a rear service exit and threw her into the swallowing void of an unmarked van idling in the shadowy alleyway while her mother waited in the food court for a daughter who would never return.

CHAPTER ONE

New Year's Eve
Lafayette, Louisiana

Amidst the revelers at Highrise, Nash Scott stood, beer in hand, a blonde under his arm, getting ready to ring in the new year, when the hair on the back of his neck rose. He stiffened. Goose bumps erupted across his skin.

Someone had eyes on him.

He'd spent too many years dodging bullets and hunting terrorists in third-world shit holes not to heed his instincts.

But this warning wasn't about danger—unless it was to his heart.

"What's wrong?" his older brother, Trees, demanded, scanning the nightclub like a man who had spent his life taking down enemies for God and country. He tucked Laila, his wife and the mother of his four children, protectively against his side. Then his gaze snagged on something that made him scowl. "Holy shit."

The band announced they were taking a break. People chatted and clinked glasses, brushing past Nash in the crowd. The activity hardly registered. His earth stopped turning. His life stopped moving. His heart stopped beating.

Without turning to see for himself, he sensed *her*. He swore he could fucking hear her breathe. He inhaled her musky amber-rose scent he'd know anywhere. His cock hardened to steel.

His date, Lissa, turned and searched the room before frowning blankly. "What?"

Nash couldn't respond to the blonde. "She's really here?"

Trees nodded. "About twenty feet behind you. What do you want to do?"

Was his brother asking if he wanted to leave? Hell no. Haisley Rowe had left town two interminable years ago. So why had she shown up here? Tonight? No clue. But he was staying to get some long-overdue answers.

He wasn't desperate to touch her again. At all.

After nearly a year of…whatever their relationship had been, she had left him with the briefest of goodbyes. No explanation, no fuck you. She'd just…gone. He'd spent six celibate months vacillating between craving her and hating her. The other year and a half, he'd tried to fuck her out of his system—when he wasn't staring like a schmuck at the engagement ring still nestled in the velvet in the box he'd never had the chance to give her.

"Who are you talking about?" Lissa demanded.

The pretty blonde at his side was used to being pursued. There was hardly a red-blooded man in Lafayette who didn't want to nail her, and she was notoriously choosy. But he hadn't worked particularly hard to persuade her to spend New Year's Eve with him. Strike one. He hadn't taken her somewhere fancy. Strike two. Now that another woman had stolen his attention? He didn't have to guess where that left him.

He didn't give a shit.

Nash uncurled his arm from around her shoulders, swallowed back the last of his beer, and tried to wire his shit tight.

He'd waited—fantasized—about his chance to lay eyes on Haisley again. He'd even made a list of everything he intended to say. Now that she was so close, he felt annoyingly stunned, tongue-tied, and blank.

"I don't think she's seen you yet," Trees assured. "Oh, wait. She just did."

Nash knew the instant Haisley looked at him. Fresh awareness sizzled across his skin. Knowing she stood mere feet away was like a double shot of Red Bull to his libido.

Fuck, Haisley had always gotten to him, from the moment they'd met at his brother's wedding. Despite the years and the hurt, he'd been bullshitting himself. Nothing had changed. He was still as hung up on her as ever. He'd give anything to touch her again.

Goddamn it.

"Are you seriously focused on another woman right now?" Lissa barked. "Um, hello. I'm standing right here."

His behavior was rude as hell, but was lying to her about his interest really better?

"Is she coming this way?" he asked his brother. *Or is she leaving again?*

"Nope. She's just hanging out with some of those girls who attended our wedding." Trees turned to Laila. "Remember?"

"Yes. She looks as surprised to see you as you are that she is here," his sister-in-law added in her lightly accented lilt.

"Wait. You're talking about some ex of yours?" Lissa stomped her little stiletto. "Seriously?"

"Yes." The only one of his exes he gave a shit about, in fact. Haisley had always mattered—even when he'd told himself she didn't. Despite two long years apart, he couldn't deny that anymore.

Hands on hips, Lissa gaped at him. "You asked me to spend New Year's Eve with you. I didn't turn down three other invitations so you could gawk at someone you used to fuck. It's her or me."

It probably wasn't smart, but Nash didn't hesitate. "Her."

In fact, he didn't care if he ever saw Lissa Hollister again. Honestly, he couldn't figure out what the fuss was about. Sex with her hadn't been that great.

His date's jaw dropped as indignation spread across her face. "Unbelievable. Don't ever call me again, asshole."

"Don't worry," he muttered as she spun away and stomped for the door. "Zero chance of that."

Trees both winced and laughed. "That's one way to lose a date. Now you'll have to find someone else to kiss when the clock strikes midnight."

Laila glanced at her phone. "You have less than twenty minutes to accomplish that."

Normally, he wouldn't need even half that much time. But he didn't want anyone except Haisley. And that woman was as unpredictable as she was sexy. She tied his balls in knots and twisted up his heart. Always had.

"Working on it. You two lovebirds find a table."

Trees snorted. "I doubt that's possible, but we can take a hint. Besides, Zy and Tessa should be here soon, so we'll keep an eye out for them."

Absently, Nash nodded, his thoughts already fixed on Haisley. If she was here with Charli and Gracelyn, her lifelong bestie, Madison Montgomery, wouldn't be far behind. Which meant her husband Matt, another of his coworkers, would be here, too. Nash figured that his housemate, Ethan Garrison, would probably follow, since he was always up for a party.

So everyone would be around to witness this eventful reunion... where he'd probably crash and burn. Fucking fantastic.

Nash could still feel Haisley's stare on him, so he let out a breath and slowly turned. Instantly, he clapped his gaze onto her. Their stares locked. Jesus, he couldn't fucking breathe.

Damn it, why did she have to look more beautiful than ever?

Suddenly, someone clapped him on the back. He whipped around with a scowl, wondering how anyone had managed to sneak up on him. But he knew. Haisley still knocked him off balance.

Nash smoothed out once he saw the interloper. "Hey, Kane. You came, huh?"

He was surprised EM Security's loner had joined them for tonight's bash...but not enough to keep his stare off Haisley.

"Yeah. Thought I'd..." Kane's dark gaze followed his as he fell silent. "Never mind. I see your brother. I'll leave you to her. Good luck."

"Thanks," he said absently, not even blinking as he visually devoured Haisley.

Her hair was longer, fiery curls now flirting with her elbows. He'd always loved wrapping his fists around her tresses when he'd bound her to his bed and thrust deep like he owned her. Her mesmerizing blue eyes—a blend of Caribbean Sea and pure, cloudless sky—were stunning when they went wide with orgasm.

The longer their stares fused, the more color drained from her cheeks. And those plump lips he missed under his or wrapped around his greedy cock were parted softly as she gaped. Her strapless black sheath hugged every one of the curves he'd memorized and ended high on her thigh, showing off the gorgeous legs he'd loved having wrapped around him.

Could he lose his damn mind just looking at her? He sure as fuck felt in danger. He needed to touch her again. It wasn't a desire or an impulse but a primal, biological imperative.

She licked her glossy lips and dropped her gaze—guiltily?—before focusing on Gracelyn, who whispered something in her ear. Then, with a nod, Haisley spun around and headed to the bar with her girls.

That was it? No hello. No conversation. No...nothing except a wordless dismissal.

Nash let out a rough breath. Anger ignited. If that woman thought she could sweep their unfinished business under the rug, she was fucking mistaken. She might not have anything to say, but he sure as hell did.

As soon as he collected his thoughts.

Matt and Madison walked into the packed nightclub moments later, their hands raised in greeting. Nash waved back, not surprised to see Ethan in tow. Ghost and Trevor had come, too? Great... Nothing like rubbing elbows with his fellow operatives while he tried not to look like an idiot over Haisley's shocking return.

Tonight was going to be a shit show.

While Madison joined Haisley and her posse, Matt approached

him, settling his cowboy hat on his head and wearing the perpetual grin he'd been sporting since rescuing Madison from her evil ex a few years ago. "Hey, man."

"Did you know she was coming back?" Nash growled, skipping the niceties.

Matt looked over at his wife and her gaggle of girls. "Haisley? She rolled into town the day after Christmas."

So she'd had a week to call…and she hadn't. Hadn't sought him out, either. Hadn't given a shit to see how he'd been since she'd walked out on him. "How long is she staying?"

His buddy winced. "This isn't how I wanted to break the news to you, but she's not going back to Cali. Her aunt passed away, and she's decided to move home again."

Elation filled him, followed instantly by dread. How much would it fuck him up to have the woman he'd never fallen out of love with less than a handful of miles away? Then again, two miles or two thousand—it didn't matter. She'd severed all ties.

Madison waved Matt over. His friend nodded, then looked back at Nash. "You coming?"

To talk to Haisley? She clearly had zero intention of reconnecting with him… A gander across the bar once more proved she couldn't even be bothered to glance his way. "No."

"Suit yourself." Matt clapped him on the shoulder. "Looks like your brother got you a beer."

Meaning he should go drink it before everyone decided he was a heartbroken sap who didn't understand that even a silent no was still no. "I'm going to need something stronger."

His buddy leaned in and dropped his voice. "There's no rule that says you have to stay. This is a party. If you're not feeling it…"

Screw that. He wasn't letting her derail his night. "Laila has been planning this for weeks. She never gets an evening away from the kids. Haisley's return was a surprise, but I'm fine."

Matt shook his head. "You're full of shit."

"Fuck off and go be with your wife."

"All right. But…maybe it would be good if you and Haisley talked things out."

Not here. And not unless she showed a willingness to take a verbal deep-dive into their past. "Eating fucking beets every day is supposed to be good for me, too. You don't see me scarfing down that crap."

Matt laughed. "Ten-four."

As he watched his buddy adjust his cowboy hat and retreat to the far side of the bar, Nash scowled and headed toward Trees and Laila, who had miraculously found a table. A cocktail waitress recited drink orders back to them as he approached. "Give me half a dozen tequila shots."

The woman craned her neck up, up, up to look at him. Since he was six-foot-seven, he got that a lot.

"You want six tequila shots?"

He nodded. "With salt and lime. There's an extra twenty bucks for you if I have them in the next five minutes."

"Done." She jotted his order on her notepad, snapped it closed, and made a mad dash for the bartender.

"You looking to start the new year with a hangover?" his brother asked.

"Looking to have a good time. It's a party, isn't it?" Nash ignored Trees's skeptical glance.

"How you doing?" Zy asked, his arm loosely around his wife, Tessa, who despite having two kids, looked amazing.

The pair of them were sublimely fucking happy. So were his brother and Laila. Matt and Madison, too, for that matter. Nash knew none of them had reached their bliss without serious strife, and more than once it looked as if happily ever after wouldn't be in their cards. But they'd fought for their women and emerged victorious against all odds. Then again, each of those women had been madly in love with the man they now called husband.

Which meant he had zero hope with Haisley.

"Peachy," he quipped. "You?"

Zy raised a brow. "You're a shitty liar."

"Fuck off."

"Listen, Trees will tell you… I was an asshole and a half when I thought I'd lost Tessa forever—"

"I'm going to stop you right there. I don't need a pep talk. I just need booze. And maybe a horny female willing to come home with me."

But he couldn't imagine fucking another woman right now. He'd only think of Haisley. Hell, just like he had more often than not over the last two years.

The cocktail waitress returned and offloaded Zy's and Trees's beers, along with Laila's piña colada and Tessa's glass of red. Then she lined up his shots on the crowded table, settled a saltshaker in front of him, and handed him a ramekin of limes. "Made it back in less than four minutes. Anything else?"

He handed her his credit card. "Check back with me in fifteen."

The waitress nodded as she inserted his plastic in her handheld device. When she presented him the screen, Nash gave her the promised tip plus more, then signed with his finger. She double-checked the transaction with a nod. "You got it."

"What are we drinking to?" Zy asked once she'd gone.

Besides drowning my sorrows? "Whatever."

Trees eyed the row of shot glasses. "Not being able to walk out of here? Puking half the night?"

Nash licked his hand, sprinkled some salt, then lifted a glass in salute. "We're about to start a new year. How about we drink to leaving the past behind?"

No one replied, and he didn't much care. He just licked the salt away, downed the first of his shots, sucked down a lime wedge...then repeated the process until he'd gulped down every drop from each shot glass.

With one last sigh, he slammed down the final one and closed his eyes, enjoying the hot, woozy rush through his veins. He hadn't meant to skip dinner tonight, but that sure as hell aided in the buzz he had going.

"Hey." Ethan Garrison suddenly sidled up to him. "Happy New Year."

Nash just grunted. What was his housemate so fucking happy about?

Ethan looked poised to say something when he began scowling at his phone. "Son of a bitch."

"What?" Maybe the kid had something work-related he could sink his teeth into. Nash prayed that would keep him from fixating on Haisley...

"I work out with one of the local cops at the gym around the corner from my apartment. We've been talking about the disappearances around that new mall..."

Nash hadn't heard much about them. Both the local press and the police chief had been quieter than expected, given the fact that women had been vanishing from that place for a while. "Was there another abduction?"

Ethan nodded. "Christmas Eve. A nineteen-year-old girl. One minute she was at the food court with her mother. The next she was gone."

Holy shit. "Eyewitnesses? Security guards? Cameras?"

As far as Nash was concerned, after the other disappearances, the mall should have implemented more measures to keep people safe.

"No one saw anything. There were no guards in that part of the mall when it happened. The cameras were all conveniently down."

"That seems negligent as fuck."

"Yeah." Ethan darkened his phone with a shake of his head. "I hope they find her."

But he didn't sound hopeful.

"As far as you know, have they found any of the others?"

"No." Ethan cut his eyes across the bar to where Haisley and her girls stood. Suddenly, he scowled before grabbing Nash by the arm and tugging him around. "If you want to get trashed, let's go someplace else. I've got a liter of good vodka and a pantry full of junk food. Highrise isn't Ghost's and Trevor's scene—too trendy—and the drinks are expensive. Let's leave it to the couples and—"

"And what?" Nash tore free and turned to see what Ethan tried to distract him from.

Haisley. Dancing with some random dude. Who apparently had a dozen hands and even more dirty thoughts, based on the way he touched her.

"Fuck that," Nash snarled, glaring through the crowd.

She said something to her dance partner that had him backing off...

but the douchebag's retreat didn't satisfy Nash's inner beast. That part of him wanted to break the little bastard.

People parted as, his pulse pounding and his nostrils flaring, Nash stomped straight toward Haisley.

CHAPTER TWO

Haisley felt Nash Scott the moment she stepped inside Highrise. She froze. Her heart tore fire through her chest.

Of all the crappy luck...

After committing the ultimate sin of falling for him, she hadn't known what to say two years ago when she'd walked away. She still didn't.

Scanning the place, she caught sight of him. Given his height and that buzz of dark hair he kept brutally short, he wasn't hard to find. Not surprisingly, he stood with his brother—also a mountain of a man. Even less surprising, Nash had a date under his arm. Of course he'd landed Lissa Hollister. Why wouldn't he have sweet-talked the local it girl into bed?

But Haisley wasn't jealous. At all. Not even a little. Maybe the fact she'd been replaced stung her pride, but she didn't feel anything else. She refused to. Her relationship with Nash had been nothing more than a multimonth hookup, right? He'd made that clear from the onset. So had she.

But during all their breathless, scorching-hot nights together, she'd surrendered more than her body to him. She'd given him her heart.

And when she'd gotten the shock of her life, she'd had no choice but to run.

"I didn't know Nash would be here tonight," Gracelyn murmured in her ear. "I'm sorry."

Haisley shook her head. "It was bound to happen eventually."

After all, Lafayette wasn't a huge town, and the number of decent nightlife spots were few and far between.

"Probably," Charli agreed, looking even less in the mood to party than she was.

Where was her friend's husband? Haisley hadn't gotten the scoop on Daniel since she'd returned to town, but she would...

"We can go somewhere else. He hasn't seen you yet." Gracelyn pulled her phone from her stylish crossbody bag. "I can text Madison to let her know there's been a change of plans."

Haisley was trying to decide—stay or run—when Lissa Hollister tore past her and stomped out the exit. What was that about? She shouldn't care. And she shouldn't be surprised. The woman was infamous for playing hard to get.

Also not shocking, Nash didn't go after her. He'd always been the love-'em-and-leave-'em type; he'd warned Haisley about that from the onset. Clearly, nothing had changed.

Then Nash turned in her direction, and she stopped caring about the blonde.

Time stood still. She felt rooted in place, blood thundering as Nash captured her gaze. Their stares fused.

Oh, god.

She struggled to breathe. Hell, she couldn't even blink. Awareness goose pimpled her skin. She tingled. Her veins caught fire.

That hard-edged face she'd fallen for looked more rugged than ever. His expression wasn't readable...but clearly she wasn't welcome.

What had she expected? She'd been a mere convenience. He'd proven that when she'd left, and he hadn't even tried to come after her. Just like he wasn't coming across the room to see her now.

She had to face facts. Whatever had been between them had been temporary on his part and one-sided on hers.

"Haisley?" Gracelyn asked again. She sounded worried.

The sweetest of her friends always meant well, but… "Don't worry. He's not chasing me away or ruining our plans. Let's get some drinks."

Since she was moving back home, might as well get used to bumping into Nash. It was bound to happen. If she acted like it didn't matter, hopefully it soon wouldn't. Fake it 'til you make it and all that.

Tearing her gaze from his dark stare took all of her will, but she managed, then turned for the bar. Both relief and crushing sadness filled her. That man had turned her life upside down, flipped her heart inside out…and he apparently didn't even know. Or he didn't care. She'd thought she was different to him. Clearly, she'd been kidding herself.

Move on, girl. It's past time.

But when she'd tried, when she had met guys in LA, something always kept her from saying yes. No, someone. Best not to BS herself.

She'd never gotten over Nash Scott. She probably never would.

"Margarita on the rocks, no salt," she told the bartender. "Make it a double."

He nodded, then took her friends' orders.

"Madison will be here any second," Gracelyn announced, tucking her phone away.

Good and bad. Her bestie would be another buffer between her and Nash…but she'd also bring her husband, who worked with Nash. Who was his friend. Would that drag Nash to her side of the room?

Five minutes later, she knew the answer was a resounding no. Madison spotted the couple the moment they walked in. Matt greeted Nash, then joined his wife again. Instead of coming to talk to her—even to say hi—Nash huddled in the corner with his brother and Laila, Zy and Tessa, along with a few others—and a line of tequila shots.

Less than a minute later, every last one of those shot glasses was empty. The rest of his entourage stared at him like he'd lost his mind.

Whatever. She had to stop fixating and start getting on with her life.

"Bestie!" Madison hugged her tight. "How are you doing? Get most of the house cleared out?"

Haisley hugged her back, grateful for the change of subject. "Yeah. Garage, too. Aunt Cynthia was a pack rat."

And a very unwilling guardian after her mother's untimely death.

Cynthia had made it very clear that she'd purposely chosen not to have children and didn't appreciate having a seven-year-old dumped on her doorstep. But since Haisley's father had walked out when she'd been a baby, her mother's sister had been her only remaining family.

"I think the word you're looking for is hoarder," Gracelyn corrected with a dimpled grin.

Haisley forced a smile. "You're right. I just trashed forty years of *People* magazine. I've donated all her clothes, cleaned out the kitchen, reorganized every closet... I even sold most of her furniture and hired a painter. It's taken me a solid week, but it's starting to feel like my space."

"That's great!" Madison encouraged. "I'm so glad you decided to move home. Nothing has been the same without you."

Haisley scoffed. "From what I hear, you've hardly come up for air since you and Matt got married. And now that you have the handsomest little boy..."

"He's so precious." Her bestie smiled like a proud mommy, then slid a hand over her belly. "He'll make a great big brother."

"Seriously? I'm so happy for you!" And a little bit envious, if Haisley was being honest. "What did Matt say when you told him?"

She blushed. "That's why we're late. He, um...wanted a celebration of our own."

"You just told him tonight?"

"A few hours ago."

"Congrats!"

"So jelly," Gracelyn said with a grin that actually held zero envy. "And super happy for you."

Charli tried to muster a smile but fell woefully short. "You deserve all the happiness."

Her voice was even more somber than her expression. Yeah, something was up, and since the dude Charli had married last year in a Vegas chapel wasn't around tonight, there must be trouble in paradise.

No shock. Love only worked out for the fortunate few. For everyone else...it was a fairy tale at best. A pipe dream. To Haisley, it had always been a bitter disappointment.

Since Charli seemed to be struggling, Haisley made a mental note to take her friend to lunch or something soon. Madison was riding high with her new pregnancy. Gracelyn was too optimistic to understand Charli's despair. So that left her to commiserate over how badly love sucked.

The bartender set down their drinks. Haisley sucked hers back. Gracelyn sipped her fruity umbrella cocktail like a woman who didn't imbibe much and couldn't hold her alcohol. Charli chugged a double mojito in less than ten seconds, then asked for another. Haisley decided to keep pace with her. Wasn't New Year's Eve for getting trashed?

Yes, and apparently now for avoiding exes, too.

Madison, clutching a cold bottle of water, just shook her head. "What are you going to do?"

Haisley shrugged. "Replace some of the kitchen appliances, the refrigerator first. That thing is a relic. Then I think—"

"I meant about Nash."

"Nothing. He doesn't give a shit." *And I hate that I do.*

"According to Matt, that's not true. Apparently, Nash was pretty torn up after you left."

"If he was sad, it was only because he lost his easy pussy." *Which I stupidly gave him whenever he wanted.* "No doubt he's moved on."

"That's what men do." Madison shrugged. "After I walked away from Matt to marry Todd, you know—"

"He fucked half the town? Yeah." She'd hated having to tell Madison something that hurt so much. "But his heart was always with you. Since you left Todd and came home, he hasn't given another woman the time of day. You're it for him, girl. Do you know how lucky you are?"

"Every day." Madison took her hands. "Don't give up on Nash. I think he still has feelings for you."

"No need to blow sunshine up my ass."

She would have said more, but Matt rolled up to the bar and settled his arm around his wife's waist. He looked at her as if she hung the moon and stars before dropping a kiss on her lips.

"Haisley." He tipped his hat.

"Hi, Matt. Congrats on your coming baby."

His smile widened. "I'm the luckiest bastard on the planet."

"I think I'm pretty lucky, too." Madison beamed.

Haisley tried not to cry. She didn't want Matt, but she craved the kind of love Madison had. Unfortunately for her, it didn't exist. She was destined to be attached to someone who'd never really wanted her.

Isn't that the story of your life?

The bartender blessed her with another double margarita and a wink. She vaguely remembered him from high school. Yeah, that was a big no thank-you. She gave him a wan smile and a nice tip, then started downing her second drink.

"Ten minutes until midnight." Gracelyn bounced with excitement.

Yippee. All the couples in this place would be sucking face when the clock struck twelve. She wouldn't. Neither would Gracelyn and Charli, so at least she wouldn't be the only sad schmuck alone.

Maybe she should order another drink so she'd have something to do when the countdown ended.

"Wanna dance?" a stranger asked behind her, his voice friendly.

She turned. He wasn't familiar—a plus. He looked maybe a year or two older—another plus. He wasn't a troll. And he had a nice smile. "Why not?"

As the music slowed, he led her onto the tiny floor in the middle of the bar. Instantly, he pulled her against his body and swayed with the romantic tune. The dance shouldn't have been awkward, but this dude was a total stranger who didn't seem interested in talking. And he'd suddenly grown ten roaming hands.

She grabbed his wrists and pulled his grip off her ass. "What's your name?"

He laughed. "Something that rhymes with fuck."

Did he think he was being clever? Was she supposed to guess? "So, Rhymes-with-fuck, do you live in Lafayette?"

"No. Visiting a college friend who grew up here."

Someone she probably knew—a minus, especially when his hands began wandering again. It also hadn't escaped her notice that he hadn't bothered to ask her name.

"Listen, beautiful, if you don't have someone to kiss at midnight, I'm your man." He copped another feel of her ass.

Hell, no. The longer they danced, the more he gave her the heebies.

She dragged his hand up to her waist again. "What makes you think I kiss strangers whose names rhyme with fuck?"

"Why should I think you don't? Jase said you were good in high school."

Haisley rolled her eyes. Jase Simmons—douchebag extraordinaire. He'd been a lying, using, trash-talking asshole back then. He'd been famous for telling a girl what she needed to hear to drop her panties, only to ignore her the next day while he told all his buddies on the football team that he'd had sex with her, subjecting her to the leers of his teammates for weeks. Adulthood hadn't changed him. It probably hadn't changed his caliber of friends, either.

"Because I don't kiss random guys, even on New Year's Eve. If you're looking to get lucky tonight, you chose the wrong girl."

The last thing she needed was romantic entanglement, especially with another player. If she wanted that, she'd take up with Nash again. But she had too much on her plate, between settling the last of her aunt's affairs, making the house hers, and starting her new social media director gig after the holiday.

"You're turning me down before I even ask?" he chided.

"I'm setting expectations. If you're getting laid tonight, it won't be by me."

Thankfully, the song—and their dance—was mercifully nearing the end. A glance around the room told her that the clock would strike midnight in less than five minutes, and Nash was polishing off another round of tequila shots.

Suddenly, Haisley wished she was anywhere else. At least if she were home, she'd be curled up with a decent book and her cat. When the new year started, she'd be stuck here in a crowd…yet still feel utterly alone. Not that her posse wouldn't try to cheer her up. They would, and they would mean well. She loved her girls. But now that she'd seen Nash, she didn't feel much like celebrating because her heart still felt broken.

She'd been kidding herself otherwise.

Rhymes-with-fuck stopped dancing and stepped away before the song ended. "If you're going to be a cunt, we don't have much to say."

Since he didn't mean anything to her, Haisley could care less that he'd called her something vile. "We have *nothing* to say. Buh-bye."

As he stomped off, she headed toward the bar where Matt and Madison were supposed to be watching her drink…but they only had eyes for each other. It was fine. She was partied out anyway. She should have stayed home with her feline, her eBook smut, and her fellow online sleuths in the Crime Solvers International group, cheekily known as CSI.

Out of her peripheral vision, she caught sight of movement from Nash's corner of the bar. She flicked a glance in his direction. When he pinned her with a hot gaze, her heart skipped.

Biting back a gasp, Haisley broke their connection and jerked back to focus on her friends. But his stare was still on her. She felt his visual touch through her whole body.

Emotion clogged her throat. Why couldn't she get this man out of her system? And why couldn't she stop herself from turning back to look his way?

Instantly, their gazes melded. The music and the loud chatter faded away. Even her friends dissolved into the background.

Suddenly, determination stamped across his rugged face. Her pulse leapt. Time froze. Oh, god. What was he going to do? She had no idea what he had in mind as he started toward her…

Around Nash, people collectively turned to look at the flat screens around the bar where the typical New Year's Eve broadcast from Times Square had entered the last sixty seconds of its countdown. As this year ended and another began, he realized one thing: he'd spent this entire fucking year without Haisley under him. Most of the last, too. He'd be goddamned if he spent next year without her.

Blindly, he reached for the beer his brother had ordered him a while back. It was lukewarm, and he didn't care. He chugged the whole thing down and slammed the bottle on the table. Unfortunately, imbibing too much had only proven that no amount of booze was going to take his mind off Haisley.

Thank fuck the tool she'd been dancing with backed off. He'd looked angry, too. Nash suspected his sassy, sexy girl had told the motherfucker to get lost, and good for her.

Good for him, too. Now he didn't have to break the asshole's arms.

He knew precisely who he wanted to kiss at midnight, and he didn't give a goddamn that they hadn't had a conversation in two years or that everything between them was in shambles.

He. Wanted. Her.

A surge of reckless determination coursed through his veins. Given the way she was focused on him as he crossed the bar, heading straight for her, he didn't think his desire was one-sided.

"Haisley," he boomed.

She didn't move. Others did, jumping out of his path. The crowd parted like the Red Sea. He ignored the whispers and the gawking. In that moment, absolutely nothing mattered but reaching her.

"Ten, nine, eight…" the crowd chanted collectively.

As the deafening countdown rang out around them, Nash didn't—couldn't—pull his stare from Haisley as, one giant step after the other, he ate up the distance between them.

"Nash? What do you—"

"Want?" he drawled.

"Seven, six, five…"

Grabbing her by the waist, he pulled her close, his dark stare unwavering. Raw, primal intensity scorched his veins. The urge to tear off her little black dress and plow his way into her doubled when her breath caught and her eyes widened.

He tightened his fingers around her.

"Four, three, two…"

"You," he growled, dragging in her familiar musky-sweet scent that had always been his undoing. "I want you."

Fuck, one look, one touch, and she threatened to shatter the walls he'd constructed around his heart.

But that's the way it had always been. The pull between them was so goddamn strong…

"One. Happy New Year!"

Nash surged forward, dragging Haisley against him. Their chests collided. She let out a whimper, her fingers tangling in his shirt. Then his mouth crashed onto her soft lips in a searing, desperate kiss. With a gasp, she thawed against him and kissed him back.

People whooped and hollered around them. Celebratory music started up. Glasses clinked and laughter ensued. All of it faded to a distant hum as he lost himself in Haisley and the sensual flavor of her mouth. Her fucking taste felled him… Sweet, light, so achingly familiar, just like her curves.

He was drowning, dying. The sensual overload threatened to undo him.

Instead of backing away, finding his breath, and collecting his thoughts before he did something really stupid—like tell her he was still in love with her—he lifted Haisley off her feet and carried her to the nearest wall. Without a second thought, he pressed her against the mirror-clad surface, pinned her with his body, and deepened their kiss.

Nash half expected her to protest. But no. She threw her arms around his neck and parted her lips wider.

That was all the invitation he needed.

He drove his tongue into Haisley's mouth possessively, thrilled as fuck when she lifted her legs and wrapped them around his hips. He gripped her ass in his hands, dying to devour her, to lose himself in her intoxicating embrace. She had to feel how hard he was for her, like he'd always been.

God, he'd give anything to erase the last two years.

As suddenly as he'd kissed her, Haisley wrenched free, her chest heaving. She stared up at him, her eyes shimmering with a firestorm of unspoken emotions. "I can't do this."

Her trembling whisper nearly took him out at the knees.

Nash brushed a calloused thumb across her cheek and searched her gaze. "Why? Tell me what the hell happened between us."

Tears pooled in her eyes. Her pain, her raw vulnerability, was like a stab to the heart. "Nash, I…"

"What?"

"I can't do this. Again. With you."

He strained to hear her whisper above the din of the rowdy crowd. But in that moment, as far as he was concerned, no one existed except them.

"What can't you do? Talk to me? Touch me? I don't understand."

Haisley bit her lip to hold back tears and shoved out of his embrace. "I know."

The loss of her touch left him frozen and aching. "But I don't. Spell it out."

She shook her head, tears falling down her cheeks. "Please believe me... It's better this way."

When she tried to push past him, he grabbed her arm. Yeah, he knew he was riding a dangerous line. No meant no, and he respected that. But he wasn't trying to force her to have sex with him; he just wanted answers.

"The fuck it is. Why did you walk away?"

She yanked free and retreated. "It's in the past. Leave it there."

Without another word, she fled, disappearing into the throng of partygoers.

Nash watched, cursing under his breath. He ran a hand through his hair, bitter regret burning his tongue. Why wouldn't Haisley talk to him, tell him what had upset her? Why wouldn't she tell him what the hell had torn them apart?

As he had for the past two years, he thought through their last days together. At the beginning of that week, she'd been as welcoming and hungry for him as she'd been from the start. By the weekend, she'd told him to fuck off. In nicer language, yes, but the end result had been the same. She'd claimed he was too rough, too overbearing, and too kinky. Since she'd embraced those sides of him for the previous twelve months, he'd intended to call bullshit and make her be fucking honest—before he proposed.

Instead, he returned from an op that Monday to the news that she'd left town for good.

Nothing in his life had been right since.

With burning eyes, he watched Haisley grab her purse, hug her girls, and leave the bar.

For the past two years, he'd sworn that if he ever saw Haisley again, he wouldn't let her go without getting answers. Then he would fight tooth and nail to win her back. But as he watched her disappear into the cold, humid night, he couldn't help but wonder if he was too late. If he'd lost her for good.

Cursing, Nash turned away, his every step weighted with despair, as he returned to his brother and his gang.

As he approached the table, Trees whistled. "That was a hell of a show."

"Bite my ass."

Laila laid a gentle hand on his forearm—a huge step forward for the woman who had once been a prisoner of a drug cartel and, until Trees crashed into her life, had known only abuse and violence at the hands of men. Thanks to his brother's protective embrace and marshmallow interior, his sister-in-law was no longer afraid. "She has feelings for you."

He turned to the petite Hispanic beauty with a shake of his head. "I know you're trying to make me feel better, but—"

"She does," Tessa seconded. "I may not know Haisley well, but women understand women."

Were they insane? "She wrenched away from me and ran as if her ass was on fire."

I can't do this. Again. With you. The finality in her tone had been like a knife sliding between his ribs, gouging out his heart, and shattering the last of his hope.

Laila sighed. "*Sí*, but how did she kiss you *before* that?"

Tessa pointed at his sister-in-law as the women exchanged a knowing glance. "What Laila said."

The reason seemed obvious to him. Every time they'd had sex, it was off the chain. Of course he loved pussy, but with Haisley it had been so much more... Every moment with her had been scorching. Consuming. Indelibly etched into his memory.

The ladies were suggesting her reason for clinging to him had less to do with her genitals and more to do with her heart. Nash wanted to believe that, but honestly, he didn't fucking know. And he needed to.

Now.

"Damn it." He spun around, bumped and shouldered his way

through the crowd, then footraced out the door, bursting outside and sweeping the parking lot with a frenetic scan.

She was gone. Goddamn it.

Nash stood there, his breath misting in the frigid air as bitter regret damn near choked him. He had been a fool, complacent and cocky, when he'd let her walk out of his life two years ago without demanding answers. And now, when she finally showed up again, she'd slipped through his fingers once more.

Never fucking again.

Clenching his fists, Nash let out a ragged sigh, his gaze fixed on the twinkling lights of the city. Haisley was the other half of his soul, the one woman who had ever truly seen him, the good and the bad. She was out there. And he wasn't letting her go a third time without one hell of a fight.

Steeling his resolve, Nash turned and headed back into the bar, scanning the crowd for Madison. Haisley might be gone…but her bestie would know exactly where to find her.

Instead, Matt intercepted him. "Hey, buddy."

"I need to talk to your wife."

His pal shook his head. "Nope."

After he'd helped his pal save Madison from her ex, Matt wasn't willing to engage in a little quid pro quo? "You're going to cut me off at the balls?"

"I'm not. I'm saving your breath. Madison won't tell you shit. When it comes to secrets, she's locked down tighter than Fort Knox. Besides, she's pregnant again, and the hormones…" Matt shook his head. "I have healthy respect for those. If you know what's good for you, you will, too."

The news was like a punch in the gut. Sure, he was happy as fuck for them. Nash had never wanted marriage, picket fences, and babies…until Haisley. Now he was jealous as hell.

"Congratulations, man. That's fantastic."

"We're over the moon, but you and I can talk about that later. Right now, you want to ask my wife how to get back in Haisley's good graces—and her bed—right?"

And how to capture her heart for good. "Yeah."

"You didn't hear this from me…but on Monday, she'll be starting a new job working for some local hotshot real-estate developer."

"What does that have to do with me?" Barging into her place of employment would only piss Haisley off.

Matt shrugged. "Thought you might know something. How about this? She belongs to an avid online sleuthing group called Crime Solvers International. Anyone can join, even anonymously. I looked it up."

Suddenly, Nash's phone dinged. He glanced at the text.

"That's the link." Matt clapped him on the back.

Nash stared at it for a minute, then a slow smile spread across his face. If Haisley wouldn't talk to him, this might be his only in. Back-door clandestine shit wasn't his first choice…but she was setting the pace. That didn't mean he couldn't bend the rules and hurry her along. "Anonymously, huh? Game on."

He was determined, now more than ever, to reclaim the woman he loved, no matter what it took.

CHAPTER THREE

Haisley couldn't get home fast enough. Thank god the streets of Lafayette weren't crowded because she drove like a bat out of hell until she made it into her newly uncluttered garage and closed the door behind her, blocking out the night.

Unfortunately, her lips were still tingling from Nash's kiss.

She had been back in this damn town for a handful of days, and already the man she'd hoped to avoid so she might save herself more heartbreak had gotten up in her personal space, flashed her those unsettling dark eyes, and kissed her. And not just a peck. Oh, no. He'd gone for the gusto. And she'd let him, wrapping her arms around him, opening her legs wide to him. Damn it. The way she'd melted into a puddle the second Nash had touched her, it was a miracle she hadn't dropped her panties for him, too.

"Pathetic," she muttered as she dropped her keys on the hall table, tossed her little bag on the nearby sofa, and sighed.

What were the odds he would back off? Two years ago, he'd let her go without a fight. But tonight, she'd tasted his desperation. No, his determination. Something was different.

Haisley didn't think for an instant that she'd seen the last of him.

She wished that didn't make her ridiculously giddy, but why lie to herself? Still, when he came sniffing around her again, she didn't dare say yes.

With a huff, she marched into the kitchen for some chamomile tea. As wired as she felt, she wasn't getting to sleep without a little calming. And she refused to scratch the itch Nash had stirred up by masturbating to thoughts of him. She'd already done that too much over the past two years.

As she set the kettle on the stove, her phone rang. Since she'd changed her number after leaving Louisiana, it couldn't be Nash. Or at least it shouldn't be. Then again, he worked for an elite group of badasses—snipers, hackers, demolitions experts, tacticians. She shouldn't underestimate him.

Cautiously, she scanned her phone, relieved to see Charli's name on her display. "Hey."

"Just checking to make sure you got home okay. I would have left with you."

She winced. Her friend hadn't been having a great time, either. Haisley had been so intent on escaping the bar before she caved to Nash's touch and surrendered her self-respect for the mind-blowing pleasure only he had ever given her that she hadn't thought about anything else.

"I'm sorry. I shouldn't have—"

"It's okay. It looked like you were dealing with a lot. Did you expect him to…"

"No. Honestly, I thought he'd look right through me. I thought he'd —" *Act as if I didn't exist.* "That kiss doesn't mean anything. He wasn't exactly sober."

"Were you?"

Haisley wanted to write off her behavior as too much tequila, but she didn't feel buzzed in the slightest. "Did you go home?"

"Right after you. I wasn't in the party mood."

Something was definitely up with Charli, and Haisley felt guilty for being so out of the loop. "Same. Listen, how about Sunday brunch? I'd love to catch up, one-on-one. It's been too long."

"That would be great." Charli sighed. "Daniel will probably be at work, so I'll be alone with the laundry I'd rather avoid."

"We'll avoid laundry together." They set a time at one of their favorite restaurants. "We'll have fun. It will be like old times. Mimosas, sugar, and shenanigans."

"That sounds perfect."

If that was true, why did Charli sound near tears?

After the call ended, Haisley locked up and wandered upstairs and took off her makeup. Then she indulged in a hot shower to ward off the winter chill before slipping between the sheets with her tablet and her latest steamy read. Unfortunately, even the erotic antics of the story's main couple couldn't hold her attention.

What was she going to do about Nash? How would she handle bumping into him again without unraveling?

Maybe she'd caved so easily and been rendered breathless tonight because seeing him had been such a surprise. She'd be better braced in the future, right?

Haisley turned out the lights and closed her eyes with a sigh. But Nash refused to go away, lurking in the dark corners, peeling off her clothes, blowing her mind, then holding her close as he pried open her heart with each wicked touch. Every time she tried to clear her thoughts, he appeared, reminding her of how she'd fallen so hard and hopelessly for him…

August
Three and a half years ago

The sun beat down from the super-blue Louisiana sky, the humid summer heat sweltering and oppressive. But that wasn't what had Haisley hot and bothered.

Nash Scott was here.

She should have guessed he would be. This town wasn't all that big, and they had more than a few friends in common.

When she'd seen him last a few weeks back, he'd escorted her and

Madison to the Houston hospital where her bestie's dad was receiving cancer treatment. The hulk of warrior had homed in on her, watching her with those shiver-worthy dark eyes that made her heart pound and flirting with a good-natured smile until her knees felt like goo.

He never bothered to hide how much he wanted her, and he constantly challenged her with one-liners that got under her skin. Still, she did her best to ignore him because if she let him too close, he'd be lethal to her heart.

Even knowing that, Haisley found herself rooted in place when he arrived at the pool party. She stared, helplessly drawn to him. How did that man get hotter every time she saw him?

"I'm here, y'all. Let's get this shindig started!" Nash set a couple of six-packs on the kitchen counter, shook hands and backslapped a few of his pals. Then he sauntered her way with a grin. "Haisley. You look gorgeous, as usual. Wanna mess around?"

Oh, how she was tempted.

She sent him a saucy hair flip. "You wish."

"You know it." He looked her up and down. "What are you wearing under that cute little dress?"

Her bathing suit, like most everyone at this party. "That's a rude question. Are your brains in your tighty-whities, horn dog?"

"Nope, but whenever I'm around you, something mighty stiff is. Wanna a peek, baby?" He winked.

Haisley rolled her eyes and faked disinterest. "I typically pass on anything I need a microscope to see."

He laughed. "Wait until I prove you so fucking wrong."

"Do those delusions make things hard for you?"

"No. But you do."

She stifled a giggle. No way would she tell him how much she enjoyed their banter. Sparring with him was dangerous, and she was playing with fire...but everything about the man excited her. He was tall, rugged, confident, muscled, tatted, and sexy as hell. That sounded shallow, but she was drawn to more than his looks. Since she'd known him, he'd proven he was also smart, resourceful, protective, and funny. The whole package.

If love wasn't mostly BS and she was looking for it, he'd be a major catch.

But it was, and she wasn't. Besides, according to local rumor, he'd blown through half the single women in his town—at least. She liked to have a good time as much as the next girl, but she wasn't eager to be the next notch on his bedpost.

On the other hand, she'd heard the whispers that he was *really* good in bed. After a string of lousy lays, she couldn't deny that she was curious—and interested as hell.

Haisley forced herself to turn away and headed to the backyard, fanning her flushed face. But it was useless. Nash always got her hot and bothered. And the way he looked at her—like she was the only woman in the world—made her heart stutter.

She definitely needed to avoid him.

Grabbing a burger from the barbecue, a beer from the cooler, and some chips from the nearby buffet table, she settled beside Charli and Gracelyn. But her gaze kept straying to Nash. And every time she looked at him, he was staring straight at her. He wasn't even trying to hide it.

Being this close to him made her feel dangerously alive. He seemed to invade every corner of her body—the pounding of her heart, the tingling of her suddenly sensitive skin, the ache throbbing between her legs.

She needed a breather to catch her equilibrium.

Once she'd finished dinner and her friends were occupied with conversations, she slipped off behind the cabana for a breath. She didn't see Nash, but he'd probably gone into the house with the other guys to shoot pool.

In the shadows behind the structure, she exhaled out her tension and closed her eyes. She could steer clear of Nash—and avoid temptation—for another hour or two, right?

"Hey, baby. Looking for me?" A familiar, gravelly purr sounded low and close.

Nash.

He was here. And no one else was in sight.

She risked a glance over her shoulder. Bad idea. He leaned against the cabana wall, his muscular arms crossed over his broad chest, watching her with those molten eyes that promised all sorts of sin. Haisley swallowed hard.

"Nope. I wanted a moment alone." She silently cursed the tremor in her voice. "So maybe you'd be a good boy and skedaddle?"

"I was here first." Nash pushed off the wall, taking a few deliberate steps closer. "And I've been wanting you all to myself." He raked his gaze up and down her body, leaving behind a scorching trail of sensation. "Looks like I succeeded."

Anticipation raced through Haisley. She opened her mouth, but her retort died as he closed the distance between them.

"This dark little corner back here gives us the perfect opportunity to…misbehave." Nash traced his finger along the low neckline of her bikini top.

His whisper-light touch raised goosebumps and turned her nipples hard. Secluded together, where all she knew was his gleaming eyes, his musky scent, and his teasing caress, Haisley was painfully aware that he was all man. "I don't need you to misbehave. I can do that all by myself."

A slow grin stretched across his rugged face, complete with a flash of white teeth. "Oh, I'd love to watch you."

Was he insinuating…? Yes, and the idea sent her heartbeat skittering. "I'm not masturbating for you."

"Then I guess we'll have to misbehave together." He skimmed his thumb over her lower lip. "You want to be bad with me, Haisley. Don't you?"

She forgot how to breathe. This man was sin personified, and she struggled to resist his magnetic pull and the undeniable spark of desire between them.

Screw it. She had to know—just once—what his kiss felt like.

Haisley grasped the front of Nash's shirt, using it to tug him even closer until their bodies were flush against each other. "If we're going to misbehave, you should talk less."

A wicked grin curled up Nash's full mouth as he pinned her against the stucco wall, his large frame caging her in as he brushed a lock of hair from her face with maddening tenderness. As her heart thudded wildly, she found herself lost in him.

"Last chance to back out, baby." He dipped his head until their lips were a breath apart. "But fair warning: once I get a taste of you, I don't know if I'll be able to stop."

She was powerless to resist the overwhelming scent and heat of him. "I don't want you to stop."

That was all the encouragement Nash needed. He swooped down and claimed her mouth. On fire, Haisley whimpered against his lips, her fingers tangling in the thick waves of his dark hair as she threw herself into his searing kiss with equal hunger.

Nash angled his head, deepening the kiss as he pinned her more firmly against the wall with the solid weight of his body. One calloused palm trailed along the curve of her hip and dipped teasingly beneath the hem of her dress, blazing a path along her bare thigh. Haisley gasped, head falling back with a moan, allowing his questing tongue to delve deeper and taste her with passion that melted her.

She raked her nails down the hard planes of his back, thrilling at the way his powerful muscles flexed beneath her touch. Nash growled low in his throat, the primal rumble reverberating through her as he seized her lower lip between his teeth in a teasing nip.

This scorching desire was unlike anything she'd ever experienced, and Haisley drowned in it. Her blood rushed through her veins, echoing the staccato cadence of her thundering heart as Nash's clever mouth trailed hot kisses to her neck.

"Haisley," he rasped against her skin, each breath fanning the flames of her need. "God, you taste so good. I'm dying to devour you."

A desperate whine escaped her. She wanted that—wanted him to consume her utterly.

Haisley surrendered to the dizzying spiral of lust and tangled her fingers in Nash's hair to pull him back to her lips. He went willingly, slanting his mouth over hers and devouring her until she couldn't breathe or think or care about anything but him touching her.

He shifted, getting impossibly closer, and lifted her thigh in his grip, sliding it up and around his hip, forcing her to grip him more tightly. Then he bent his knees and notched something big and steely between her legs, rocking exactly where she ached.

Digging her fingers into his shoulders, she whimpered.

"Does that feel like you'll need a microscope, baby?"

"No," she gasped out.

"I want to fill you with every inch while you fill my ears with more of those panting little whines. I want to plow into you while your fingernails rake my back. Yes…just like that." He groaned against her mouth, his face full of pleasure. "You going to let me make us feel so good?"

He punctuated his question by sliding his thumb inside her bikini bottoms and skating the digit across her slick clit. Haisley couldn't find a reply. Plastering herself against him and deepening their kiss didn't count.

When he circled her sensitive button lazily, she cried out, breaking their kiss.

His laugh was a low rumble vibrating under her skin. "That's it. You're so wet. I want to eat this pussy, violate it, pet it, worship it." He curled his fingers in her hair and tugged until she was forced to look at him. "I want to tie you to my bed and edge you for hours, until you beg. Until I drive you so high, you surrender your will to me and take my cock over and over. All you have to do is say yes, baby. We'll leave this party, and I'll make you feel everything…"

God, she couldn't look away, couldn't not want him, despite the fact she was the one who usually loved them and left them. "Make me come."

"Go home with me, and I'll do that as many times as you can handle. I'll keep doing it until you beg me to stop. We'll see if I have any mercy."

Holy hotcakes, this man had a silver tongue and—if his thumb was anything to go by—skills that made him more than capable of satisfying her.

In high school, she'd been looking for love and stupid enough to sleep with guys who offered her far less, serving up her heart again and again. She was older and wiser now. She knew that, for most, love wasn't lasting, so she took the pleasure and ran. Even if it was fleeting, it didn't break her heart.

This man just might have the ability to do both.

"Nash…" She meant to refuse him.

But he bent and pressed a kiss on the swell of her breast exposed above her dress while his thumb slid across her sensitive clit again. She swallowed a groan.

"Is that a yes?"

"What if it was?"

"I'll have you on the back of my motorcycle, speeding toward my place in the next thirty seconds. In the thirty seconds after you hit my bed, you'll be having the first of countless orgasms."

Yes. Despite the fact climbing in his bed was a hundred kinds of bad idea, the word was perched on the tip of her tongue. No man had ever made her blood boil the way he did. That alone made him dangerous.

On top of that, he ticked all her bad-boy boxes. Seductive? Check. Risky profession? Check. Tats and attitude? Check. Hot motorcycle? Check. Not from around here? Check. Able to melt her with a single glance? Check, damn it.

"Oh, fuck!" a woman's unfamiliar voice slurred as she stumbled around the corner, clutching a sloshing beer in one hand and her stomach with the other.

As she and Nash jumped apart and whirled to face the blonde—a friend of a friend she barely knew—the woman heaved and unloaded her booze-laden stomach into the unsuspecting soil two feet from them.

Talk about a mood killer.

But maybe that was a good thing. Now that Nash wasn't touching her, she could breathe again. And think.

She didn't dare succumb to a player like Nash. He'd probably thrash her heart until it felt like he'd shoved it through a meat grinder.

Nope. No thanks. She was too smart for that.

She just had to remind her libido of that.

The aching parts of her protested, but she did her best to squelch the throbbing between her legs and pretend that Nash's kiss and his wandering thumb didn't have her so needy she was ready to scream.

Maneuvering around the upchucking party guest, she distanced herself from Nash. "I'll find her boyfriend so he can take care of her."

He frowned. "After that, you'll come with me?"

Even with someone retching and moaning between them, she was still tempted. That was scary as hell—and her reminder of all the reasons she'd been avoiding him in the first place. He was like every other guy she'd been involved with. He'd hit it and quit it. While casual sex could be fun and she wasn't looking for forever, she didn't like being treated as if she was disposable.

"Actually, I think I'm partied out. See you around, hotshot."

Before he could talk her out of it or—god forbid—touch her again and make her lose her head, she dashed off, whispered a quick word to the upchucker's boyfriend, then hauled ass to her car.

That night, sleep was a long time coming, and erotic dreams of Nash plagued her.

Back in the present, her feelings were every bit as stirred up. Haisley turned off the lights with a sigh, worried as hell she was doomed to repeat their dangerous cycle now that she had returned to town.

CHAPTER FOUR

Present Day

To let his buzz wear off and his desire cool, Nash hung out at Highrise with Trees, Laila, Zy, Tessa, Ethan, and Kane as the New Year's Eve festivities wound down. Drinks flowed as readily as the laughter while everyone enjoyed the party vibe, swapping stories and finishing their drinks.

Nash wasn't in the mood for any of it. His thoughts kept wandering to Haisley and the searing kiss they'd shared.

How the hell could he get through to her? Coax her into talking to him again? Find out what the hell went wrong between them?

Despite two years apart, their chemistry remained an undeniable force. No doubt about that. Two hours after their blazing kiss, Nash's body still thrummed with insistent need, the echo of Haisley's soft whimpers and the taste of her ripe berry lip gloss lingering on his tongue. No amount of booze or pretty, two-legged distractions could possibly dull the fever she ignited in him.

Was Haisley lying awake right now, too, replaying the feel of his hands skimming her curves? Remembering how perfectly they'd fit together?

Shortly after midnight, the crowd started thinning. Ghost and Trevor split for someplace less hip. Melancholy Charli called it a night a few minutes after Haisley's abrupt exit. Something was up with that girl...

Trees and Laila headed for home around one to relieve their sitter. The rest of the happily married crew followed suit over the next twenty minutes.

Once Matt and Madison left, Gracelyn, Haisley's perky brunette gal-pal, gravitated to his table and started a surprising flirtation with Kane. The team's lone wolf eye-fucked her hard in return.

With an inward grin, Nash watched the sparks flare between the two. Kane deserved someone warm and bubbly like Gracelyn to counterbalance his stoic nature...but did she know what she was getting into? Nash had heard whispers about Kane's proclivities, and they were all filthy. Then again, maybe under her good-girl exterior, Gracelyn liked it down and dirty. He certainly wasn't one to judge.

About quarter till two, Ethan left arm-in-arm with a barely legal college girl he intended to sex up for the night, Kane hit the can, and Nash found himself alone with Gracelyn, who'd looked a bit tipsy. If Madison wasn't going to talk...would one of Haisley's other friends?

Maybe he should feel guilty for taking advantage of her inebriated state. But his need to gather intel on Haisley outweighed any qualms.

"Having a good time?"

She smiled, her eyes slightly glassy. "Yeah, I don't usually let loose like this, but it's been great catching up with everyone. So...what do you know about Kane? I can't believe we've never met. He seems like a solid guy."

Wow, she didn't waste any time. Good. He couldn't afford to, either.

"How about we tit for tat? I'll fill you in on Kane if you tell me about Haisley."

Her face shuttered closed. "I can't."

Translation: Gracelyn knew exactly what had gone down to make Haisley peace out of his life—a secret she and her girl-posse were guarding fiercely. He squashed his growing frustration. He could hardly be mad that Gracelyn was loyal. "I'm not asking for her deepest, darkest confidences, just a little info. The last time we... Well, before she left, she had an apartment downtown. But that was a couple of years ago. Where is she staying now, her late aunt's place?"

Gracelyn hesitated, then bobbed her head. "She's fixing up the house. She intends to live there."

He'd ask where it was, but why waste his time with Gracelyn? Now that he knew her plans, he could easily figure out the address, along with her new phone number, on his own. "Is she...doing all right? She's not, like, broken up or anything?"

"About her aunt? No, nothing like that. Those two were never close."

Even though the woman had raised her? Odd...

Nash filed away that tidbit for later.

Haisley had always been so guarded when it came to her family, deflecting his questions about her parents or childhood with a skill that used to low-key frustrate him. Not enough to cause real friction. He'd learned to avoid that landmine and instead explored Haisley's other fascinating layers.

Still, her evasiveness had bothered him, because she'd been an open book in almost every other way. God knew she'd been sexually adventurous, but their relationship hadn't all been tie-her-up, tie-her-down fucking. Surprisingly, they'd talked—a lot. Slowly at first. But they stayed up more times than he could count until the gray light of dawn just...talking.

Inevitably, they'd become tangled in each other's lives, their connection transcending the hook-up they'd started with. Over the months, she'd become his best friend, his lover...and the woman he'd pictured building a life beside. He'd known exactly how she felt about friends, jobs, marriage, kids, politics, religion, and more. They weren't always aligned, and that was fine. They had similar opinions where it mattered most.

At least until he'd changed his mind about one crucial issue. Was that why she'd bolted without warning? Had Haisley found the engagement ring he'd bought for her and freaked out? The excuse she'd given him was BS, and he couldn't think of another reason she'd run from him, fled the state, and cut off all contact for two years.

"Is Haisley...upset with me?" He couldn't hold back the question anymore. "We didn't get to talk much tonight. Or since she's been back in town."

"She's not mad, Nash. Just..." Gracelyn sighed. "I think you two really need to have an open, honest conversation. Clear the air."

The brunette was absolutely right. How to make that happen was a whole other question, especially since, every time he came near Haisley, all he wanted to do was drag her against his body, throw her onto his bed, and never let go.

"I intend to. I need to make her see how much I..." His desperation wasn't Gracelyn's problem, and he had to keep her talking. "You get it. Is she seeing anyone these days?"

"No. She dated off and on in LA, but nothing serious. She was too busy as the social media manager for a local TV station out there. Apparently, it was a twenty-four seven job, so she's looking forward to her new gig. She's hoping it won't be so demanding."

Nash breathed a sigh of relief. At least Haisley was still single.

He opened his mouth to ask more questions, but Kane emerged from the men's room and started shouldering his way toward them with his usual quiet confidence.

Gracelyn's stare locked on the other man like a magnet to metal.

Nash fought back a grin. "Kane is a good guy. Honorable to the core but a loner. He's tough as nails, smart as hell, and, according to rumor, kinky as fuck. As far as I know, he's not dating anyone. Then again, I don't think he dates."

She gave a long-suffering sigh and downed the last of her drink. "Another guy who just wants to hook up? I'm getting too old for that shit. When do you Peter Pans grow up and want more than empty orgasms?"

Nash couldn't answer that question for his teammate. Kane was older so maybe never. Then again, Nash never imagined he'd want till death do us part. At least until Haisley had come along and turned all his preconceived notions upside down. "I think it takes the right woman. Give him a shot. If it's any consolation, I've seen the way he's watched you all night. I don't know if he's ever looked at a woman like that."

That perked her up. "Really?"

"Really."

Kane reached their table again and sidled close to Gracelyn with a searing glance. "Your drink is empty. Did they already shout out last call? If not, I'll get you another."

"They did, so I'm out of here." Nash clapped Kane on the back, then winked her way. "Gracie-girl has had too much to drink to drive herself home."

Gracelyn gasped. "Oh, I'm okay. I don't need—"

"I'll make sure you get home safely," Kane rumbled in a deep, gravelly voice as he slid a protective arm around her.

"Great." Nash palmed his keys. "I'd do it, but I'm on my motorcycle. I only brought one helmet, and it's chilly. Kane will make sure you get tucked in proper, though. Won't you, buddy?"

His face flickered with amusement. "I got her six, man."

"You two enjoy the rest of your night." Nash saluted them. "Happy New Year."

With a wave, he left the pair, feeling lighter despite his unresolved shit with Haisley. At least she was back for good. He intended to use that to his advantage and remind her every single day of the connection they shared until he wore her down and she fell into his arms again.

Striding out into the crisp night air, he pulled out his phone and quickly located her new place—a little craftsman bungalow just two point six miles from his own rental. He couldn't resist taking a detour for some quick recon, but all the pretty blue cottage's windows were dark and still. No car in the drive, so it was probably in the garage around back.

Nash restrained his urge to pound on her door, kiss his way between her legs, and start the new year off right. She wasn't open to being with him again—yet. But he was determined. No more volunteering for the riskiest ops or using other women to try and fill the Haisley-shaped hole in his heart. He would win her back and slide that diamond on her finger once and for all.

As he kickstarted his bike and peeled away into the starry night, Nash felt a surge of clarity. Of purpose. For his future. All he had to do was break through her walls and coax her back into his arms...and his life. Not that she would make it easy. Haisley was one obstinate woman. Good thing he was a stubborn son of a bitch, more than ready for the sweetest battle of his life. Haisley was a prize worth sacrificing everything to reclaim.

Nash gunned his engine and headed home, vaguely wondering what was happening between Gracelyn and Kane. Maybe nothing. Maybe a one-night stand. Maybe more. After all, he and Haisley hadn't started out as more than a scratching of their mutual itches.

That night seemed like forever ago, and he wished like hell he could go back and change so many things...

January
Three years ago

Saturday night, and Nash was fucking spending it alone. Yeah, he could go to one of the bars around town and find some temporary company, but he couldn't muster the enthusiasm.

Because he didn't want just anyone. He wanted Haisley Rowe. He cursed the obnoxious party guest who had drunkenly interrupted their kiss. Since that August night, he'd thought about her a lot. But life—and Haisley herself—had conspired to keep them apart.

Nash had been away protecting a senatorial candidate in DC, a paranoid internet influencer in LA, and a federal judge receiving death threats in New Orleans. Then he'd spent the holidays in West Virginia with his folks. When he'd been in Lafayette, he had glimpsed Haisley a few times since they'd locked lips—and every single time she'd invented excuses to run away like her very fine ass was on fire.

After Christmas, the first thing he'd done was hunt her down at Highrise. Goddamn if she hadn't given him the cold shoulder again—

while eating him up with those pretty blue eyes. Oh, she'd pretended to flirt with some local redneck, but she clearly hadn't meant it because she hadn't left with him.

And that was the real reason Nash wasn't at a random bar tonight, getting his drink on and hitting on a more willing female. He and Haisley had unfinished business. Besides, no other woman measured up.

Fuck, he had it bad.

A knock on his apartment door interrupted Nash's musings. He wasn't expecting company. He was suspicious by nature, and caution had saved his ass more than once, so he tucked his SIG in his holster and slowly opened the door.

Well, well, well... Speak of the devil.

Haisley stood on his doorstep, one hand gripping an unopened bottle of whiskey, her fiery hair curled and tousled. His hungry gaze dropped, snagging on the rosy pout of her lips. His eyes nearly popped out when he took in the tiny black dress that molded to her lush curves, revealing glimpses of her creamy, toned thighs.

Damn if she didn't look like she'd stepped straight out of his most scorching fantasies.

"Hey, hotshot."

Her seductive murmur, along with a cocky grin, had him hard in two seconds.

"Haisley Rowe. Just who I wanted to see." He leaned against his doorframe. "What's up?"

"Nice to know you haven't forgotten me." She peeked around him, nosing into his apartment. "You alone?"

"Not anymore." He stepped back and invited her inside with a sweep of his hand. "I got back from an op at two this morning and spent most of the day sleeping. Have a seat. Sorry the place is a mess."

Her smile turned sly. "I heard you were back, and I didn't come to critique your housekeeping."

"Good. I have other, more critical skills that might interest you," he rasped out in a low tone as she brushed past him and entered his living room.

"So you've told me." She placed the bottle on the coffee table and settled herself on his sofa.

"How did you know where I live?"

"Matt is full of helpful information."

After months of running, she'd gone out of her way to find him, dolled up, and appeared on his doorstep. Why?

Staring as if her expression would give him the answer, Nash sat in the oversized chair near her. "Remind me to thank him later. To what do I owe this pleasure?"

She nibbled her full lower lip between her teeth, batting those baby blues at him through a fringe of mascaraed lashes. "I've been thinking…"

"Should I be afraid?" he teased.

"Depends." Haisley pretended to study her nails as she uncrossed and recrossed her legs, giving him a tantalizing glimpse of her soft inner thighs. "Do I scare you?"

Nash swallowed and tried to focus on their conversation. But it was too late. His thoughts had disappeared straight between her legs. "Not even a little. Maybe I should ask if you're afraid of me."

"Is that what you think?" She scoffed. "No."

That's not what Madison told me… Granted, she'd said that a couple of years back, and maybe things had changed. But Haisley's evasive maneuvers since August backed that up. Either way, Nash wouldn't betray Madison's confidence. But he intended to figure out why—until now—Haisley had been reticent to even be in the same zip code, much less the same room.

Clearly, she'd come tonight for a reason. What did she want?

"You just drive me a little crazy," she added.

"Yeah? You always drive me crazy, baby," he drawled as his molten gaze roamed over her, slow and blatant.

"Please." She rolled her eyes. "You were crazy long before you ever laid eyes on me."

God, he'd missed bantering with her. Desire simmered low in his gut as she leaned closer. Her nearness and the intriguing musky-floral scent of her skin…hmm. Even being next to her felt like delicious foreplay.

Damn it, if she'd come here purely for help or information, he'd be crushed.

"You're not wrong." He gave her a self-deprecating grin. "But I won't bite…unless you ask me to."

She raised a fiery brow. "What if I was asking?"

Oh, holy shit. Her impromptu visit was a booty call? What had changed her mind?

Nash didn't care. Whatever her reason, he was totally on board.

He swallowed hard as images of her spread out before him, her satiny skin under his lips while they lay tangled together, fucking with wild abandon, pelted his brain. He itched to grab the scrap of silky dress in his hands, rip it from her body, and explore every luscious inch of her.

But Haisley was waiting for an answer, her face rife with a hunger that matched his.

"I'm game, baby." Somehow he resisted the urge to yank her onto his lap and see if her lush mouth still tasted as sweet as it had during the shimmering height of summer. "For you, I've got lots of game."

"But there are rules."

In bed, he always called the shots. She'd learn that quickly enough. In fact, he'd enjoy the challenge of coaxing her to submit. But for now, he entertained her. "Like?"

"I'm here for a good time, not for a long time. This happens tonight—and tonight only. I'm not interested in repeat performances, much less—god forbid—a relationship."

Nash wasn't interested in permanence, either. But why was she so anti-entanglement? He suspected the answer would help him solve his Haisley riddle, but that wasn't a problem for now. "Works for me. I have a strict no-strings policy. I'm down for a short-term, friends-with-benefits situationship. But I'm out on marriage, and I'm never having children."

She frowned. "Got something against kids?"

"No." They were adorable. "But after helping to raise five younger siblings, I feel like I've already been through fatherhood. I'm not looking to repeat the experience. And with my crazy schedule, I don't need the responsibility. So no Nash Juniors for me."

"I never had the nuclear family thing, and I turned out all right." Haisley shrugged. "I think it's overrated."

Not necessarily. He had a lot of fond memories with his parents and siblings—holidays, camping trips, even playing in the sprinklers and tossing footballs. If he was looking for forever, he'd want it to look like that...minus the harried, overworked parents and the living in poverty. But he was never getting hitched or procreating, so it wasn't an issue. "You didn't come here to discuss your philosophy on family."

She shook her head slowly. "I came here to make you lose your mind."

After avoiding him for months, now she was laying it all out? What the hell was she up to?

"All right. But fair warning..." He dropped his hand on her thigh. "If you stay, you'll be the one losing your mind."

Her pupils flared with naked hunger. "Those are big words. How do I know you can back them up? Last time we got close... Well, let's just say you didn't follow through."

"*I* didn't?" Nash raised his brow in challenge. "You jumped away from the puking chick, tucked your tail, and ran. I would have been more than happy to tear off your clothes, fill every inch of your pussy to bursting until you begged, and fucked you until you screamed my name."

"What makes you think I would have let you?"

"You panted. You whimpered. You clung to me. Your eyes begged."

"That's not true." She crossed her arms over her chest.

"We both know it is. You loved every minute of it. You were wet."

"You can't possibly know that."

"I can. That night taught me exactly what you smell like when you're aroused."

She sucked in a sharp breath, leapt to her feet, and grabbed her bottle. "Coming here was a mistake."

Haisley could say all she wanted that she wasn't afraid of him, but something was spooking her. Something she'd allowed to keep them apart since meeting a few years ago. She obviously wanted to be wanted, but it was almost as if she viewed her desire for him as a weakness.

Why?

"It wasn't." He approached cautiously. "We've been circling each other for a long time. I've just been looking for a sign that you were ready to take this past banter and flirtation."

"That's why you didn't shoot your shot? It wasn't because…" She shifted uneasily from one foot to the other, not quite meeting his stare. "Never mind."

"Because I didn't want you? Is that what you thought?" Haisley didn't answer, but the way she bit her lip and half shrugged, Nash knew he'd hit a bull's-eye. "You were fucking wrong."

Her gaze skittered up. For a moment, he saw her insecurity and hope. But she blinked and covered them with a brazen stare. "All right. You going to stop talking and prove it?"

CHAPTER FIVE

"I'll do more than prove it. I'll fuck you until you can't remember your own name, baby." Nash seized Haisley's nape in one large palm. The other, he curved around her hip and yanked her flush against him. The shock of her softness nestled to his solid frame wrenched matching groans from their throats. He drilled down into her eyes. "I've waited so long to touch you. I'm going to ruin you utterly for anyone else."

He had no fucking idea what made him vow that—the heat of the moment?—but even imagining another man's hands on her made him homicidal.

A needy shudder rocked her body. She arched closer in blatant invitation, silken curves melting to his hard edges. They fit perfectly together. Desire scorched Nash's veins.

In the moment, he swore she'd been made for him to fuck. God knew no other woman had ever twisted him in knots like this one. He loved that she not only kept him on his toes, but sometimes had him sprinting to catch up.

The thought evaporated when she wound her arms around his neck and dragged her nails against his scalp with a low moan. Something primal and ravenous unleashed itself from his mental chains.

This woman might just be the death of him...but what a pleasurable way to go.

As his fingers crept up to fist her hair, he sealed his mouth over hers in a searing clash of lips and questing tongues. She tasted sweet, but her flavor had a darker, richer edge he'd never forgotten that was pure Haisley.

With a groan, he hauled her even closer as he bent and angled his throbbing cock against the soft heat of her pussy.

If she backed out now, he'd be hard-pressed not to toss her over his shoulder and cart her caveman-style into his bedroom. Even imagining burying himself in Haisley's slick, soft cunt had his control fraying. And now that he'd gotten drunk on another taste of her lips, Nash didn't think he'd survive tonight without her.

What about tomorrow? Whatever this was between them burned so fucking hot. What were the chances they'd be able to extinguish the fire before dawn? For the rest of their lives? Nash wasn't convinced the ferocious ache she stoked would be snuffed out in a single encounter.

But that was a future-him problem. Nothing was stopping him now.

Haisley dragged her nails down his back in scorching trails, her lithe body writhing shamelessly against him as their tongues wrestled for dominance. Her satin rasped against his denim, filling the quiet only broken by their harsh, panted breaths and long moans. Nash cradled her lush ass in his big hands, squeezing and kneading as she hooked one silky thigh over his hip in blatant invitation.

With a low, guttural growl, he hoisted Haisley up until she straddled his waist. He pinned her against the nearest wall as she arched and gasped, grinding against him in a maddening tease.

"Naaash," she moaned.

Mindless with desperate desire was exactly how he craved her.

"I'm here. You've got me," he vowed, his lips making a molten trail down her soft throat. "All of me. As many times as you can take me tonight."

Haisley responded with a full-body shudder, her thighs tightening as she writhed against his aching cock. Electric sparks of sensation licked across his nerve endings, driving his hunger higher.

Nash captured her plush mouth again in ravenous possession, trailing his hands down the curve of her hips and over the velvet skin of her thighs. He bunched her dress in his fists and tugged the shiny fabric up to her waist. And as he thrust deeper into her mouth, he rocked his erection between her legs. Through her flimsy underwear, he could feel how hot and wet she was.

Whimpering, Haisley clung, her soft arms clutching him as she surrendered to him kiss by shuddering kiss. But Nash feared he was the one losing it. She still had all her clothes on, and he was already a goddamned goner. After tonight, after he'd mapped Haisley's every lush curve and tasted every delectable inch, would he really be able to walk away?

She tore free from their kiss, panting roughly, and met his stare. Her eyes were dilated and dark with need. The way she visually consumed him ignited something ferocious inside him. A flame impossible to put out.

Then she licked her way up his neck. An explosion of tingles sent a shudder rolling through his body. Before he'd recovered, she nipped at his lobe, rubbing against him again and supercharging his demand.

He wanted her naked and under him right now.

With a growl, he lifted her away from the wall and gripped her tight against him, carrying her to his bedroom. Once inside, Nash maneuvered her onto the mattress, then covered her body with his own. He slanted his mouth over hers again, his big palms skimming her silky panties and even softer thighs until he reached the dress bunched around her middle. With a ruthless tug, he dragged it farther up her body.

Haisley writhed and twisted under him, eyes closed, legs parted, as he dragged the fabric over her flat stomach and delicate torso. Beneath him, she gasped and gave another sensual roll of her body, rubbing her sweet pussy against his straining hardness. At the blistering friction, a harsh groan tore loose from Nash's throat.

Fuck, she was fraying his restraint. If he didn't strip her down and get inside her soon, he was going to combust.

"Off." He plucked impatiently at her little dress.

Together, he yanked and she pulled until the garment cleared her body, and he hurtled it to the floor in a forgotten heap. He drank in the sight of her clad in nothing but a scanty black bra and matching lacy underwear.

In the moonlight slanting through his windows, her skin glowed such a pearly, unspoiled shade of pale, especially against the dark lingerie. He'd never seen a woman look so velvety perfect. Damn. He was rarely speechless, but just looking at her tied every part of him up in knots, including his tongue.

His brain shut down. Instinct took over, and it told him to bury himself deep, claim her, and never let go.

He ripped her panties down her thighs and tore them free from her body, flinging them who knew where. At the same time, she tugged at her bra, arching to unfasten the hooks behind her back. Then she tossed the lace-and-wire scrap to the floor. Every inch of her body was blessedly bare.

Haisley caressed her breasts in shameless flirtation and parted her thighs. "That look on your face…"

"You're beautiful." Utterly perfect in her flushed, tousled desire for him.

"Yeah? I would have sworn you intend to nail me into the mattress."

"Oh, I do."

But he had to get these jeans off first—before they strangled his cock.

When Nash vaulted off the bed and reached for his fly, Haisley spread across his mattress provocatively. He damn near swallowed his tongue.

"Like what you see, hotshot?" She raised one dainty foot and trailed her sole over the ridge of his denim-clad arousal.

Her teasing rasp was pure sin as she applied toe-curling pressure, massaging him with her foot. Heat detonated through Nash's veins at the erotic contrast—her cool challenge against his scorching want. Her soft caress against the rough texture of his denim.

A feral growl rumbled up from his chest. "Fuck."

"That's the plan. But it's your turn. Get naked."

Nash shed his shirt and ripped at his fly before kicking away his jeans. Her hungry stare unabashedly consumed him, tracing his wide shoulders and his heavy, inked pecs before dropping to the bulge in his boxer briefs. "What about the rest?"

"Once these come off, I'll be inside you. And before we start that, there's so much of you I want to savor. Starting with those nipples…"

Everything about Haisley appealed to him, from her fiery hair and saucy smile to her little painted-pink toenails—and all the delectable parts of her in between.

Since she thought this was their one and only night together, he needed to heap so much pleasure that she changed her mind. And forgot any other man who had ever touched her. Saying he wanted to ruin her for every other guy hadn't been an idle threat. He didn't want to think about why.

Nash sank onto the mattress, caressing her silken thighs and nestling against the shock of red hair between them as he covered her with his own body in a tangle of legs, rough to smooth. Groaning, he fell onto her breasts, cupping them in his big hands, and worked his lips across her soft, pure skin. He teased her, laving and circling close to her sensitive nipples, but never quite touching them.

Under him, she writhed and arched. Her breathing roughened. Her legs grew restless. Her moans turned louder.

Haisley scorched him to the core.

He skimmed a tormenting thumb just under her swollen tip, brushing tantalizingly close. "Want something, baby?"

"Stop playing games. You know what I want."

"Yep. I know exactly what your body craves. But I won't give it to you until you spell it out for me—every dirty detail."

Her lashes fluttered up to reveal dilated blue eyes. Knowing he'd aroused her torqued up his desire another notch.

"You want me to explain how you should pleasure me?"

Oh, she was being her sassy self—and playing with fire. He skimmed his thumb close to her steely peak again. "Does it really feel like I need you to teach me?"

"N-no, but—"

"No. I just want to hear you beg me for what I know you need."

She frowned. "We're exchanging pleasure; you're not bending me to your will."

He wasn't budging until she lowered her walls and at least tried to be vulnerable. "Is that what you think? Since I'm not the one on the bottom, hungry for orgasm, I'm calling the shots. And I can do this all night, baby." He rocked his rigid cock against her pussy, reveling in the way she burned him with her damp heat. "How about you?"

"Bastard."

"Did you think I was a nice guy?" He dragged his knuckles over her distended nipples and delighted in her gasp.

"I didn't think you'd torment me for fun." She tried to sound angry, but her voice came out as somewhere between a groan and a plea.

"Give me what I want, and I'll relieve that ache throbbing between your legs."

She pressed her lips together mulishly. "I don't beg any man for anything."

"I'll be the one to change your mind." He climbed over her, reached into the nightstand drawer, then withdrew a pair of padded cuffs. Before she could even sputter, he had them attached to her wrists with the chain attaching them looped around the decorative slats of his headboard.

Her eyes widened. "What the hell?"

"Are you scared?" If she was, he'd let her go instantly.

"No." She scoffed.

"Good. I would never hurt you." He kissed his way up her throat and hovered over her pouting mouth. "But you sure do look pretty bound and at my mercy. Be a good girl, and I'll reward you in ways you've never imagined."

Nash punctuated his promise by exhaling hotly on one stiff nipple. He followed up by slowly dragging his tongue over the engorged tip.

Her breath caught. Her body stiffened. In the next heartbeat, her back arched. A whimper slipped from between her lips. "Nash..."

He did the same to her other nipple, then murmured against her skin. "Yeah, baby. Something you want to say?"

"I'll get you back for this."

"I look forward to it. But if you want more, you know what I need to hear."

Haisley dragged in choppy breaths, her cheeks now red. The flush spread to her chest. Another moan escaped her throat as she tugged at the cuffs. Fuck, she looked stunning. And her needy sounds were some of the sweetest he'd ever heard.

But Haisley was a stubborn thing, biting her lip to hold in the surrender on the tip of her tongue.

"I'm waiting," he whispered.

"Fuck you."

"No, baby. I'm going to fuck you. And you're going to both beg me and thank me for it." He nipped at her first stiff peak again, then followed it with a teasing suck—a moment of relief before he pulled away again. "Unless you want me to stop?"

"Don't you dare."

"Are you sure?" he taunted. "I'll uncuff you, help you get dressed, and send you on your way, wet and aching."

"I own a vibrator."

"You really think that will satisfy you better than I can?"

Haisley let loose a long whine and shook her head. She was so, so close to giving in, he could almost taste it.

"That's what I thought," he drawled, thumbing her nipple. "You going to stay?"

"Yes, goddamn you," she gasped. "I'm staying."

Triumph filled him. "Then you know what I want to hear. Say the filthy, magic words, and I'll give you all the orgasms you can handle."

Again, he sucked one of her nipples, rolling it across his tongue, tugging on it with a gentle nip of his teeth.

She grabbed the headboard with a whine that dripped need. "Please."

"There it is… There's my good girl." He rewarded her by plucking her other nipple between his lips and dragging it in deep.

Haisley twisted and moaned, halfway to mindless. "Please…"

"Anything you want, baby. Spell it out for me."

"Your lips. Your tongue. Your teeth." She lifted her torso in offering, presenting him her engorged nipples. "Suck them. Give me more. Make my toes curl. Don't stop."

Normally, he'd remind her that she wasn't running the show, but since her request dovetailed with his plans, he didn't push back. "My pleasure. That's one thing you'll learn about me. Play nicely, and I'll be a giver."

Then he stopped using his words and unleashed the ferocity of his desire on her tender nipples—sucking, nipping, laving, pinching, squeezing, tormenting—until her skin flushed a beautiful, head-to-toe rosy red. She spread her legs wider and encouraged him with writhing hips.

Fuck, she exceeded every fantasy of her he'd ever dreamed up.

"Nash," she panted. "Nash...please. I can't—" She sucked in a shocked breath when he curled his tongue around one of her plump points again and caressed his way down her body. "Oh, god. I need..."

"What? Tell me, baby, exactly what you want and how you want it."

"I need to come."

"I know." He rolled her clit under his slow-churning fingers. "Give me details. Beg me. Sweetly."

She panted, meeting his stare with desperate eyes. "You're being an asshole!"

"Tsk, tsk. That's not going to end your torment." He circled her most sensitive nub again.

"Why?"

Nash knew exactly what she was asking. "Do you need me to spell out that I like to be in control in the bedroom?"

Her eyes widened. "This torture isn't a one-time thing?"

"No. It's not even punishment for stringing me along and making me want you for years." He lowered his head and kissed from the graceful arch of her neck to her breasts heaving with every breath. "It's because I can. And because you look so pretty when you tell me how much you want me."

Then he stifled whatever she'd been about to say by crushing her plump, gaping mouth under his.

He was drawn to her spirit. He liked the fact she knew her own mind. He adored her sassy streak, and he wouldn't want her any other way. But damn if he didn't want her to need him so badly she was willing to plead for her pleasure…

Haisley tore her mouth free. "Fine. Please, Nash. *Pleeeaase…*"

"What, baby? What can I do for you? Tell me. The dirtier the better."

"Stop messing with me and make me scream."

The frustration in her voice was delicious…but it told him he was approaching her limits and he'd pushed her enough. Next time—and there would be one—he'd go harder. She'd learn that when she asked him for exactly what she wanted, he delivered in full.

"Please?" he taunted.

"Yes. Please. Please now. Please stop tormenting me," she nearly sobbed. "Please…"

He bent his head and sucked each of her nipples again, one after the other, loving the way they'd swelled and stood hard in a silent plea for more. He nipped and laved…all the while rubbing her clit in leisurely circles, driving her higher until she closed her eyes tightly, her entire body trembling and taut, shuddering and on the edge.

"You're so fucking beautiful," he praised as he scrambled up long enough to drop his underwear and reach for a condom.

"You can't leave. You didn't make me come yet. I begged—" She gaped at his cock. "Oh, my god. That's huge."

He grinned. "I'm six-foot-seven. I'm…proportional."

She blinked. "You're going to split me open."

"I'm going to make you scream, just like you asked. And since you weren't specific about how I should do that, I'm doing it my way."

Nash donned the condom and vaulted between her legs, catching each thigh in the crook of his elbows and settling the stalk of his aching cock against her wetness. He rooted around until he found her clit.

Then he smiled—and dragged his length up the sensitive nub, gratified when her eyes flared wide again and she cried out in high-pitched supplication. "Nash?"

"You still want to come?"

"Yes!" She tossed her head back and gave herself over to him.

He loved her reaction. "Tell me. Ask me."

"Please. Please..." She repeated her plea like a mantra, her eyes as full of surrender as the feminine whine in her voice. "I need you. Inside me. I need—"

"Hard? Slow? Soft? Fast?"

She gripped the slats of his headboard and begged with her eyes. "Yes!"

Clearly, Haisley was done talking. Good thing. So was he.

Nash balanced himself on his elbows and dragged his cock through her wet slit, groaning at the silken, juicy feel of her against his length. Then he stroked up again, slowly rubbing himself against her needy nub until she arched, her mouth flying open in a silent scream.

He allowed her no respite as he repeated the motion over and over until she scratched at his headboard and stared at him as if he were both God and the devil himself. Her slack jaw, the look of sensual agony on her face, the rosy flush of her cheeks... If he'd ever had a more beautiful woman in his bed, he didn't remember.

This one he would never forget.

As he pressed his erection against her cunt again, he slid through her wetness. He smelled her need. He lost himself in her mounting bliss.

With a keening little moan, she closed her eyes. He stopped midstroke, inciting a gasp of protest. "Nash!"

"Eyes open. Look at me. I want to remember your face the first time I make you come."

Instantly, she obeyed. Triumph spiked. Thrill swelled. And as their gazes fused, he fell into her eyes, drowning in her darkening blue as her breaths roughened. His heart rate picked up, along with the pace of his strokes and his desperation to be inside her. Beneath him she rocked, legs spread. Her body tensed and surrendered to him.

"I...I—oh. That's...oh, my god. *Yeeessssss!*"

Under him, her body bucked and jolted as ecstasy overtook her. But she never blinked, never looked away. Watching her come undone for him as he stroked her passion and sent her soaring damn near dismantled his restraint.

"Give it to me. That's my girl. Fuck, baby..." He stroked her to the height of climax, then reared back long enough to check that his condom was still in place. "Yes."

He had to get inside her. He'd had grand plans to wring a handful of orgasms from her before he buried himself in her pussy, but the need to feel her, be surrounded by her, be closer to her, couldn't wait.

"Nash!"

The way she writhed under him and her naked, vulnerable expression was too much to resist. He angled his hips to settle his sheathed crest at her clenching opening and began tunneling his way in.

"Take me. Take all of me. Every inch. I fucking need you, baby."

As he slowly impaled her, Haisley's eyes widened. She let loose a hoarse, warbling cry and nodded frantically. "Yes. More. Oh, my god. Oh, my god!"

"That's it." He worked his way in and out in insistent, unhurried strokes. Fuck, she was so hot. So tight. "So perfect. How does that feel?"

"I'm so full, it burns." But the mewling note in her voice told him she loved it.

"I still have more to give you." He inched in deeper.

"More?" Her strangled cry thrilled him. "Oh…"

"We'll do this together, a little at a time."

She gave him a shaky nod, biting her lip as he reached up to entwine his fingers with hers. She squeezed him back.

He loved how brave and willing Haisley was. Honestly, she was more delicate than the women he typically fucked. Not that he didn't love the way she was built, but he was big and rough…and he didn't want to break her. So he had to go slow, even if he was sweating with the strain and everything inside him growled to shove his way in to the hilt and fuck them both into oblivion.

Inching back, he gritted his teeth against escalating need and began easing forward. "I'm going in deeper."

"Yes…" She lifted her hips to him, and her eyes slid shut as he filled her even more.

"Good?"

"Amazing," she moaned. "I feel you everywhere."

"Only a few inches to go."

Her breath caught. "Seriously?"

"Relax." He pressed a kiss to her lips and rested his forehead to hers. "That's it. Good girl…"

As he eased a bit more, his heart started revving. God, she was like silken fire wrapped around his cock, all tight, rippling heat. With her, the sensations were mind melting. He felt like a king.

"Nash!"

He eased back again. "Almost there, baby. You're doing great. Still burning?"

She breathed against his lips. "Yeah. You're…big. There's so much of you inside me."

He heard that a lot.

"Oh, my god!" Haisley gasped as he surged inside her again.

"Baby, baby… Fuck, you feel so good. We're almost there. Tilt up. Yes, just like that." He rocked into her, shoving his cock in deeper still. "Amazing…"

"Yes," she panted. "I've never felt anything like this."

"So why have you been avoiding me?"

Haisley flashed him glassy blue eyes. "What?"

"After our kiss at the pool party. I wanted to see you again. You ran from me."

"I didn't."

They both knew that was a lie.

He pulled back—almost completely withdrawing—and refused to move. "You did. What made you change your mind?"

"Nash…"

She wanted him to sweep this question under the rug. Not happening. His timing was shitty on purpose. He wasn't giving her another inch until she answered. "I'm trying to understand, baby. The last thing I want to do is scare you."

"We'll talk about this later. *Please.*"

"We'll talk about this now."

Haisley whimpered. "I'm not thinking straight."

"I know." So he was more likely to get the truth. "Do your best."

"I like to be in control, all right? With you…I'm not."

Exactly what he'd suspected. She dated guys she could take or leave, dudes she could walk all over. That wasn't him. Never would be. She could deny it all she wanted, but he scared her.

That made them even. She scared the shit out of him, too. Other women he enjoyed but didn't crave. This one…fuck, she was already in his blood, and he didn't even know why. Her sassiness? Her challenge? Something else entirely? He'd figure it out.

After he rewarded her honesty and put them both out of their misery.

"Thank you. I've got you, baby. You don't have to be in control with me."

"I want to be."

Did she not know who she was sexually? He sure as hell did, and all her saucy one-liners and don't-give-a-fuck attitude were her defense mechanisms. Deep down, she was a woman built to kneel—but only for the man she trusted.

"With me, you don't have to. Close your eyes." He waited until she obeyed. "Exhale. Yes… Now let go and take the rest of me."

She smiled—until he surged forward, completely burying his cock inside her in one insistent stroke.

"Nash!"

"Oh, fuck, yes. There it is. Every inch of me is stuffed inside you…"

She writhed under him, flushing as he withdrew, then plunged in again, nudging her G-spot with his crest until she gasped. "That's *so* good. What are you doing to me?"

Grinning, he did it again. And again. And again, until her mouth gaped open and her cunt clasped him so tight, he had to fight his way inside her.

"How. Do. You. Feel?" He pumped her hard, punctuating every word with a bed-shaking thrust.

"Oh! I'm…I'm going to—"

"Come," he snarled. "For me. Now."

She did, screaming out her pleasure as her body convulsed.

Nash felt his control slipping. He'd wanted Haisley for too long to hold back. Every touch between them was too combustive. The way she gripped him, pulsing and clenching, blew his goddamn mind.

He gave in with a long, hoarse growl, slamming into her with fast, demanding strokes as he relinquished his self-control and gave everything to her.

Nash exploded. Fireworks shot behind his eyes. His head swam. His limbs seemed to weigh a thousand pounds. But the ecstasy... Holy shit, this woman had blazed her way through his restraint and burrowed directly into his soul.

Together, they panted until they recovered. Finally, Haisley opened her eyes, blinking and looking stunned. "What the hell just happened?"

"I don't know exactly. But I want to do it again."

As usual, Haisley was a contradiction. Those so-blue eyes of hers teared up, but she grinned. "What are you waiting for?"

Nash rushed to divest himself of the condom and grab another. In seconds, he took her mouth again, losing himself totally in her tangy-sweet kiss, her silky skin, and her soft vulnerability.

When she began digging her nails into her palms and pleading, Nash delved inside her again—and lost himself. Before he went under completely, he had one realization: when it came to Haisley, all bets were off. After the years of insane tension between them, the dam of primal desire had burst and swept them both away. There would be no sparing her the kind of searing, possessive bliss he intended to lavish on every lush inch of her body every chance he got.

As their passion ratcheted up to another feverish climax, Nash silently vowed that this night with Haisley wouldn't be his last. He was staking his claim. He would be the only man plowing her sweet pussy and reaping the rewards of the soft heart she hid under her barbed-wire exterior.

From tonight on, Haisley would be his. He just had to convince her.

CHAPTER SIX

Present Day

Dreams both erotic and heartbreaking starring Haisley plagued Nash until he gave up on sleep. After a handful of hours, he vaulted out of bed, took his usual five-mile run and lifted weights before he grabbed a shower and a cup of coffee. Then he sat down in front of his computer.

Today began a new fucking year, and he'd be damned if he started it with regret. He'd get Haisley to speak to him again and tear down the barricades around her heart—no matter what he had to do. Thankfully, Matt had given him the means.

"Dude…" Ethan stumbled into the kitchen bleary-eyed. "What time did you get up?"

Most days he didn't mind sharing a house with Ethan Garrison. His fellow operative could be loud. He didn't always have a great filter, so he ran his mouth more than he should. But the kid was smart, and he had a good heart. Besides, someone had to watch out for him.

"Six. Just brewed a pot of coffee."

Ethan sighed as he poured a cup. "If I was into dick, I'd marry you."

"No, you wouldn't, because I'd never say yes."

"I can be persuasive." He winked as he poured a dash of creamer into his java.

"I've seen." Ethan got laid a lot. Must be the kid's flash, tattoos, the bad-boy vibe, and snark.

"But you're not my type."

Nash scoffed. "Ditto in double for you, asshole. Your...date still here?"

"Yep. Out cold. When I was done with her, she rolled over with a happy sigh and hasn't moved a muscle since." As he crossed the room, he grinned like he was damn proud of himself. "Orgasm overload can do that. Hey, since Haisley seemed so pissed off last night, maybe you should take notes. I can't believe you were stupid enough to flatten her against a wall and drunk kiss her."

"Fuck off."

"No, thanks. What's your plan?" He bumped Nash's shoulder. "You do have one, right?"

"I've been piecing a plan together all morning. I'm getting Haisley back."

As Nash filled Ethan in, he clicked the link Matt had sent him. Since she'd said she couldn't do "this" with him again...maybe she could do it when he was someone else. At the very least, maybe he'd get answers.

Using the name of his childhood dog, Jasper, he went through the approval process to join Crime Solvers International. Once in the group, he scanned various cases the members were trying to solve. Not surprisingly, there were subgroups working on infamous murders—Jack the Ripper, JFK, the Black Dahlia, JonBenét Ramsey, Tupac...all the usual suspects.

Other subgroups were hard at work on more recent murders and disappearances. He glanced through a few, happy to see that a couple of their theories had been proven true. One even led to an arrest and conviction in Florida. Good for them.

"Let me get this straight." Ethan scowled. "She's into solving cold cases with people online, and you're going to connect with her again through a shared love of murder?"

"No." Nash rolled his eyes as he found the handles of all the members and started scanning for a familiar redhead. Among a few thousand people, this could take a while. "I'm going to connect with Haisley through a common interest. Of course I'll flirt with her, too. Let her get to know me again while I regain her trust."

"By lying to her?" Ethan shook his head. "Dude, once she finds out you've been chatting her up using a pseudonym, she's not going to appreciate the subterfuge any more than she's going to welcome you invading her online space."

"It'll be fine." Nash hoped.

"Youre funeral," Ethan quipped.

"Okay, dipshit, if you were in my shoes, what would be your smooth move?"

Ethan tossed up his hands. "Off the top of my head? I don't know, but it wouldn't be lying to her."

"You don't understand how Haisley works. She's stubborn as the day is long, and right now she's not speaking to me."

"Because she doesn't want to, and I'm guessing it's because you screwed the pooch somewhere along the way. Figure out what you did, then try to talk to her when she's not in a crowded bar with her girls and you're not drunk. Maybe invite her out to dinner or—"

"I can't invite out a woman who's blocked my messages on every conceivable platform and pushed me away last night, so fake name it is."

"Boy, you *really* pissed that girl off. What did you do?"

"Honestly, I don't know." And that was the rub. "We didn't fight. She just...mumbled some BS excuses, pulled back, and ran off to Cali."

Ethan scowled. "It's been a couple of years, but I remember that woman being really into you. I would have sworn you two were headed to the altar. And the maternity ward, the way you went at it all the time."

"Me, too." And a possibility that had once scared the hell out of Nash had felt like a happy eventuality—until Haisley fled. "That's why I need to figure out what happened. And if I have to be a little underhanded...isn't that how intel works?"

"On a job, sure. In relationships? That seems like dangerous ground, but you do you." Ethan swallowed the last of his coffee and stood. "Since I intend to start my New Year off right, I'm going to escort my horny little sorority princess out the door, get in a workout, meet her for lunch, then bring her back here for round two. See you later."

Nash shook his head. "See you, man."

When Garrison disappeared into his half of the house, Nash rededicated his effort to finding Haisley among the thousands of people in the online group. Finally, he located her. At least he thought she was RedHotSavvySleuth. Her avatar wasn't her face but a cartoon of a curvy bombshell in a trench coat, but her bio claimed she was a feisty redhead who lived in Lafayette. How many could there be in this group? Then he tracked her latest posts, noting the cases that interested her most tended to be the ones that needed attention.

That gave him an idea.

As JasperThePrivateDick, he agreed to the group rules, posted to the newbie forum, fielded welcome messages, then did a little digging on the disappearances happening at the nearby mall. Shockingly, he couldn't find much. Finally, he asked the general forum if anyone was looking into this case. Since he claimed to live in New Orleans, he asked if anyone living locally could shed some light.

Thirty minutes later, RedHotSavvySleuth welcomed him and said she hadn't heard of the case. But she said she'd been to that mall many times, so she'd love to hear more.

Grinning, Nash immediately slid into her DMs. "I'm coming for you, baby. Let's connect."

His eyes narrowing in concentration, he typed out a response, trying to strike the right balance between curious and friendly with a tinge of flirt. Once he hit Send, he leaned back in his chair, his gaze fixed on the screen. Anticipation coursed through him.

The soft ping of an incoming message made his pulse jump.

> RedHotSavvySleuth: Thanks for bringing this case to my attention. I'm hoping the police are all over the disappearances at that new mall, but Lafayette's finest aren't all that great, in my experience. Tell me more.

> JasperThePrivateDick: I couldn't find a lot online, which seemed odd. So I started thinking… CSI seems like it's tackled some tough cases and had some successes. Because this is a local issue, any chance you're up for tackling a mystery in your own backyard? I'll provide all the help and backup I can. And be your sounding board, of course.

Tense minutes ticked by as Nash waited for Haisley's response. He hoped like hell she didn't shut him down. Finally, the soft ping of a new message broke the silence. His breath caught in his throat as he read it.

> RedHotSavvySleuth: I'm a bit out of touch locally since I've just moved back home after being away for a couple of years. Admittedly, I've been looking for a good distraction. The thought of taking on a local case is intriguing. I've never investigated one before. Anything else you can share?

Gotcha. Nash's lips curved into a wolfish grin. Haisley might have played hard to get last night, but online, when she had no idea who he was, her curiosity and her unwavering sense of justice would give him the in he needed. Drawing her in deeper would require an admittedly deft touch—and a delicate balance between flattery, facts, and intrigue.

> JasperThePrivateDick: Beyond the fact young women are disappearing—five in the last year or so—I can't find much. Nothing about an official investigation. But I only got a tip about these disappearances last night. They piqued my interest. Have you heard much locally?

> RedHotSavvySleuth: Nothing. Now that I think of it, that's weird. The city's rag usually reports any sort of criminal behavior, even a stolen bike or garden tools out of someone's garage. I can't imagine why they haven't reported on something this big.

> JasperThePrivateDick: Maybe someone is trying to keep it hush-hush? Possible corruption at play? Seems to be plenty of that everywhere these days. This case is something I'd love to sink my teeth into, but I live too far away to do the legwork. Since we started talking, I've read some of your posts. You're insightful, and you have a can-do attitude. Your local knowledge would be invaluable. I think we'd make one hell of a team. I have experience working disappearances, and I'm tenacious. You game?

> RedHotSavvySleuth: You make a compelling pitch, but I'm starting a new job tomorrow. I don't know how much time I'll have.

Fuck. Had he come on too strong? Or maybe she'd been hit on by a fellow crime solver before.

> JasperThePrivateDick: I get it. My schedule is erratic, and my job is demanding, too. I swear I'm not a perv hoping to send dick pics or ask you for nudes. I really want to get to the bottom of these disappearances, and I'm not close enough to do it myself. Don't these women deserve our help?

> RedHotSavvySleuth: They do. Clearly, someone taught you how to pack extra-heavy bags for that guilt trip.

> JasperThePrivateDick: Don't we all have grandmas? And I did mention that I'm tenacious. It's one of my charms…

> RedHotSavvySleuth: Charms? Is that how the people in your life would phrase that quality?

> JasperThePrivateDick: No comment. LOL! But I'm relentless when I'm in pursuit. Once I sink my teeth into something juicy, I won't let go until I'm fully satisfied. You'll find I can be insatiably thorough.

> RedHotSavvySleuth: My, my, Jasper. Is that silver tongue of yours making promises it can't keep? I hope you can back up that bravado with actual skill.

Haisley might be fuzzy on just how skilled his tongue was, but he'd be more than happy to remind her.

> JasperThePrivateDick: Hang around and find out.

> RedHotSavvySleuth: You are smooth and every bit as tenacious as you claimed. I'll give you that.

> JasperThePrivateDick: Yep. The question is, can you keep up?

> RedHotSavvySleuth: And you're cocky, too. Obviously, you don't know me. But trust me, I can keep pace without breaking a sweat. I love solving a good mystery. And I believe in justice.

That was such a Haisley answer. Good to know that, even if she was barely speaking to him, she hadn't changed.

> RedHotSavvySleuth: So tell me your angle. What about this particular case interests you?

> JasperThePrivateDick: I'm a protector by nature. This kind of crap shouldn't be happening. Women who want a new pair of shoes or whatever shouldn't have to fear for their lives.

> RedHotSavvySleuth: It sucks that more men don't feel this way. But you didn't answer my question. Why this case?

Nash grinned. Haisley was testing him, probing for ulterior motives. She was smart as hell, but he didn't intend to give up until he won her over and she agreed to partner with him on solving these disappearances. Slowly, he'd coax her, then, at the right moment, he would reveal himself...

> JasperThePrivateDick: Let's just say I believe in justice, too.

> RedHotSavvySleuth: You a cop? Or a PI, as your handle suggests?

> JasperThePrivateDick: Neither. I hate red tape, and I hate criminals. I also have a healthy appreciation for a woman who isn't afraid to dive in headfirst and get dirty for the right reasons. Since we have justice in common, I think we'll make one hell of a team, Red. My skills complementing your local expertise? We'll have this case spread wide open in no time. What do you say?

As he hit Send, anticipation rippled through Nash. He was playing a dangerous game. But the thrill of the chase, the delicious tension already simmering between them, was intoxicating.

> RedHotSavvySleuth: This case has piqued my curiosity, I'll admit. Why haven't I heard a peep about these disappearances? On the other hand, I never said I was looking for a partner.

> JasperThePrivateDick: You never said you weren't, either. C'mon…

> RedHotSavvySleuth: I should probably have my head examined, but tell me how you propose we tackle this case together?

Nash fist-pumped the air. Haisley was slowly but surely taking his bait. He licked his lips and carefully contemplated his next move.

> JasperThePrivateDick: How about we start with a little reconnaissance? I can dig through public records and see what I can uncover about these disappearances while you carefully see if anyone locally can shed some light. Then we'll circle back together and come up with a working theory or two. It will be exciting.

And if we happen to find ourselves in need of a private debriefing along the way—with our clothes off—I can think of worse fates.

As he waited for Haisley's response, Nash savored this delicious moment. The game was on, and he had no intention of backing down until Haisley was his again. He'd advance on multiple fronts until she waved her white flag and surrendered to him.

> RedHotSavvySleuth: I'm probably crazy, but it's a New Year. Why the hell not? Let's do it!

The aroma of freshly brewed coffee and warm pastries wafted through the cozy Sunday brunch spot as Haisley settled into the plush booth.

Across from her, Charli looked as gorgeous as always—a tumble of rich, dark curls spilling over her shoulders, skin so perfect it would make an esthetician cry, and a body that owed its shapeliness to good genes and a faithful gym habit. Before Haisley had moved to Cali, Charli had been full of party, snark, and grab-life-by-the-throat fun.

She barely recognized this version of her friend, subdued and almost painfully quiet.

It had been so long since they'd spent quality time together. Guilt filled Haisley for letting too many months slip past them. Naturally, she'd attended Charli's Vegas wedding last year...but Haisley hadn't seen much of her—or the rest of her girl posse—since. Thank god that, regardless of the miles or years that once separated them, their longstanding friendship made getting together feel as if almost no time had passed.

"Thanks for inviting me this morning. I was itching to get out of the house." Charli smiled, but her hazel eyes dimmed with a troubling sadness. "I know the circumstances that brought you home aren't ideal, but I'm glad you're back for good."

"Thanks. Losing Aunt Cynthia shocked me. She'd been sick for a while, from what I understand. Not that she ever told me."

"You two were never close."

They hadn't been, no matter how much Haisley had wished otherwise when she'd been a kid. "So being back here... I'm dealing with lots of memories and not many of them good."

For the grieving girl suffering the sudden loss of her loving mother, Haisley had hoped her mom's younger sister would fill that gaping hole in her heart. Instead, her aunt had given her a decade of chilly resentment before kicking her out.

"I know, sweetie." Charli's expression softened as she reached across the table to squeeze Haisley's hand. "I was surprised you moved back but selfishly happy. You really think you're staying for good?"

"Yeah. Aunt Cynthia owned the house outright, so I have a free place to live for life. I hate that we never resolved our differences, but I'm lucky. A house without a mortgage is something many people will never have."

"You're right about that. Daniel and I have been saving for a down payment since the day we got married. He's obsessed."

Something about that clearly made Charli sad. But her friend didn't elaborate, and her face closed up. Questions filled Haisley, but she hated to pry. Charli seemed so fragile, so Haisley steered the conversation elsewhere.

"LA was cool...sometimes. But I missed home. When I got the call about my aunt's passing, my lease was about to expire. It felt like the right time to leave Cali and put down roots. Besides"—she dropped her gaze to the steaming coffee their waiter slid across the table—"I missed everyone."

"We missed you."

Quickly, the women placed their orders, both choosing favorites, heedless of calories. Once the waiter left, Charli slanted a skeptical gaze her way. "Are you sure there isn't more to your decision to move home? Did Nash have anything to do with it?"

Haisley tried not to feel the stab of pain in her heart. "That's over."

Charli raised a brow. "It didn't look that way on New Year's Eve."

"Just the celebratory moment. Besides, we'd both had too much to drink."

"You were once head over heels for him."

"Ancient history." Haisley willed herself to believe it. "We weren't meant to be. We wanted different things."

"I get that." Charli's gaze grew distant, her shoulders slumping as she heaved a melancholy sigh.

Prying now was too much...but Haisley couldn't resist some gentle nudges. "You don't look happy. What's going on with you and Daniel? Don't tell me nothing. I know better."

She shrugged as if the weight of the world were on her shoulders. "I don't even know. One day, everything was perfect. The next, we were like strangers living in the same house."

"Oh, honey. I'm so sorry. If you want to talk about it, I'm happy to listen. Where was he on New Year's Eve?"

"At home. In bed. Asleep." Charli shook her head despondently. "I thought we wanted the same things. But lately, it feels like we're living two different lives."

Haisley ached for her friend, the raw anguish in Charli's voice resonating in her own bruised heart.

"If he had another woman, my decision would be simple. I would just leave his ass. But no, he's always working, always talking about getting ahead, saving to buy a house, and preparing for the future so we can support the children we'll have someday. I know he's right... but it feels like he's putting his job first. And when he is home, he's exhausted. He barely pays attention to me unless he wants sex. It's like he's not really there, you know? Like I'm a pretty fuck doll he feels a responsibility to take care of. Decoration instead of a flesh-and-blood wife. I can help. I work, too. I contribute. But he insists that looking out for me is his responsibility. I can't fault him. He takes care of everything...except my heart."

Haisley squeezed her friend's hand. She understood disappointment too well. Love, she had learned the hard way, was typically painful. All the fairy tales lied.

"Have you talked to him?"

"Of course." Charli sighed, her shoulders sagging with defeat. "But it's like he doesn't hear me. Or understand. He just goes on like I didn't say I'd rather have him home than for him take on a special project that will get him promoted faster. I feel like background noise in his life."

Haisley felt a surge of protectiveness and clenched her free hand into a fist beneath the table. To see her confident, vibrant friend so defeated was like a knife to the heart.

"Listen to me. You're way more than 'background noise.' You are an incredible woman, and you should be his queen. If Daniel can't put you on his throne, then he's an idiot."

"Hais, I..." Charli teared up. "I don't know what to do. When we got married, this isn't at all the life I pictured."

"Don't cry. We'll figure it out." She gave Charli's hand a reassuring squeeze. "Together. Like we always have."

As she nodded miserably, Charli's tears fell. "My disintegrating marriage is all I think about."

"Then you need a distraction until you two can work it out. Maybe you should join my online sleuthing group, Crime Solvers International. CSI works together to solve cold cases, share theories, and put our detective skills to the test."

Despite her tears, Charli smiled fondly. "Of course you'd join a group like that. You always had a knack for putting together puzzles and solving mysteries."

"It's a lot of fun, and it will definitely help to occupy your thoughts. And you'll make some cool new friends…"

"I already have cool friends. You, Gracelyn, and Madison are the best."

"Naturally." Grinning, Haisley sent her an exaggerated hair flip. "But seriously. Join us for an evening. I just jumped onto a new case. It's local, which makes it even juicier."

"I don't know. With everything going on with Daniel…"

"That's exactly why you should join. He has purpose. Since you're not married to your job, you should find one, too." So she wouldn't have to focus on her sadness so much. "Then maybe you'll find some balance. And if you don't"—she gave Charli's hand a reassuring squeeze—"solving crimes with me will be fun."

"I'll think about it. Have you made new friends in the group?"

"Tons. The guy who runs it is a retired cop from Vegas. Super interesting. The moderators either have law enforcement, legal, or military background. The members are all super smart. And the group is growing. In fact, a new guy just joined yesterday. Jasper is the one who talked me into helping him with the case happening right here in Lafayette. Something about young women disappearing from the new outlet mall up the road?"

"Interesting." Charli arched a brow. "Is Jasper cute?"

"I don't know. It's an online group."

Charli waved a dismissive hand. "Details. Was he flirty?"

"More friendly than flirty, but that's the way I want it. I'm steering clear of romance."

"Maybe you should flirt with him. Jasper might be just what you need to get over Nash once and for all."

"I wish." Haisley wasn't convinced that was possible.

Before she'd left LA, she'd been so certain she was finally over that man. But after one amazing, toe-curling New Year's Eve kiss, he'd destroyed that hope.

Charli's expression softened. "You deserve happiness. And who knows, maybe your online mystery guy will help you find some."

"Maybe." Haisley shrugged. "Or maybe there's no such thing as happily ever after, at least for someone like me."

"Someone like you? You mean someone awesome? You're more lovable than you know. The right guy will come along."

"Sure." She told Charli what she wanted to hear. "Now, tell me all the gossip around town I've missed..."

As their conversation drifted to lighter topics, Haisley fought encroaching sadness.

No man had ever gotten to her the way Nash did. She didn't think another ever would. Living almost two thousand miles from him had been painful enough. Living around the corner from him, so to speak, was bound to be agony. What would happen when he finally lost interest in her and focused on someone else? What if, heaven forbid, he got married, and she had to see the happy couple around town?

It would crush her.

Why hadn't she seen heartbreak coming when she'd started hardcore flirting back with him all those months ago? Why hadn't she foreseen how totally falling for him would break her heart?

CHAPTER SEVEN

On Sunday afternoon, Nash stretched out on his battered leather couch, nursing a cold beer as the Packers-Vikings game flickered across his TV screen. Despite the fact nearly forty-eight hours had passed since New Year's Eve, his thoughts kept drifting back to the scorching kiss he'd laid on Haisley. Even mass amounts of tequila couldn't dim the memory of her soft curves molded against his body, those sinful lips under his as he devoured her for the first time in two agonizing years.

His blood ran hot, despite the lingering chill of the winter morning. Then again, the gorgeous redhead had always set him on fire. From the moment he'd met her, Haisley's saucy aloofness had ignited him. During their year together, his instant and burning need to give her pleasure had become a never-ending urge to make her his.

The shrill ring of his cellphone shattered his reverie. Nash frowned at the familiar number flashing across the display and braced himself. "Hey, boss. Happy New Year."

"Yep. Same to you." Hunter Edgington was a former SEAL, and, as usual, the man's gruff tone signaled that he had no patience for pleasantries. "We've got a new job, and you're up."

So much for a lazy afternoon indulging in fantasies about Haisley naked in his bed as his lips blazed kisses across her skin, down to focus on her sweet, dripping pussy. Nash sat up straighter. "What's the op?"

"Heard anything about young women going missing from that new mall?"

Holy shit. Someone had hired EM Security to look into this case? And Hunter was assigning him? After Nash had agreed to study it with Haisley? Talk about ironic…

If his hunch was right, Nash understood why Hunter had prefaced his new assignment with that question. The disappearances had barely made a blip in the local press. In the last couple of days, he'd looked. All he'd found were a few vague bulletins quickly buried in the local news cycle.

"Not nearly as much as I should be. I'm smelling a cover-up." Like someone rich and powerful was working overtime to keep a tight lid on the whole sordid mess.

Hunter grunted in grim agreement. "That's my read, too. After the most recent disappearance, the mall's developer, George Benedict, hired EM Security to get to the bottom of the incidents. I think we're his out with the press and law enforcement so he can claim he's doing 'everything possible' to stop the abductions."

Nash frowned. He didn't know much about the wealthy local real estate mogul, just whispers—mostly that Benedict was a blowhard whose sole concerns were making money and preserving his interests. Dealing with him and his BS wasn't something Nash was looking forward to, but business was business.

"Know if he's done anything to stop the abductions prior to hiring us?"

"From what I can gather, the minimum for optics. He upgraded the tech some and hired a few new guards. That kind of shit. Nothing actually likely to stop the kidnappings."

Hunter was rarely wrong, and Nash agreed with his boss's assessment. "Think Benedict has anything to do with these disappearances?"

"Anything is possible."

"We doing recon on him, too, or just running a straightforward op?" Nash scrubbed a hand over his stubbled jaw.

"For now, we play nice and keep this aboveboard," Hunter insisted.

"EM Security will handle the investigation into those missing women, end of story. But if the trail leads you to Benedict, we'll start sorting his dirty laundry. Quietly, mind you. He can't know."

Nash huffed, resigning himself to navigating the situation with kid gloves—at least for the time being. Looking for angles and ulterior motives was second nature to him, but he couldn't deny the urgency of this case. Five young women had gone missing under very suspicious circumstances from the same spot in the last handful of months—and since powerful players were doing their damnedest to keep that buried, Nash suspected the case would be rough.

Under his online alias, he'd have to be careful about feeding Haisley and her inquisitive spirit too many details. The last thing Nash wanted was to put her in harm's way, especially if this case turned as insidious as his gut warned. She was clever—sometimes too much. She loved to snoop and dig, so he'd have to keep her part of the investigation chewing on theories and information while she stayed safely at home. Unfortunately, he couldn't shake the worry that she might push to get deeper. Or worse, start her own investigation.

"Understood," he said at length. "What are my marching orders?"

"Report to Benedict's office at ten hundred tomorrow for briefing and standby. I'm slotting Ethan to partner with you. He needs the experience of dealing with difficult clients and not just saying fuck you to authority all the time. I'm counting on you to make sure he doesn't trip over his own dick out there."

A reluctant grin tugged at Nash's mouth. No surprise that Hunter wanted him to babysit Ethan. His housemate had slowly become a friend, but Nash knew the kid's weaknesses. One of them was his short temper, especially when he perceived injustice...or when someone in a position of power tried to tell him what to do. He could balance Ethan. And together, they'd proven that, despite bending the rules occasionally, they got results.

"Roger that."

"I need you to listen." Hunter's insistent bark pulled Nash from his musings. "This must be an airtight op. We'll be dealing with the press and some powerful people in this town. No deviating from protocol or pulling that shady, back-alley shit you two loose screws seem to favor."

Nash held back a mirthless chuckle. So much for operational flexibility. "I read you loud and clear, boss. We'll be model fucking Boy Scouts."

"Sure you will." The muffled sound of feminine sarcasm filtered through. No doubt that was Hunter's wife, Kata.

"I'm serious," Hunter insisted. "Handle this clean and by the book, or there will be hell to pay."

"We're on it."

Hunter ended the call with a grunt of a goodbye, leaving Nash alone once more with his swirling thoughts. He strode toward the bathroom for a much-needed, scalding-hot shower. If today was his last day off before the grim case started sucking up most of his time, he wanted to see Haisley.

They had some talking to do.

If she gave him a chilly reception, he wouldn't be daunted. He'd simply drop in to her CSI online group as JasperThePrivateDick and engage her about theories. No doubt, she'd already started sifting through whatever information she could find. Besides, now that he'd be working this case, might as well start piecing together what information he could.

As the pounding stream rinsed away the residue of his earlier workout, Nash steeled his resolve. One way or another, he would unravel the secrets behind the disappearances of these women while rekindling his connection with Haisley. He wouldn't quit, wouldn't stop, wouldn't give up until everything was right.

And no offense to Hunter, but whatever rules Nash had to bend—or outright break—to make it happen... Well, like always, he'd do what needed to be done.

Haisley smoothed her hand over her sleek black skirt as she strode into the historic building in downtown Lafayette, hoping her nerves didn't show. Today marked a fresh start for her, a chance to establish herself professionally in her hometown. Her new employer might deal in land acquisition, development, and maintenance, but their online presence was somewhere between old school and nonexistent. It needed a strategic overhaul and a fresh approach. She was determined to give it to them and up her own stock in the process.

The expansive lobby, a blend of old and new world charm, gleamed with polished marble and glass, providing an air of understated luxury. Haisley drew in a steadying breath and approached the curved reception desk where a stylishly dressed young woman offered her a warm smile.

"Good morning."

"Hi, I'm Haisley Rowe." She repositioned her purse strap higher on her shoulder. "I'm starting with Benedict Land Development today."

The receptionist's smile brightened. "Mr. Benedict is expecting you. Take the elevator to the fourth floor. I'll call up there and let someone know you're coming."

"Thank you," Haisley called back as she hustled to the elevator.

After the ding and the doors opened again, she stepped off. Another receptionist sitting behind a giant desk emblazoned with the company name in big, gold letters pressed the phone to her ear and jotted a message while waving her into a nearby chair.

Crossing one leg over the other, Haisley managed a tight smile as the butterflies dive-bombed her belly.

An imposing, broad-shouldered man in a tailored charcoal suit strode toward her, hand outstretched. "Ms. Rowe?"

When his gruff bark cracked through the quiet opulence of the lobby, she shot to her feet and plastered on her most confident smile. Despite the graying at his temples and the faint lines around his eyes, he carried himself with a robust vitality. Clearly, this man was a doer. If that was their corporate culture, she should fit right in.

"Mr. Benedict?" She shook his hand.

He gave her a cursory once-over, then nodded. "Welcome aboard. After our phone interviews, it's good to meet you in person. Welcome to Benedict Land Development."

"Thank you. It's great to put a face with a name. I'm thrilled to be here—and back home in Louisiana."

He sauntered past the reception desk and motioned her to follow before he turned toward a maze of workspaces. "Come with me. I'll introduce you to a few key players and show you to your desk. The rest of the team can fill in the blanks as you get settled."

Haisley fell into step beside him, her kitten heels clicking against the gleaming floors. Along the way, Mr. Benedict pointed out various workgroups. Each stopped to give her a polite smile before resuming their work. She did her best to commit their names and locations to memory.

"In that corner, next to the window, is your desk. You'll have an assistant once we hire someone. I thought you might want to be part of the process."

"I would. Thank you."

"The rest of your team—Angela, Curtis, and Blake—is looking forward to your fresh perspective and the experience you gleaned in LA."

The trio glanced up, offering tepid nods of acknowledgment. Clearly, she would need to earn their respect. She'd been there and done that when she'd first arrived in LA. She'd eventually win them over.

"Mila!" Mr. Benedict hollered as they veered down a hall lined with offices.

"You bellowed, husband?" A lilting feminine voice drew Haisley's attention toward the open door of a nearby office.

A petite, polished woman about a dozen years the boss's junior emerged with a warm smile, blue eyes crinkling at the corners. Dressed in a smart blazer and slim-cut trousers, Mila Benedict projected a friendly, effortless elegance.

"I'm showing Haisley the ropes." Mr. Benedict's intimidating edges softened as his wife sidled closer. "Mila, this is Haisley Rowe. Haisley, my wife, Mila."

"It's lovely to meet you." The woman enveloped her hand in a gentle squeeze, her delicate ring finger adorned with a huge, glimmering diamond. "Hopefully, you'll breathe some fresh life into our branding."

"That's my goal, Mrs. Benedict. I'm excited to get started."

"Oh, please, call me Mila. The last thing we need around here is more formality. Isn't that right, George?" She sent her husband a teasing glance, laughing when he huffed. "Why don't you get settled in, then we'll debrief you on everything. I'm sorry to say we've got something of an emergency on our hands, so today will be a bit of a fire drill."

"In my last position, change and chaos were constant. I'm used to it, and I'll contribute in any way I can."

George grunted, then doubled back and began leading her toward the open room full of desks.

Frowning, she called to Mila over her shoulder, "Let me know when you're ready, and we'll convene."

As the woman nodded, she and Mr. Benedict rounded the corner. Was he that impatient for her to get started? Or was he always dismissive of his wife? The politest way to describe his demeanor during their interview was brusque. Just now, he'd all but tugged her away. The whole thing felt borderline rude.

No wonder the job had come with such great pay. Her new boss had a reputation for being an asshole. Haisley suspected he'd earned it.

"Tell me something, Miss Rowe," he muttered as he stopped in front of the coffeemaker tucked in the corner and began brewing a cup. "Coffee?"

"I had a cup at home, thanks."

Mr. Benedict sighed. "What do you think this company's greatest social media challenge is?"

She hadn't expected to be put on the spot so soon, but she'd already given this question a lot of thought. "I see a couple of areas of opportunity for you. First, the average person doesn't have a great opinion of land developers and real-estate moguls in general. I mean, everyone wants to be rich, but no one likes people who *are* rich."

He barked out a laugh. "That's true, but—"

"Not your biggest problem, I know. The second issue is that you've made a career out of creating retail spaces all over the South, but a lot of them are malls…which are slowly dying."

"Because you Gen-Z and Millennial types would rather shop on your phones than change out of your pajama pants, comb your hair, leave your houses, and interact with actual people."

It was Haisley's turn to laugh. "Guilty. But right now, your biggest problem is something else entirely. Something you don't know how to stop."

George paused. "I'm listening."

"You're struggling with the disappearances of those young women at Oakfield Mall, right?"

Surprise crossed his face. "You've heard about that, huh? Tell me what you know."

"Only what's trickled out: that a handful of young women have gone missing these past few months, but nothing comprehensive or detailed. I'll bet that's by design. You've largely kept a lid on this situation. Normally, the local press would have screamed these salacious headlines. But they've barely reported on the incidents."

Still, if the disturbing string of missing persons became common knowledge, the shit would hit the fan. Mr. Benedict had to be prepared for that possibility. The best defense was a good offense—or however the saying went.

"Because I've done everything in my power to keep the situation contained. For reasons that should be obvious."

George Benedict was clearly more interested in saving his financial ass than the young women who had vanished without a trace. He'd squelched their stories and buried their search efforts under a thick veneer of silence. How long before the victims faded from public consciousness altogether, leaving those captured without hope?

Haisley understood his decision from a business perspective—but she hated it. How could he live with himself as a man? As a human being? "I see."

"I told the local press I would pull my significant advertising budget if they didn't keep their mouths shut. In the rare instances that didn't work, I threatened to sue. So most of the reporting has been page-six stuff, and my name has never been mentioned." He scowled. "You disapprove."

Haisley wasn't surprised that her face gave her away. "People aren't stupid. You're well known in this part of the state, and I'm sure they remember the fanfare when the mall opened last spring. The most recent disappearance happening on Christmas Eve was particularly heartrending. That terrified moms everywhere. Has foot traffic been down since?"

"Yes. But I expected that. Christmas is over."

"Still, these problems must be making an impact." And whether she disapproved or not, he'd hired her to do a job. "You need an image rehab that shows you're concerned about customers' safety without admitting culpability. We've got to get you positive community vibes. That's where I come in."

And while she devised spin all day because he paid her to, she'd spend her evenings working with JasperThePrivateDick and her CSI group to hopefully solve this case and stop these abductions. Her penance for doing business with the devil.

She had no idea who Jasper was or if that was even his name, but he seemed smart. He was definitely tenacious. Together, they might be able to blow this case wide open. Then there would be no more victims, and she'd have so much positive press to dish out for her new boss that Mr. Benedict would happily reward her. Maybe they'd even be able to find the women who had been abducted. A win all the way around.

And Jasper made her smile. After her New Year's Eve debacle with Nash, she desperately needed a distraction, especially since she seemed to be on his radar again.

After the way he'd kissed her that night, she wasn't foolish enough to think he'd given up. She'd have to devise creative ways to keep distance between them. Otherwise, it would be too easy to give in to her feelings. She'd tried to purge him from her heart…but she still missed him way more than was smart.

She had instigated their split for his own good. Why wouldn't he just accept that?

Her boss's jaw tightened. "What are your plans for these positive vibes?"

"I have a few thoughts, but I'll need more information before I can develop a solid plan."

"Oakfield Mall is one of my most valued—and problematic—properties. Those incidents you're aware of? Those five missing women? There were three other thwarted attempts that never reached the press. Unfortunately, those women who got away never saw anyone or noticed anything helpful. All these incidents occurred on the mall's premises, despite the upgraded tech and security guards I pay through the ass for. Somehow, every measure fails. The cameras blipped for twenty minutes on Christmas Eve, just as Kaylee Wright was abducted. It's like someone knows the property's weaknesses and can guess my every move. If I can't stop this, it's going to ruin me. Two of the missing girls' families are threatening to sue."

A chill skated down Haisley's spine. Having such sinister crimes happening in her own backyard, to young women just starting their lives… It was terrifying and unthinkable. "I had no idea the situation was so dire. So seemingly…deliberate."

"Neither did I—at first. Not until the latest victim. But that phone call was a gut punch. It destroyed my wife's Christmas. I knew I had to take more drastic measures."

Haisley risked a sidelong glance at her new boss. His expression remained impassive as he gazed out the floor-to-ceiling window. Did this incident bother him beyond the financial?

Maybe she was being too harsh. She hardly knew him, and some people didn't wear their emotions on their faces.

"So what 'drastic measures' did you take?"

"Follow me."

He led her toward the contemporary U-shaped desk he'd pointed out earlier. A laptop sat waiting as he gestured her into a black ergonomic chair. This was where she'd be spending most of her waking hours. It wasn't fancy, but at least she was near a window.

She opened the lid on her laptop and was immediately prompted for a password.

"Before I say anything else, do you have any recommendations from a PR perspective?" he asked.

"Attacking the problem head-on. We can continue spinning your social media. You didn't ask me, but you should consider hiring someone more competent than the local police and mall cops to solve the problem quickly and discreetly."

"I'm a step ahead of you. I didn't just hire 'someone.' I hired highly trained operatives from one of the most elite private security firms in the region, if not the country. They'll get to the bottom of these abductions, utilizing every resource at their disposal."

At least he was done fucking around. "Good. Once they've accomplished their mission, we'll go wild with the press."

He nodded in approval. "I'd like you to work with these security experts, provide them whatever information they need from this office, and stay apprised of what they're doing so that if anything is press or social-media worthy, you can start getting Oakfield—and us—some wins with the public."

Resolve buoyed Haisley. These cases dredged up the worst of today's world, but she couldn't deny the sense of purpose at the prospect of putting her skills to meaningful use. In order to help end this horrible string of crimes and make the world safer—even if it was just her hometown—she'd give it her all.

"You can count on me, Mr. Benedict. I'll do whatever it takes to assist their investigation and highlight their progress through all our media and public channels."

"Good." He smiled faintly. "I hired you for your spirit and gumption."

"When will I meet the operatives you hired?"

From behind, she heard heavy footfalls approach. Haisley turned as a broad-shouldered silhouette emerged, backlit by the blinding morning. The world dropped out from beneath her...

CHAPTER EIGHT

A painfully familiar figure filled Haisley's vision. She couldn't breathe.

Nash.

Oh, shit.

Her heart rattled in her chest as she took in his rugged features, all chiseled angles and battle-hardened edges. He looked just like he had the night of their heated kiss—powerfully built beneath the snug black tee that hugged the sculpted contours of his physique and gripped his tatted biceps. A black leather cuff encircled his thick left wrist. His inscrutable onyx stare landed on her, scorching her from across the room.

She licked her suddenly parched lips, assailed by visions of their kiss at Highrise, of Nash's body pressing her into the unforgiving wall, of the slick heat of his mouth trailing a searing path down her throat, of the steel bands of his arms engulfing her in his embrace while he drank her in like a man dying of thirst.

Haisley swallowed hard against the sudden, visceral rush of bone-deep attraction.

Recognition sparked in Nash's gaze. A flicker of something deeper Haisley couldn't decipher crossed his face. His brow furrowed with a primal dare that raised the fine hairs along Haisley's nape. Then his expression shuttered closed.

Mr. Benedict stared between them, frowning as if trying to grasp the sudden undercurrent. "Are you Nash Scott? This is Haisley Rowe, our new social media director. Haisley, Nash is one of the operatives who will be leading EM Security Management's investigation into the…situation at the mall."

Several beats of charged silence stretched between them, thin and taut.

Suddenly, Mila appeared, her giggle slicing through the tension. "Looks like you two have already met."

Nash turned a scorching gaze on the boss's wife. Mila's playfulness vanished.

Haisley gave herself a mental shake and forced a smile. She was not about to clue in her new boss—or his nosy wife—about her old flame. "Nice to make your acquaintance once again, Mr. Scott. I look forward to assisting your team in any way I can."

Another heavy pause hung between them, rife with all the things they couldn't say. Not here. Not with witnesses present. Not with their tangled history. And definitely not with the secrets she was keeping.

Then Nash's jaw took on a stubborn set, his expression an impassive slab of granite. "I'm sure you do, Ms. Rowe. I look forward to working very closely with you."

His words rang like a vow—equal parts unspoken promise and veiled threat. Despite the perspiration prickling along her hairline, a reckless thrill jetted through Haisley's veins. A matching excitement pooled between her legs.

The man did that to her every damn time she saw him.

Nash's burning expression launched a thousand memories of him kissing her, of him peeling off her clothes, of him with his head buried between her legs as she pleaded for release, of him fucking her relentlessly until she saw stars.

She felt herself blushing and tried to look away, but his intent stare wouldn't let her escape.

Mr. Benedict cleared his throat, shaking off the awkward air that had settled over them. "Yes, well, you two can become…reacquainted after we've addressed a few critical matters." He turned to Nash and lifted his jaw in a gesture of brisk authority. "As soon as you're able, I want a status update on the investigation into the missing women. Have you started your preliminary look into this? Made any headway yet?"

"I'm still gathering information, sir. My associate, Mr. Garrison, is interviewing potential witnesses today. I'll be reviewing the information you passed on and combine it with whatever Ethan finds. We'll pursue every available lead—official channels, underworld sources, whatever it takes. I'm even extending some online feelers into the more...unconventional spheres. And I'll factor in anything Ms. Rowe passes my way."

Nash slanted her a hooded stare, causing the fine hairs along her nape to prickle again. A frisson of tension slid through her, adding to the lingering thrill of his proximity.

When she hadn't heard from him all weekend, part of her had hoped that kiss was the booze and the festivities talking and that he'd keep distance between them. His expression told her the chance of that happening was zero, especially now that they'd been tossed together by her boss and dangerous circumstances.

Nash planned to pursue her again; it was all over his face.

What the hell was she supposed to do?

"Leave no stone unturned," Mr. Benedict demanded, his voice low. "I didn't spend all this time and money to bring your outfit here on a lark. I need results before this situation spirals out of control. Another incident like that poor girl on Christmas Eve, and I'm concerned I won't be able to hold back the press. They'll have a field day, never mind the liability..."

"Of course. You have my word. EM Security will do everything possible. Whoever is behind these abductions won't be able to fart without us knowing."

"I expect you to keep that promise. And work closely with Ms. Rowe." Mr. Benedict sighed—a weary, bone-deep exhalation—before he turned toward her once more. "And you, Ms. Rowe, I trust you'll cooperate with Mr. Scott, whatever he needs?"

His words fed treacherous impulses—of her stripping for him, kneeling for him, spreading her legs for him—like she'd done at least a hundred times in the past. Haisley stamped out the visions before the sparks ignited into a blaze. "I'll do everything I can to aid in damage control and information flow on the public relations front pertaining to this case, yes." She risked a glimpse at Nash through her lashes. "In that regard, I'm at your operative's disposal."

She chose her words carefully, but if the sharp tic in his jaw was any indication, he got the message. Since they'd been thrown together, she intended to keep their interaction purely professional.

"I'll devote myself to making this partnership with Ms. Rowe work. That's a promise."

Haisley tried not to panic at Nash's innuendo. He was a shiver-inducing magnetic force of nature—distracting enough from afar. But to have to work with him day in and day out, when the temptation to give in to him would be so strong?

She. Was. Screwed.

No. Innocent lives and her employer's reputation hung precariously in the balance. She couldn't allow Nash to be more than a working partner—no matter how deliciously her body burned to rekindle their connection.

The past would haunt them. The truth would only destroy them. Next time he tempted her—and he would—she needed to keep all that in mind.

Haisley's boss retreated to his office down the hall, finally leaving them alone—if Nash didn't count her curious coworkers unabashedly staring.

He turned his gaze to her. "Well, Ms. Rowe. What a surprise. I didn't expect to see you here."

But he'd hoped. And he was damn glad his hunch had been right, especially after he'd worked up the courage to stop by her place and knock on her door last night. She hadn't been home. Or she simply hadn't answered. And he must be a perverse SOB because, despite everything, having her this close again, yet so far away, made him want her more than ever.

She stiffened, her pulse visibly jackhammering. Nash felt a primal sense of satisfaction that he could still rattle her.

"Let's get coffee." She grabbed his arm and all but dragged him into the cubby on the other end of the floor, away from everyone else. Her hands trembled as she poured herself a cup from the pot. "For the record, I didn't expect you here, either."

"Well, you're stuck with me."

"We need to set some ground rules. This will be a strictly professional relationship."

Nash stepped into her space, reaching past her to grab a Styrofoam cup and deliberately brushing against her. He watched her swallow hard. "You think? I distinctly remember our relationship being anything but."

Her pupils blew wide. God, he'd missed seeing desire war with restraint on her beautiful face…usually before she gave in to him.

"Those days are over," she insisted, though she sounded breathless. "I told you on New Year's Eve that I can't do this again. We're not repeating ancient history, understood?"

It was hard to take her seriously when her nipples hardened and poked the front of her blouse.

He grinned, loving that she was still so responsive to him, to the molten chemistry simmering between them, no matter how much she wanted to pretend otherwise. "Trying to convince me there's no fire between us is futile."

"Whatever you think is between us is in the past—and it's staying there. So we'll divide and conquer on this case. You pursue leads and see if you can figure out who's behind these abductions and how to stop them. Keep me posted on whatever you find. I'll handle research and everything PR-related. Anything I come across that I think might be helpful to your investigation, I'll email you. Thanks for the chat." With that dismissive quip and an accompanying pat on the shoulder, she abandoned her cup of coffee and broke for her desk.

Nash wrapped his fingers around her arm and dragged her back flush against his chest. "We'll try it your way, but I know you, Haisley.

So let me be clear. Though we're a team, you will *not* poke your nose into anything that could potentially turn ugly. You don't put yourself in danger. I'll handle all that. Step a toe out of line, and I'll spank you."

She whirled, her eyes flaring with anger. "Like hell you will! You're not touching me, and you're not treating me like some wilting damsel. I can handle myself."

Unable to resist pushing her buttons further, Nash bent closer until his lips were a scorching whisper from her ear. He could feel the blistering heat radiating from her, could smell her arousal as her breathing turned shallow.

"Maybe so, but I'm not taking any chances when it comes to your safety. End of discussion."

No matter how capable she was, he wouldn't allow her to put herself in harm's way. An image of her falling into the hands of whoever was abducting these young women, of them brutalizing her body, flashed through his mind. He clenched his jaw and shoved away the vision.

"Ugh." She tossed her hands in the air. "This is exactly why we shouldn't be partners. You make me insane."

"Can't handle the tension between us?"

"I can handle anything you can dish out, but you're already trying to dictate terms. I'm not putting up with it, and I'm not risking my professional future."

Nash dropped his voice to a gravelly murmur, knowing she could feel his words like a physical caress. "You not taking risks? We both know you're a divining rod for pushing limits. Why fight it now?"

Her face tightened. "Can you at least pretend to respect my boundaries?"

"Sure. When you stop pretending there's nothing between us."

"Who says I'm pretending?"

"You forget how well I know you, baby."

When she opened her mouth to protest, Nash silenced her by trailing a scorching fingertip down the side of her exposed neck. The shudder that rolled through her revealed her body's blatant betrayal. She didn't want to admit that she still wanted him, but on a primal level, she did.

He leaned even closer to savor her intoxicating scent, wishing he could kiss her. Even the thought sent heat straight to his cock.

Haisley's shallow breaths mingled with his own in the charged atmosphere. He could practically taste the tension pinging between them. Part of him knew he should stop this cat-and-mouse game, guard himself and not give her a chance to shatter his heart again.

But her eyes still burned with that same reckless spark that had drawn him in all those years ago. The same spark that made rational thought fly out the window whenever he was around her, consequences be damned.

"You're playing with fire," she whispered, but her tone carried more breathless excitement than warning.

She was right. Last time they got close, this heated friction ended in a scorched trail of wreckage. It might end that way again.

Right now, Nash didn't care.

"I can stand the heat. How about you?" He watched her resolve waver as he closed the infinitesimal gap between their bodies and settled his mouth against the delicate shell of her ear. "Admit it. You've missed the friction between us."

"No."

"Liar." He grazed the sensitive skin below her ear with his lips, watching a shiver wrack her and her eyes slide shut as she seemed to lose herself in sensation. "What are you afraid of?"

Nash wished like hell he knew the answer. For two years, he wondered what had driven her away. He'd combed through their final few nights together. Had she really been horrified by what they did in bed? She'd never given him any indication of that…until she'd ended things. Why hadn't she just talked to him? Haisley had never been shy about speaking her mind.

"I'm not afraid of anything, especially you." She placed a firm hand on his chest and shoved him back. "We've been back here too long, and people are going to talk. It's my first day, so could you please not screw this job up for me with your caveman crap? Whatever you think this was, it's over. We're here to solve a case, not rekindle our old flame."

"Is that what you really want, to walk away from this heat between us again? Without talking this out or seeing what could be? Look me in the eyes and tell me you don't feel this same desire to fuck your little rules and see what's left."

Haisley's chest heaved. She opened her mouth, no doubt to issue another bullshit denial, but the words seemed to stick in her throat. They both knew she felt something for him. The exhilarating, forbidden pull glowed in her blue eyes.

What the fuck was holding her back?

The tension between them thickened. Nash could practically taste her inner turmoil. Would one more well-placed touch have her throwing caution to the wind—and herself into his arms? Or would it drive her away for good?

"It's over, Nash."

It wasn't. Every part of her body—from her beseeching stare, to the way she licked her lips, and ending with her shallow breaths—told him that.

The only question was, what should he do about it?

Pushing her now wasn't the answer. He couldn't risk ruining whatever chance he had with her. Besides, they both had jobs to do, and like him, she took hers seriously. He had to find the willpower to resist stepping over the line and change tactics. Since he wanted to win her back, he needed to find his goddamn patience and play a long game.

"We'll see." He set his cup down and stepped away with a raised brow full of challenge. "For now, I'm going to confer with Ethan and start interviewing the existing security staff at the mall, look at their cameras and the rest of their tech setup, and see what I can find. You dig up the architectural plans for the structure and any outbuildings. I want permits, schematics—anything you can give me. I'll let you know what I find."

His chest constricting as he forced himself to leave her, Nash turned away—only to be stopped short when her fingers wrapped around his forearm in a desperate grip.

"Wait."

The urgent note in her trembling voice stopped him. He turned back, his gaze locking onto her beautiful face as he fought the urge to take her in his arms and soothe her. "Yeah?"

"Be careful. These people are clearly dangerous. Depraved, even."

"I'll be fine. I'm hardly their usual target."

"I'm serious. I...I don't want anything to happen to you," Haisley confessed in a hoarse whisper.

A wave of tenderness crashed through Nash. Despite her protestations and anger, she still cared. If he'd truly been too rough or kinky or whatever fill-in-the-blank excuse she'd had for breaking things off, she wouldn't be staring at him like her whole world would fracture if these twisted monsters took him down.

Of their own accord, his feet carried him back to her. Nash nudged her into the cubby again, out of her coworkers' sight. Cupping her face, he drank in every delicate angle and curve. He gently stroked the silken skin of her cheeks with his calloused thumbs as her worried eyes searched his.

"Don't worry, baby," he rasped in a voice thick with emotion. "You haven't seen the last of me."

CHAPTER NINE

The rest of the day passed in an emotion-filled haze. Nash walking into her office to be her counterpart investigating these disappearances at the mall had knocked her world off its well-ordered axis. The trio of people in her group—the ones whose trust she needed to win—had all stared at her when she'd returned empty-handed after a full ten minutes in the refreshment cubby with Nash.

Angela lifted her pierced brow. "No coffee, huh? Were you back there getting something other than a steaming cup of java?"

She ignored the woman and went about her day, setting up her computer, her voicemail, and meeting the other important people in her office. But she felt scattered. No, rattled by the thought of investigating so much as a missing paperclip with Nash.

She also hated him jumping into the middle of this dangerous investigation. Which was silly. Or she tried to tell herself it was. His job was dangerous as hell. She'd always known that. It hadn't bothered her much in the past. He was strong, intimidating, well-trained, and capable. When they'd been together in the past and he'd left on a mission, he had always let her know he would be gone for a few days. He'd checked in when he could and called her as soon as he made it to safety. Yes, to make plans to hook up again, but she'd been able to breathe once he'd assured her he was on his way home.

What was different now? The fact that she knew how perilous this case was...or that she'd finally admitted she was still in love with him?

Her afternoon wasn't any better. While out at lunch, something had pissed off her boss. He came ranting into the office, slamming doors and rattling windows, growling at a handful of her coworkers to hustle their asses into the conference room. Reluctantly, they complied. Afterward, his wife hid in her office for the rest of the afternoon. Mila seemed so bubbly and sweet that Haisley felt sorry for the woman having to endure Mr. Benedict's bad mood and verbal abuse.

In the meantime, she dug into the company's social media and started rounding up the things Nash needed. Reluctantly, she knocked on Mr. Benedict's door.

"What? This better fucking be important."

Wincing, Haisley stepped in. "I've found the schematics and other associated documents Nash asked for. Is it okay for me to send them on?"

"Nash?" Benedict barked.

"Mr. Scott."

"What's up with you two? Today wasn't the first time you met."

"We know each other through mutual friends." Not a total lie...but she didn't owe her boss information about her personal life, especially when he was in a crappy mood.

"Is that all?"

"We've butted heads a few times, but that won't be an issue here. We're professionals, and we'll act accordingly."

"See that you do. You can start by doing your damn job and sending the operative whatever he needs."

"Of course, sir." *Asshole.*

Yeah, it had been a fab first day.

With a sigh, she unlocked her front door, glad that it was over, and shouldered her way into her bungalow. Ugh. Why the hell was she despondent and weepy? Worried?

She'd love to blame hormones, but Nash was back in her life. He always wreaked havoc on her heart.

What she needed was some girl time to get her mind off him so she could focus on getting her shit in order. Her friends always helped her screw her head on straight.

But when she texted Madison, Matt answered, saying her bestie had a raging case of morning sickness that had lasted all day, so she'd taken her green, vomiting self to bed. She'd call tomorrow. Haisley wished her well, then DoorDashed her expectant friend some ginger ale and ice cream.

Next, she'd reached out to Charli...who had typed back that she couldn't chat now because she and Daniel were talking. No elaboration, which seemed like code for the couple arguing. With a heavy heart, Haisley told her gal pal to call if she needed an ear.

Finally, she'd tried Gracelyn, who was a glass-half-full kind of girl and saw everything in a far happier light than Haisley's cynical outlook. She finished dinner and half an episode of some real estate show on Netflix before her optimistic friend texted back that she was "hanging out" with Kane but could chat in the morning.

Yeah. No thanks. She didn't want to talk to Gracelyn while the woman was cozied up in her lust bubble with one of Nash's teammates. Talk about awkward.

She thanked her friend for getting back to her and promised to call soon.

But that left her little house too empty, too quiet. Even her feline housemate, Miss Priss, was crashed on the back of the sofa, tuning Haisley out. She felt lonely—and that was dangerous because she was so, so tempted to call Nash and beg him to come over. Hell, before he'd left her office, she'd almost hoped he would kiss her again. He'd certainly looked as if it had crossed his mind.

How the hell was she going to work with him indefinitely without giving into the undeniable pull between them?

Haisley had no idea, but she had to get her mind off Nash now—or she'd do something she would regret. As tempting as it was to invite him to fill her night, nothing good could come of it. Well, other than amazing, incendiary, blow-her-doors-off sex. But by morning, he would be crowding her space, demanding more of her body, and inadvertently prying open her heart.

No. Not happening.

Besides, her secret would always be between them. She didn't dare give him the opportunity to worm it out of her. The truth wouldn't do Nash any good, so why bother? Maintaining distance was the only way she could protect him.

Thank god she had CSI. Maybe she should check in on a few of the cases she'd been assisting with. Yeah, and if she was going to do that, why not see if JasperThePrivateDick had made any progress?

Haisley nuked a frozen dinner and poured herself a generous glass of wine, then settled onto her sofa with a recent playlist and her laptop. Two minutes later, she propped her feet on the coffee table and scarfed down her dinner with one hand while logging into CSI with the other. She opened her private chat with Jasper, somewhat surprised to see he was also online.

> RedHotSavvySleuth: Hi, Jasper! How was your Monday?

> JasperThePrivateDick: Hey, Red! It was a little crazy, but I feel good about my accomplishments. You?

> RedHotSavvySleuth: It was crazy for me, too. I don't know that I feel good about anything I accomplished, but I do have information to share.

> JasperThePrivateDick: Same. But before we dive in, do you want to talk about whatever happened?

> RedHotSavvySleuth: I appreciate the offer, but I just want to put it behind me and see if we can focus on helping these victims.

> JasperThePrivateDick: I completely understand. And normally, I'd agree. But when my mind is full of heavy stuff, I find it really tough to concentrate. We might do these victims more good if we sift through whatever's upsetting you first. I'm a willing ear...

> RedHotSavvySleuth: That's very sweet, but I doubt you want to hear my BS.

Besides, she barely knew this guy.

> JasperThePrivateDick: Don't assume. I'm rattling around this big house alone tonight, and all I can think about is my beloved. She's been gone a couple of years, but I still miss her every day. Life has been so empty without her. So if I can focus on someone else's problems and make any difference at all, you'd be doing me a favor.

His words hit her straight in the heart. OMG, had his wife left? Died? Haisley didn't want to pry, but... Was Jasper sitting alone, missing the woman, despite the years since she'd gone? He must have loved her so much. His woes were none of her business, but losing a spouse or significant other made her own problems seem paltry by comparison.

> RedHotSavvySleuth: I'm so, so sorry, Jasper. I know what it's like to miss someone you can't have anymore. Mine was a breakup and not anything as permanent as your loss sounds, but I saw my ex today. At my new job, of all places. Long story short, life is crazy, and not only did I learn that I'm actually working for the man who built and still runs the Oakfield Mall, where these women have disappeared, but my new boss hired my ex to get to the bottom of the incidents. So now I'm going be stuck with him indefinitely.

> JasperThePrivateDick: That sounds challenging. How are you handling that?

> RedHotSavvySleuth: Not well. But enough about me. I have the schematics of the mall, as well as all the associated permits.

> JasperThePrivateDick: Does your ex say or do things that upset you?

> RedHotSavvySleuth: Not in the way you mean. He's just a flirt, and it's my fault for thinking I meant more to him. But honestly...I'd rather not talk about it. Let's focus on the case. Before I left the office, I stumbled across a list of all the security measures that have been in place since the mall opened, along with new ones they've implemented since the abduction started.

> JasperThePrivateDick: Are you at liberty to share all that with me? If you're not, I completely understand. This is your job and your livelihood. I would never want to risk that.

Funny, before he'd asked her to share, she'd decided not to leak Mr. Benedict's information to Jasper. But his respect for the delicate situation she was in and his understanding soothed her. Besides, Mr. Benedict behaved like an asshole. Was it possible he'd just been having a bad Monday? Sure. But that didn't make his barking, growling, unpleasant nature any better.

True, but his crappy demeanor didn't make betraying the man's confidence okay, either.

> RedHotSavvySleuth: I appreciate that. I'm not comfortable sharing what I have right now. I hope you understand.

JasperThePrivateDick: Absolutely. Maybe if I ask questions, you can answer them, based on your information?

RedHotSavvySleuth: Let's do that. You found something today?

JasperThePrivateDick: I did. I have a former associate who happens to know someone retired from the Lafayette PD. He called some buddies who still work on the force and were willing to chat.

RedHotSavvySleuth: Wait. You just happened to have a friend in New Orleans who knows cops in Lafayette?

JasperThePrivateDick: I know a lot of people. Anyway, the Lafayette PD officer talked to my former associate off the record about the case. I didn't get a lot of information, mind you. But he's willing to let this former associate ask him questions on our behalf, so…hit me with your thoughts.

RedHotSavvySleuth: Really? That's great. Let's think about this… Did you find out anything about the case in general? Anything we should pick apart and question? Does Lafayette PD have any suspects?

JasperThePrivateDick: The officer played everything pretty close to the vest, I'm told. But what I did get is that, so far, they're confounded. Malls are public spaces, so anyone can be there during business hours, which is when all the abductions have occurred. Every victim has been female, between sixteen and twenty-nine. Two were alone. Three were with others. Apparently, there were several more targets who got away.

Since that was something her boss had told her in confidence, Haisley had to admit that Jasper seemingly had a reliable source of information.

> RedHotSavvySleuth: That's my understanding, too. I don't know anything about the girls who got away, just that they supposedly didn't see or hear anything before they escaped.

> JasperThePrivateDick: Each one of them described leaving the bathroom by the food court and finding themselves alone in the adjacent hallway before someone grabbed them from behind and tried to drag them out the service doors that lead to the dumpster area in the parking lot behind the mall.

That was more information than she'd gotten out of Mr. Benedict. Then again, she hadn't wanted to risk his wrath on day one and ask.

> RedHotSavvySleuth: Did the cop mention any cameras or other security measures they checked for information?

Granted, her boss had mentioned that all his measures failed during the last abduction, but what about the others?

> JasperThePrivateDick: When the mall first opened, there were static cameras in public points of entry and exit, and of course in the customer-facing parts of the mall. But areas that were designed for mall staff and other employees? No. Cameras were added in those parts of the facility after the second disappearance. But apparently, they're proving unreliable for some reason. Entire days have passed where nothing is recorded, including the disappearance of the third victim and the first foiled attempt. The tech was upgraded again after that, but it still goes on the fritz occasionally.

Haisley frowned. On the fritz...or someone intentionally turned it off when they plotted to grab the next target.

> RedHotSavvySleuth: Anything else you can share?

> JasperThePrivateDick: Not that I can think of. But I have questions about the layout of the mall, since I've never been.

> RedHotSavvySleuth: What do you want to know?

> JasperThePrivateDick: What's in that part of the mall? I understand it's the food court, but that's all I heard.

> RedHotSavvySleuth: The design of that area is very odd, at least in my opinion. The bathroom is down a hallway behind one sit-down chain restaurant. If you're facing the food court itself, that's on the right side of the area. To the left of the hallway is a pastry shop known for their cinnamon rolls. They do a banner business on the weekends and make a mean hot chocolate. But I digress.

> JasperThePrivateDick: Do you like cinnamon rolls and hot chocolate?

> RedHotSavvySleuth: Am I female? LOL! Love them. Anyway, the remainder of the restaurant storefronts all fan out to the left of the pastry shop before a nasty pizza place curls back toward the main aisle on the far left.

> JasperThePrivateDick: No point of entry or exit by the bad pizza joint?

RedHotSavvySleuth: No. Just more shops. Did your cop connection say any of the other abductions were in a different part of the mall?

JasperThePrivateDick: No. All in the same spot. Which begs the question, why doesn't your boss do something about that location? Is he not concerned?

RedHotSavvySleuth: He's deeply concerned. At least that's what he says. Between you and me, I think he's mostly concerned financially. He's worried this will ruin him. But according to him, he's tried to beef up security to no avail.

JasperThePrivateDick: Besides the parking lot, what's behind that mall? It looks like a main thoroughfare with several highways close by.

RedHotSavvySleuth: Exactly. So once these kidnappers get someone out the door and into their vehicle, they can be on the freeway, headed to almost anywhere, in less than three minutes.

JasperThePrivateDick: That's disturbing, but optimal for scum like these kidnappers. I also looked at a county map. I see a couple of private airstrips not too far away.

RedHotSavvySleuth: That's possible. To be honest, I never paid attention to them. I'm not flying any sort of airplane myself, except maybe paper. LOL!

JasperThePrivateDick: A private airstrip is the easiest way to get a victim out of the area and ultimately anywhere in the world where there's a waiting buyer.

The idea made Haisley sick to her stomach. Yes, she knew such things happened, but knowing it was taking place so close to where she laid her head every night? So close to a place she'd been shopping? It was deeply unsettling.

> RedHotSavvySleuth: So you think they're being sold rather than being a kill trophy for a single sick perpetrator?

> JasperThePrivateDick: Either is possible, but no one has found any bodies. The rate of the abductions and the fact they're getting more frequent suggests this is likely a burgeoning business model rather than a sick thrill. Of course, serial offenders need their high more and more often, so I won't take that possibility off the table, but it seems awfully organized for one perpetrator. And correct me if I'm wrong, but the curb just outside those double doors is a no-parking zone.

Haisley had never looked herself, but she opened her scan of the mall's schematics and verified with the satellite footage available online. It led her to one obvious conclusion.

> RedHotSavvySleuth: You're right. That suggests this guy isn't working alone. The bricked-off area where the dumpsters are housed protects anyone driving on the street west of the mall from seeing whatever's going on at the curb. The east side isn't really visible either since the mall curves around. Even the main drag encircling the mall is probably half a football field away. So unless you're in that specific area—which almost no one is—or you're looking at those double doors—which, again, why would anyone do that?—then no one would see a victim being dragged out against their will.

> JasperThePrivateDick: Precisely. It almost makes me wonder if the mall was designed with this vulnerability.

Was he suggesting her boss had purposefully designed the building as the perfect place for abductions? She didn't know Mr. Benedict, and she didn't like him so far, but being gruff hardly made him evil. It also didn't make him a saint.

> RedHotSavvySleuth: I don't know. That seems like a big leap. I mean, it would still be hard to take someone from that area without anyone hearing. Victims surely screamed... Did your cop contact say anything about witnesses hearing cries for help?

> JasperThePrivateDick: No. But I didn't ask specifically. Our conversation was cut short since he got an urgent call. I'll add that to my list for what I hope will be our next conversation. You make a good point, though. My guess is that, with road noise and whatnot, it's a noisy area in general, so any screaming might get drowned out or ignored. And that assumes the victim isn't being gagged or drugged as she's being hauled into the offenders' vehicle.

> RedHotSavvySleuth: True. And if I were doing this, I'd use some sort of industrial vehicle that looks like a delivery van or trash truck—something most people would never question.

> JasperThePrivateDick: Yes. That would also explain why some of these abductions have been in broad daylight during very busy times, but no one saw anything.

> RedHotSavvySleuth: Exactly. Did the cop say he'd talked to any of the regular food-court employees?

> JasperThePrivateDick: It's not actually his case, but he hears things... I'll add that to my list. I'm sure they have but who or what was asked, I don't know.

> RedHotSavvySleuth: If we could get our hands on that information, it might be really helpful.

They filled the message screen for another ten minutes before realizing they'd hit something of a dead end with the information they currently shared. Questions had few or no answers, and they could speculate themselves in circles, but that helped no one, least of all those poor women who had been abducted and had now been missing anywhere from eighteen months to ten days.

> JasperThePrivateDick: I wish we knew more.

> RedHotSavvySleuth: Me, too. I feel helpless. I really want to drive out there and poke around. They don't close for another couple of hours. Maybe I can find some security guards or restaurant employees to ask our questions.

> JasperThePrivateDick: No! It's too dangerous. For all we know, the assailants are watching and waiting for either another opportunity or anyone who could thwart them. I've gathered from your profile that you're female, and I'm going to guess that you fit into the victims' age range. Am I right, Red?

> RedHotSavvySleuth: Yes, but I can take care of myself.

> JasperThePrivateDick: Do you think there's ever been a victim of such a crime who didn't feel the same way?

> RedHotSavvySleuth: Point taken. You sound a lot like my ex. He forbade me to do anything even slightly dangerous.

> JasperThePrivateDick: I don't know if I like being lumped in with someone stupid enough to let you get away. And before you read that as any sort of flirtation, I promise you my heart is too broken to pursue anyone else. You don't have to worry about me. I'm here to fill my time, and if I find a friend…I'm happy about that. If we just solve a case, I'll be happy about that, too. All that said, I think your ex might be onto something. Besides, you may only get one opportunity to interview these people. You want to do it when you have enough facts to ask the right questions. Not on a Monday night when you'll be rushed and you're still grappling to understand what's going on. Not to mention the fact you don't know whether they're working today. Or hell, if they're working there anymore at all.

> RedHotSavvySleuth: You have valid points. Sometimes, I'm impulsive and it gets me into trouble. When I see something that needs to be done, I tend to want to do it right this minute and cross it off my list, you know? Or am I the only crazy one like that?

> JasperThePrivateDick: I'm all for getting things done, but I tend to be somewhat measured. But maybe that's age. I seem to recall a few years ago—well, maybe more than a few—that I was fairly gung ho, too. But I do agree with your ex on one thing. You need to stay safe. You can't do anyone any good if you're hurt—or worse.

He wasn't wrong, Haisley supposed. She wasn't trained for interrogation, much less combat. If someone needed a boost to their Instagram, she was the woman for the job. Sure, she liked investigating murders…from the safety of her living room. She wasn't afraid of life, but she wasn't stupid, either. She knew her limitations.

RedHotSavvySleuth: Point taken. I'll stay in tonight. It's not like I don't have a lot to think about.

JasperThePrivateDick: Got your ex on your mind?

RedHotSavvySleuth: Yeah. I mean, I'm thinking about this case, too, but I haven't seen him in a couple of years. All of a sudden, he's popped up twice in the last few days. I wasn't braced to see him either time.

JasperThePrivateDick: You in love with him?

RedHotSavvySleuth: It's complicated. And pointless to dissect now. I was just a fun convenience for him.

JasperThePrivateDick: Are you sure it wasn't more?

RedHotSavvySleuth: Positive. The feelings were all one-sided, but whatever. When he figures out I won't be his anything with benefits again, he'll give up…and that will be that.

JasperThePrivateDick: From where I sit, you deserve more than to be someone's occasional toy. Are you sure he's not more serious about you?

RedHotSavvySleuth: Trust me. But the good news is, we're both dedicated to solving these abductions, so we'll work well together. Thanks for listening.

Now if I can just figure out how to keep my feelings out of it…

JasperThePrivateDick: Anytime. But one piece of advice? Don't write him off yet. Take it from someone who would give everything to spend even another moment with his beloved. Cherish every day. You never know what tomorrow will bring.

CHAPTER TEN

The next morning, Haisley hustled into the office—latte in one hand, briefcase in the other—with a lot on her mind.

Her conversation with Jasper played on repeat in her head. She'd almost called Nash last night to fill him in on everything she had learned, but setting a precedent where they talked after work hours, even about work, seemed…risky. Heaven forbid, he wanted to chat about personal stuff or persuaded her to get together to examine some clue she found in the future. Where he was concerned, she was already weak. Relying on her restraint was a recipe for disaster.

This morning, Nash was apparently eager. When she stepped off the elevator and around the reception desk, he was already leaning against her desk with steaming coffee and a smile. At least she'd arrived before Angela, Curtis, and Blake. Now she prayed Nash would respect the boundaries she'd set yesterday so she wouldn't have to haul him back to the coffee cubby for another chat.

"What are you doing here so early?" She set down her java and bag, then gave her totally professional attention to Nash. She didn't at all notice his well-muscled body as he oozed masculinity in a hunter-green T-shirt, distressed jeans, and steel-toed boots.

"Morning. I wanted to tell you about progress I made in the case yesterday and see if you'd discovered anything new I should be aware of. I only need a few minutes of your time."

His response took her aback. No flirting? No innuendo?

"Sure. What did you learn?"

"About an hour ago, I tracked down the detective assigned to investigate these disappearances. Haskins is very experienced, over twenty-five years with the force."

"That's good." But his face said otherwise. "No?"

"My read? He's a few months from retirement, and he'd rather slide by and hand this case off to someone else. So he's doing the bare minimum to avoid negative scrutiny. Last year, he went through a divorce. His kids barely speak to him." Nash shrugged. "I think he's burned out and we're not going to get much help from him."

That was a blow she hadn't seen coming. "Damn it. I'd ask if he just doesn't give a crap about all the women who have been taken and what they're suffering, but I'm guessing after a quarter century of crimes, he's numb to that."

Nash nodded. "His attitude seemed to be that none of these women would survive long, and after what they've probably endured, they'll wish they were dead anyway."

"That's a horrible outlook."

"Yep. I was able to get some information out of him that we can run with…" Then Nash proceeded to tell her pretty much everything Jasper had imparted last night.

"So I heard."

He scowled. "How?"

"An online source. Someone I know who happens to know people. He did some digging, too. But corroboration is good. What else?"

"I swung by the mall and checked out the area near the food court. I don't like anything about the way that alcove was constructed. The lighting is almost nonexistent, and unless you happen to be standing directly in the hallway, you can't see what's happening near the women's room."

"You're right. And I'm confused. If Mr. Benedict can pay for extra cameras and security guards, why didn't he pay for better lighting. At least maybe victims could see their assailants coming and have a fighting chance."

"Oh, there are light fixtures. Someone removed the bulbs. I checked—before I got caught by one of the maintenance staff, who threatened to call the mall cops on me." He grinned. "I shut his ass up by threatening to have the police drag him to the station for questioning as a suspect in the abductions."

Haisley gaped. "For real? What did he do?"

"Sputter. He claimed he removed the light bulbs after they went out, and he swears he hasn't replaced them yet because they're on backorder due to the holidays and supply-chain issues. I asked to see the purchase order for the replacement bulbs. Shockingly, he couldn't put his finger on it."

"In other words, he either didn't bother replacing the bulbs or didn't bother ordering them in the first place."

"That's what I think. He promised to follow up today. Of course that was after he threatened to call Mr. Benedict. I encouraged him to do just that. He was less ballsy after I pointed out the man had hired me to investigate."

"Naturally." But that got her thinking. Did Mr. Benedict have any idea how the Oakfield Mall actually functioned day-to-day? That people over there weren't doing their jobs? That the area by that restroom was almost pitch black? "I'll speak to my boss, get his take."

"Yeah. I'd love to know his thoughts. I suspect that if I ask him, he'll see it as some sort of interrogation or threat, and I'll get nothing but bluster."

"I don't know Mr. Benedict well, but I agree." She dropped her voice so the accounting folks a few rows over couldn't hear. "Obviously, I just started working here, but I don't think my boss takes 'helpful' suggestions from others well."

"He's the sort of man who wants to be right all the time, and when he's not, he finds a way to pretend that he was right all along and every good idea was his."

"Which means he'll take credit for anything good I do while I'm here." Haisley sighed. "My boss in LA was a lot like that. It's exhausting."

Nash looked like he had something to say, but he merely sipped his coffee and swallowed it down.

Yesterday, she would have sworn he wanted anything she would give him—time, information, attention—and most of all, sex. Today he seemed purely professional...and not at all interested in her personally. That was what she asked for. What she'd said she wanted. What she'd demanded, even.

So why was it bothering her? Why did she feel an irrational pang of disappointment at his sudden aloofness?

"What's your next move?" she asked as she booted up her laptop and tried to act like his about-face wasn't flustering her at all.

"This morning, I'm going to see if I can speak to the mother of the victim abducted on Christmas Eve. The girl's father, when I talked to him last night, was a mess. He wants to help, but he wasn't there, so he can't add anything. Instead, he's going to do his best to bolster his wife so she can tell me everything she remembers."

Haisley's heart hurt for the woman. "I'm sure she's beating herself up for not stopping the kidnapping. Just like I'm sure the police grilled her, and every time she has to answer questions, she relives the tragedy."

"Exactly. And there's no way to be gentle."

Not when they needed cold, hard facts and time was of the essence. "Unfortunately."

"I'm also going to talk to two of the girls who managed to escape, see how closely their stories match and make sure Detective Dipshit didn't overlook something crucial. The other one who got away is still out for the holidays. Then this evening, I'll head back to the mall. Two of the teenagers who work at the food court's pastry shop will be working. I have permission from their manager to ask them questions. She's very concerned about the situation over there and has refused to let any of her female employees go to that restroom without an escort."

"Good for her."

"Sad it has to come to that, but yes."

"Anything else you need from me?" As soon as the words left her mouth, Haisley wished she could snatch them back. She'd left herself wide open for one of Nash's flirty suggestions that would be so tempting and damn near impossible to refuse.

But he surprised her by keeping things aboveboard and professional again. "The list of facility employees I have is dated December first. Can you see if Benedict has something more recent? I want to see if anyone has left their job in the last thirtyish days and find out why."

"Actually, Mila told me yesterday afternoon she's working on that. I'll get with her as soon as she's available and forward it to you."

"Thank you. See if you can also find out if there's any employee handbook for the people who work for the mall itself, especially management and maintenance. The general manager and I played phone tag yesterday. By the end of the day, it started to feel intentional. From what I gather, he's a slimy little bastard who cuts corners. No one likes him."

"Got it. I'll also find out why Mr. Benedict hired him and what his qualifications are."

"Good call. I think that's it."

Haisley frowned. Seriously? Not a single innuendo-laden comment or a double entendre from Nash? Not even a wink? If he had behaved this way yesterday, she would have been convinced that their New Year's Eve kiss was alcohol-fueled, but that sober Nash wasn't interested at all. The thought made her chest tighten.

"Yeah. Um, do you need me to go with you to the mall tonight?" As soon as the words were out, Haisley winced. OMG, that sounded desperate. "I mean you're going to be talking to teenagers and—"

"I'd rather not have you near the mall." His voice dropped. "Bad shit is happening there. I already hate that your job has involved you in this mess. Unless it's necessary, I don't want you in deeper."

"But you're in."

"Like I said, I don't fit the victim profile, and I'm trained for this."

"But it's dangerous for you, too." The words slipped out before she could stop them.

"Ethan will back me up."

"He's a fukboi. How can you take him seriously?"

"Since we started renting a house together, I've gotten to know him better. He's more serious than you think, and he's damn good at his job. I did some digging. His dad and three uncles are all local legends in Vegas for taking down a mob boss terrorizing the city. He learned from the best."

She trusted Nash's judgment since he obviously knew Ethan better, but she was miffed that Nash had flatly refused to spend any part of the evening with her. And yes, she realized she was being contradictory. But the fact that he suddenly didn't seem interested in her except as a partner in this case rattled her more than she wanted to admit.

"All right. Um…maybe you could call me after your interviews tonight to tell me what you found?"

He chugged back the last of his coffee, trashed the disposable cup, then shrugged. "Unless it's something earth-shattering, there's no reason for me to disturb your evening. I'll catch up with you tomorrow."

Now she was downright annoyed, a twinge of hurt pride mingling with her exasperation. "You're right. I guess…I'll talk to you tomorrow."

Nash pushed away from her desk and gave her an impersonal salute. "Talk to you then."

With that, he sauntered out the door. Haisley watched his fine ass retreat until he disappeared.

Shaking her head, she sighed, trying to ignore the confusing ache in her chest at his abrupt departure. He'd given her exactly what she asked for—a purely professional relationship. She hated every second of it. What was wrong with her? Or maybe the better question was, what the hell was up with him?

January
Two years ago

> Happy Friday. At six, let yourself in my front door, go straight to my bedroom, and strip off your underwear. Leave them on my pillow and wait beside my bed with your dress lifted so your pussy is exposed. Is that clear?

Haisley reread Nash's text with a rough sigh as she texted him back.

> Yes, Sir.

Wondering exactly what he planned for her tonight got her almost as hot and excited as her certainty that, whatever it was, he'd make it deliciously terrible and drive her to the edge of her sanity until she was a shuddering, pleading mess.

Sometimes she had to pinch herself. In bed, Nash was creative, intense, indefatigable, and amazing. She loved every second she spent with him. She melted when he touched her as if nothing and no one else mattered. She felt her heart race when he kissed her until her toes curled. She lost her mind when he took command of her body and turned her inside out. But most of all, she just loved being with him.

Haisley did her best to hide her growing feelings with an occasional cool brushoff or snarky comeback. If he knew how attached to him she'd become, he'd probably classify her as a stage-five clinger and cut her loose.

Sometimes she almost believed he was falling, too, especially when they cuddled on the sofa for a movie marathon, swapped bad jokes, or shared meaningful conversations about family, philosophy, and dreams... Who did all that with a mere hookup? But Nash had never budged on his stance against marriage and children. And she'd broken their cardinal rule.

She'd fallen in love.

Haisley didn't know what to do. Come clean? Or break it off before he broke her heart?

She did neither. He was only home sporadically between missions, and she'd sworn she would never revolve her life around some man's. But...she always made herself available to this one. She couldn't help it. Each time Nash commanded her body, she obeyed, putting off her day of reckoning until some nebulous "later."

During their very first night together, he'd vowed to ruin her for all other men. She hadn't believed him. She'd even laughed a little to herself, thinking he was ridiculously overconfident. Nearly a year later, Haisley hated to admit that he'd succeeded.

And she didn't know what the hell to do.

Shoving down her worries, she grabbed a few things from her apartment, tossed them in a bag, then headed to Nash's place. As usual, it was on the messy side. No surprise since he blew in and out of town a lot. Now that he was on his way home from his latest op, she brought him a cold six-pack, turned on the heater to ward off the January chill, washed the dishes soaking in his kitchen sink, and tidied up.

At five till six, she scurried back to his bedroom and tugged off her panties, draping them across his pillow as he'd commanded. Her heart raced, even as her brain asked what she was doing. They needed to talk more than they needed to fuck. But her body didn't care. She'd been a long ten days without Nash, and she was achy and needy for the pleasure he alone could give her. And to give him the affection he would accept from her.

Across the silent apartment, Haisley heard the key fit into the lock. The knob turned. She fluffed her hair, bit her lip, and lifted her skirt as he shut and locked the front door. While his heavy footsteps encroached down the hall, her heart thrummed.

The instant Nash saw her, he dropped his duffel onto the hardwoods, his dark, hungry eyes brushing her lips, caressing her nipples, then fixating on her pussy, which grew wetter with every second he stared. A shiver rippled through her. She needed him so badly...

"Hi, baby. You look beautiful." He closed the distance between them in two long strides, cupped her nape in his giant palm, and took her lips in a greedy kiss that delved straight into her soul.

She melted into Nash as dark need twisted in her belly and gathered behind her exposed clit. She knew better than to let her skirt fall. He would spank her for that. She might like that...eventually. But right now she'd missed him too much to do anything but obey.

As he pressed another demanding kiss to her lips, he overwhelmed her senses. His scent—a heady blend of hot, masculine musk, danger, and solid man—enveloped her. She breathed him in greedily, savoring the taste of his lips—slightly salty from adrenaline and sweat with an underlying sweetness that made her crave more.

His hands roamed her body with a practiced confidence that sparked her desire. The roughness of his calloused palms contrasting with the silkiness of his fingertips as they trailed over the exposed skin above her blouse made her shudder. As he unfastened the buttons one by one, his featherlight touch descended, igniting her with every sweep.

Haisley whimpered into his mouth. The wet glide of his tongue stroking hers flooded her with desire so sharp it was almost painful. She anchored herself against him, a slave to the dizzying onslaught of sensation and emotion only Nash could heap on her.

This man undid her utterly—mind, body, and soul. With each ragged breath, every erratic thump of her thudding heart, Haisley poured her unspoken love into the all-consuming fire between them she could neither douse nor deny and lost herself in Nash. It was the sweetest torture.

Suddenly, he pulled back and fastened his demanding stare on her. "Did you play with my pussy while I was away?"

"No, Sir," she breathed.

"But you wanted to, didn't you?"

She licked her lips. "I ache when you're gone."

"I wanted to touch you, too, baby. But I'll reward your obedience and make your wait worth it." He dropped to his knees and exhaled against her mound. "What a pretty pussy. I hope you're hungry, because I sure am. Keep lifting that skirt for me."

Haisley's breathing roughened, and her heart rattled against her ribs as Nash delved face-first between her legs, his tongue unerringly finding her clit. Ruthlessly, he drove her up, then kept her hovering at a fever-pitch, forcing her to both stand still and expose every one of her secrets for his play and her pleasure.

"Nash..."

"What, baby?"

"Let me lie down and spread my legs for you."

"No. You take the lash of my tongue. You stand still like a good girl so I can worship you. You come when I tell you—not before. When I want you on your back, legs wide for me, I'll put you there myself."

Then he dipped his head and returned to slowly driving her insane.

Her yearning grew as her anxiety did. "Nash. Nash! I—"

"Need to come?"

He knew she did. Sometimes he knew her own body better than she did. "Please."

"Oh, you know I love manners." He took a long, leisurely swipe through her slit, then leaned back. She watched him lick his lips before he parted her folds with his thumbs, smiling as he exposed her even more. "Come for me."

When he lowered his head again, Haisley couldn't resist. Couldn't hold out. He dragged the flat of his tongue across her clit again, then sucked it deep.

She was gone, her head lost to a realm of sensation that had her swimming in tingles and dissolving into shudders as she hoarsely screamed his name.

The moment her orgasm ended and her replete body sagged with a sigh, Nash lay her across his mattress, tore away the remnants of her blouse, unzipped his pants, and seated himself to the hilt inside her with one roaring thrust.

"Nash!" Through his charcoal-gray T-shirt, damp with sweat, she dug her nails into his back.

"Take me. Take every fucking inch of me," he growled as he pinned her wrists to the bed and invaded her still-sensitive pussy over and over with his girthy cock.

Mercilessly, he ratcheted her up as he stared down into her eyes, plunging deep, then deeper, until she couldn't catch her breath. Her clit felt as if it were on fire, and her heart surrendered again to him, as she did every time he touched her.

"I need to come again," she wailed into his cotton-clad shoulder.

"Ask me. Beg me."

"Please," she gasped out. "Please, Nash. Please… I need you."

"Goddamn, baby. Yes. Oh, fuck, yes. I need you, too." He

pounded at her until his bed frame rattled, until he panted against her lips, until his face tightened with bliss. "Come with me!"

Impossibly, he hardened inside her. His thrusts roughened as he banged her faster into the mattress. Her senses soared. Blood rushed through her body, catching fire in her veins. Her desire tightened and twisted before the dam burst in a flurry of heat and fireworks. Black spots danced behind her eyes as Nash let go inside her and she screamed out her release.

Slowly, they came back to earth together in a tangle of clinging limbs and panting breaths. Neither seemed inclined to move, and Haisley loved it that way. She nuzzled her face in his neck, closed her eyes, and inhaled his salty, manly musk.

There was no place she'd rather be.

"Happy I'm home?" he rasped out, his voice still thick with passion.

Haisley knew what that question meant. Tonight would be an orgasm marathon, and she was giddy for it. "Very. I missed you."

As soon as she admitted that, she winced. Nash didn't want her heart, just her body. She had to be careful or she'd scare him off.

"Did you? Or were you just getting horny without me?" He lifted a cynical brow. "I know your kitty gets cranky when I don't pet her often enough."

Unfortunately, he wasn't wrong. Since Nash had stormed into her life, not only had he forbidden her from self-pleasuring, she didn't enjoy it anymore because it didn't really satisfy her.

Haisley craved him, and she worried all the time it would bite her in the ass. Despite that fear…she couldn't stop.

"Yeah? Your 'dog' gets pretty snarly when I don't take him for frequent walks."

He busted out laughing. "True that. God, it's good to be home. What a fucking horrible op that was. I hate being schlepped out to urban shitholes for stupid-ass reasons."

"What happened?"

Nash sighed. "I can't say. Political ramifications and all that."

"Was it dangerous?"

"Isn't it always? But I'm careful. And why wouldn't I be? I've got a good reason to come home…"

"Yeah?" Her heart lodged in her throat. "Are you BSing me?"

"Never. And I'm not going soft, either. When I have pussy this good, it's impossible not to be hard as fuck."

On some level, she knew he meant that as a compliment…but it was hardly a confession of love. Then again, she hadn't expected one. By unspoken mutual agreement, they kept emotions beyond desire to themselves.

God, the silence made everything between them feel tenuous. Uncertain. Their communication was shit. But Haisley wasn't ready to be brave enough to tell him how she felt. Getting attached to anyone—even family—had never worked out for her. And Nash had been very clear that he wasn't interested in permanence of any kind.

So Haisley did what she could—held him close, tracing lazy patterns on his back as she inhaled him and tried not to dread the moment it would end.

The air smelled like sex. Her head was filled with him as he tightened his grip, drawing her closer. "I have a very important question for you, Rowe."

Her heart leapt. Was there any chance he felt something more for her? That he was ready to say something? "I'm listening."

"McDreamy or McSteamy?"

That's what he wanted to know? Stifling her disappointment, she snorted. "Neither. Give me Cristina and Owen any day."

"Really? I pegged you for a Meredith and Derek fan."

"Too obvious. Cristina and Owen had that fiery passion, that delicious tension." She glanced up at him through her lashes. "You know what I mean."

Nash grinned. "I do."

They lapsed into a charged silence. Haisley ached to ask him what they were, to put a label on this incredible thing between them. But the words stuck in her throat.

He tried again. "What about Carrie and Mr. Big?"

She forced a laugh. "God, no. That whole relationship was a toxic mess."

"True." He toyed with a strand of her hair. "But they had chemistry. Their connection was undeniable, even when they were apart. You know?"

Haisley's breath caught. Was he hinting at something? Or was she just projecting her own hopes onto his meaning? "When you put it like that...your argument has merit. How do you know about all these fictional couples? Have you actually watched *Grey's Anatomy* and *Sex and the City*?"

"Not much, but you know I have three sisters who love both shows. On long plane rides to my next hotspot, I sometimes sneak in a few episodes so we'll have something to talk about."

She narrowed her eyes. "You're lying. You like those shows."

"I plead the fifth on *Grey's*. And Carrie is too self-absorbed and self-sabotaging for me to take *Sex and the City* seriously. Miranda annoys me. Charlotte is vapid and—"

"Of course you prefer Samantha. It figures you'd identify with the one whose motto is nail everyone hot and move on."

"At least she's honest. But I like her more because she's driven and fearless. Like someone else I know." He tapped her nose. "But if you think I've been nailing anyone and moving on these days, you haven't been paying attention."

Was he saying he hadn't been with anyone else lately? Haisley hadn't been since their first time together, but she'd never asked what or who else he did. She'd been too afraid of the truth, and neither of them had ever breathed a word about exclusivity. "Oh?"

"Don't look shocked. I'm way too into your body to mess with anyone else these days." He dropped a lingering kiss on her lips. "Want me to show you again?"

"Please," she breathed. "Sir."

"Oh, there are your good manners. I'll definitely reward those..." He rolled to his side, propping his head on his palm while trailing his free hand between her breasts, over her stomach, then down, down, down between her legs where she was already aching again. "Be a good girl and spread your legs."

Instantly, she complied, moaning when he circled her hardening clit lazily.

"Hmm." He nuzzled her neck. "You want me to make you beg before I make you feel good?"

Her breath hitched. "Yes, Sir. Please."

He licked his way up her throat to nibble on her lips. "Then tell me your favorite TV couple. What's the perfect romance to you? Ross and Rachel?"

Haisley shook her head, already fighting to string her thoughts together as he cranked up her need. "No. Too neurotic and indecisive. Too unable to get it together. Too...oh, that feels *so* good."

Nash laughed and brushed his lips over hers before leaning in to suck her nipple with long, strong pulls. She gripped the sheets and closed her eyes. God, he knew how to undo her so easily, and she loved it almost as much as she loved him.

He popped her hard tip from his mouth, then dragged his knuckles across it before cupping her breast and squeezing.

"Ouch." She jerked involuntarily.

"Sorry." Nash shifted his squeezing into a caress. "Too rough?"

"It's one of those you-don't-know-your-own-strength moments."

"I get excited, baby. *You* get me excited. Every minute I'm with you." He kissed her until she lost her breath and her brain threatened to melt.

Did he mean that as romantically as it sounded? "Nash..."

"Baby..." he crooned back, then rubbed her needy clit again in slow, torturous circles. "C'mon. Give it to me."

"You want me to come?"

He scoffed. "We're nowhere near ready for that."

Not true. She was, but... "Then—"

"Tell me your favorite TV couple."

"Jim and Pam," she gasped out. As far as Haisley was concerned, this duo from *The Office* were who every couple aspired to be. Friends before lovers. Funny, lots in common, considerate of each other, patient. Most especially, she loved that they'd finally overcome the bad timing, their awkwardness and shyness, and declared their love for each other openly, honestly, and without fear.

But she didn't ever see that being her and Nash.

"The ultimate will-they-or-won't-they couple?"

"That's one way to look at it. All those longing looks, that slow burn…" Haisley wriggled and tried to focus on the conversation. Something in her brain told her this might be important, but his fingers and the dark weight of his stare was driving her wild. "It's romantic."

"He proposed to her at a gas station."

"He loved her too much to wait."

Nash stopped rubbing her to stare down into her face. "I thought you didn't believe in love."

"Jim believed enough for both of them until it came true. Their relationship was sweet. Don't you think?"

"What about real life?"

Haisley's heart started chugging. What was he saying? Had he changed his mind? "I never said I didn't believe in love, just that it only happens for some people. The lucky people. Your brother and Laila. Zy and Tessa. Matt and Madison. Hell, even your bosses seem to be happily married."

"So you *do* believe in love?" His voice dropped an octave, drizzled with a tone as sweet as syrup on a stack of fluffy pancakes. "Do you want love? Is that what you mean?"

Jim had the courage to tell Pam how he felt about her. With Nash pinning her to his bed and staring down at her, she had no place to hide. And her courage deserted her. She'd never remotely been in love —until Nash—and being the one to utter the words first terrified her. All his attention, affection, and pleasure could be gone in a snap if she spilled those three little words.

"I mean that I like good TV as much as the next person." She shoved at him until he backed away. Then she vaulted off the bed, scrambling to find her clothes.

"Where are you going?" He rose from the sheets, his body so solid and beautiful, his cock standing at attention, pointing at her like a divining rod.

For months, she'd been telling herself that the way he wanted her constantly must mean something. He had to have some feelings for her, right? He'd even admitted he'd been faithful since they started hooking up.

But that wasn't a declaration of love.

Feeling exposed, she grabbed her dress and held it over her nakedness. "What about you? Do you believe in love?"

"I never said I didn't."

What did that mean? Maybe nothing, and she didn't want to find out the hard way.

"I think I should go." Haisley grabbed up the rest of her things he'd strewn across the floor when he'd undressed her and ran to the bathroom, slamming the door and locking it behind her.

With shaking hands, she tugged on her clothes, sniffling back tears that stubbornly insisted on leaking from her eyes.

He pounded on the door. "You okay?"

"Fine."

But she wasn't. Every time Haisley got around Nash these days, she felt emotional. She hated feeling so off balance.

It was another reason to put distance between them. In fact, maybe she ought to think about doing it for good because sooner or later, he was going to shatter her heart. And she wasn't sure how—or if—she'd survive.

CHAPTER ELEVEN

Present Day

After a hectic day, Nash was exhausted when he sat down with a cheeseburger near nine p.m. and opened the lid on his laptop.

The disappointment on Haisley's face this morning had haunted him all day. His best read on her mood? While it was possible she'd awakened grumpy, she'd clearly been confused when he'd refused to engage with her beyond the professional. Did that maybe mean she missed him?

"You're finally home, asshole?" Garrison padded barefooted and bare-chested into the kitchen, a discarded T-shirt slung over his inked shoulder.

"Hey, fuck face."

"Aww, I love our pet names for each other. They're almost romantic," he quipped as he poured himself a glass of milk.

Nash rolled his eyes. "I'm eating here. Don't make me hurl. I'd never want to be romantic with your hairy ass."

"Same. So...do you know where your girl is tonight?"

That taunt made Nash freeze. "Haisley?"

"Who else?" Ethan quipped with an I-know-a-secret smile. "I ran into her less than an hour ago."

If she'd been at Highrise flirting—or worse, sneaking around the mall—he'd spank her ass a spectacular shade of red. "And?"

Ethan chortled. "Listen to you, trying to play it cool. Dude, your face is telling me you're desperately worried about what she's up to…"

Nash tossed down his burger and stood. "Okay. Ha ha. You've had your laugh at my expense. You want me to tell you that woman drives me crazy? I admit it. She does. You got me. Now tell me where you saw her."

"Chill, bro. I ran into Haisley at Matt and Madison's. She stopped in to check on her bestie, who's apparently having a real bitch of a time with morning sickness. She was worried."

"Oh." Nash sat again, relieved that he didn't have to chase her down and have it out tonight. "Did she say anything about me?"

As soon as the words fell out, Nash wished he could bite them back. Fuck, that sounded so junior high. But he was out of restraint.

Not flirting at full throttle with Haisley went against everything in his nature. Being so close to her this morning while forcing himself to behave like she was nothing but a counterpart in this case—rather than the woman he loved—had almost killed him. Changing tactics with her had seemed like the best option after she'd confided in Jasper that their past relationship had felt like nothing more than an extended hookup. She genuinely fucking believed that she hadn't been his everything. That he'd merely viewed her as a good time.

She'd be shocked to know he'd been ready to propose.

None of that helped him now. Jasper couldn't tell Haisley that she had everything wrong. But Nash could. And he could win her back, starting by respecting the boundaries she'd set yesterday—no matter how much it killed him.

He'd use Jasper as recon, to check in with her, make sure she was staying safe, getting the emotional support she needed…and then hope like hell that when the time to come clean rolled around, she understood he'd been trying to help and support her, not bullshit and hurt her.

But either way, he refused to lose her without putting up the fight of his life. Somehow, someway, he would convince Haisley Rowe that he loved her. Once she knew the truth... Well, what happened next was up to her.

Ethan laughed. "She might have mentioned you once or twice. What's it worth to you?"

Nash slanted his roommate an annoyed glance. "What do you want?"

"You do my laundry for a month, and I'm an open book."

"You're a rat bastard. I'm not washing your sweaty underwear or sticky sheets."

"That's the deal. Take it or leave it."

"Motherfucker." Nash wasn't looking to be the kid's bitch, but he would absolutely bend his pride for help in winning back Haisley. "Fine. But I'm not folding."

Ethan laughed. "Sucker."

Nash hurdled the sofa and crossed the kitchen floor in a handful of steps, grabbing the kid by the throat. "You better not tell me you punked me."

"Lighten up, dude." When Nash let go, Ethan rolled his shoulders. "I'm just yanking your chain. To be honest, I didn't hear that much, just that you being all straight-up business this morning confused her. She doesn't know where she stands with you."

As he'd suspected. "Thanks. Give me your laundry."

"I'm not going to make you do it. I just wanted to see how much this woman meant to you."

"Son of a bitch." Nash stomped back to his dinner.

Ethan trailed after him. "Sorry. You okay?"

"Fuck, I don't know." He scrubbed a hand through his hair. "You want to know what Haisley means to me? Everything. When she left, it fucking crushed me. I thought we were on the same page—until she took off. Why is communicating with that woman so hard?"

"It's not like you've been lonely without Haisley, dude. You get laid a lot." He grinned. "Almost as much as me."

"And it's all empty. It's all..." His insides twisted. "Meaningless. That's great for a while. But...man, once you have someone who means something, it's different. And going back to those empty fucks? It's just... You're going to fucking laugh, but some mornings, I'd wake up and roll over and think—for just a moment—that I had Haisley back. Then I'd open my eyes and see someone else. No matter how sexy or sweet or snarky or whatever the woman beside me was, she still wasn't Haisley. And I kept wondering what the hell I did to not only drive a wedge between us, but to make her flee two thousand miles away."

Ethan dropped onto the sofa beside him. "Shit, man. I'm sorry. I just thought... Hell, everyone thought you were just hooking up. You didn't take her out or bring her to the company parties or act like you had a thing for her. So I thought—"

"That I just wanted to nail her. Apparently, that's what she thought, too." And Nash felt like an idiot. He'd so zealously guarded his time alone with her that he hadn't stopped to think about how she might perceive his behavior. But she'd never pushed back, never asked him to take her out or show her a good time that didn't involve his bed, some cuffs, and his stiff cock. She'd been so fucking perfect for him in every way.

And he'd been an idiot.

Of course Haisley had assumed she was his favorite hookup, not his treasured submissive or his girlfriend. He hadn't given her any reason to think he loved her or wanted to marry her. It seemed so fucking obvious now, but in the moment...he'd only thought about being as close to her as possible.

Well, that wasn't the whole truth. The very first night they'd spent together, she'd been adamant that she wasn't looking for a relationship. For months, he'd been searching for a way to tell her that he wanted more than sex with her. And he'd been afraid of being too honest and losing her.

"What are you going to do now?" Ethan asked.

"Everything I can."

"I'd ask if you need relationship pointers, but I'm the guy who lost his high school girlfriend to his dad, so—"

"You're making that up." He had to be.

"I'm not. My dad married Havana right after her eighteenth birthday. They have three kids now. I tease him all the time that he needs to stop knocking her up. It's embarrassing."

Nash laughed, mostly because it felt nice for a few seconds not to think about how badly he'd fucked up. "Wow."

"It kind of sucks, but they're happy, so…" Ethan shrugged. "Listen, about earlier today, at the mall—"

"It's not your fault the girl working at the pastry shop wouldn't talk to us. She wasn't going to."

Ethan sighed. "I didn't think Abby would be so skittish."

"Same." And Nash felt bad for not realizing that he and Ethan were probably intimidating, especially in light of the abductions happening less than a hundred feet from her. "And that other kid…"

"I guarantee he's stoned more than he's working. Did you see his eyes?"

"Yep. That's my read, too. And the fact he refuses to wear his glasses… Jesus, he shouldn't even be driving."

"No wonder none of the police reports mention that guy. Then again, I don't think Detective Haskins gives a shit about anything these days except his upcoming pension, his gold watch, and endless days of fishing."

"It sucks. I'm not sure where to turn from here. We need to sit down with a list of facts and unknowns, then start asking the right questions, rule out people who couldn't possibly pull this off, then start narrowing down to a list of suspects who could."

Ethan nodded. "We'll hit it first thing in the morning."

"You going out tonight?"

The kid grinned as he pulled on a T-shirt. "I've got two booty calls, and I'm already late to the first. See you in the morning."

"How are you going to get any sleep?"

That made Ethan laugh. "If that's your first priority, you're getting old, dude. See you."

"I'm not fucking old," he called to Ethan's retreating back.

The door slammed. Nash cursed, then focused on his laptop.

Putting on his Jasper hat to talk to Haisley tonight was probably reckless, but every part of him needed to make sure she was okay. Nash wasn't in a position to reassure her yet; she wouldn't listen to him. But Jasper was. *If* he could be fucking delicate—something he absolutely sucked at.

He hated lying to her, and hopefully, this subterfuge wouldn't blow up in his face. He'd come clean eventually, and using a screen name to get close to Haisley wasn't his first choice, but she hadn't left him more appealing options.

Sighing, he navigated to the CSI site and logged in. He already had a message waiting from Haisley. Eagerly, he opened it, but it didn't say much more than hello and a tacked-on hope that he had a good day.

He answered right away.

> JasperThePrivateDick: Hi, Red. My day sucked. I hope yours was better.

> RedHotSavvySleuth: Nope. Day two of my new job, my boss is still an asshole and this case is still an enigma.

> JasperThePrivateDick: Sorry to hear that. What about your ex? See him again?

> RedHotSavvySleuth: Yes. Don't remind me. No offense, but why are men so confusing?

> JasperThePrivateDick: Ha! We ask the same thing about women all the time.

> RedHotSavvySleuth: But you mastered it once. You had someone you clearly loved.

> JasperThePrivateDick: More than she'll ever know.

Nash hated how true that seemed right now.

> **RedHotSavvySleuth:** Ugh. Let's not talk about the past. I wish I could say I'd made headway on the case, but it's hard when I'm stuck in the office, and I can't actually investigate beyond the paperwork inside those four walls.

> **JasperThePrivateDick:** You're safer that way. Presumably your ex and the others working on the investigation have been trained for danger. Isn't it better to let them do their jobs?

> **RedHotSavvySleuth:** You mean sit on my ass while other women are in danger? Shouldn't I be doing something helpful?

> **JasperThePrivateDick:** Supporting the people in the trenches is doing something helpful.

> **RedHotSavvySleuth:** Not enough. And you're sounding like my ex again, warning me away from a potential paper cut.

> **JasperThePrivateDick:** Getting abducted by these people would be a lot more perilous than a paper cut, Red.

> **RedHotSavvySleuth:** I know. Doesn't mean I like it. Did you learn anything new today?

> **JasperThePrivateDick:** I'm afraid not. Today was hectic, and none of it as productive as I'd like.

Not that Jasper could share any of today's findings with Haisley. That would all have to come from Nash. At least he'd have things to tell her, even if all the news was terrible. At least he'd get to spend more time with her.

Fuck, he had it bad.

> JasperThePrivateDick: Did your ex make any progress on the case?

> RedHotSavvySleuth: Some. He tracked down the lead detective, but the old fart is basically useless.

> JasperThePrivateDick: Hey, watch that old talk. I identify with not being as young as I once was.

Not a total lie. After all, his age started with a three now. Nash was still wrapping his head around that.

> RedHotSavvySleuth: You're not useless in any way, shape, or form, so don't go there. I meant that this detective is burned out and coasting to retirement. 😒

> JasperThePrivateDick: That's frustrating. I'm sure your ex isn't thrilled, either.

> RedHotSavvySleuth: He isn't. But he's pushing forward, following other leads. Talking to witnesses, victims who escaped, that sort of thing.

> JasperThePrivateDick: Sounds like he's as dedicated to solving this case as you are. Good. Those victims deserve someone in their corner. How are things between you two? Any more communication now that you're working together?

Yes, he was fishing.

Haisley paused for a long time before responding.

> RedHotSavvySleuth: Yes and no. Yesterday, I was irritated with all his flirty innuendos and smoldering looks, so I asked him to behave more professionally. Today, he was strictly business. It was actually too professional. 🙄 It's like he did a complete 180 overnight and decided to treat me like any random coworker.

> JasperThePrivate Dick: Isn't that what you wanted, though? For him to respect your boundaries and keep things aboveboard?

Another lengthy pause. Nash could practically see Haisley worrying that plump bottom lip between her teeth as she mulled over her response.

> RedHotSavvySleuth: I mean, yeah. I did. I do. It's just… I don't know. It felt weird. Unsettling. Like I said, men are confusing. ☹

> JasperThePrivateDick: Sounds like maybe you're not entirely sure what you want from him.

> RedHotSavvySleuth: I want to solve this case. I want to stop more women from being abducted and who knows what else. That's what matters most.

Nash's chest tightened at her evasion. She was dodging the real issue, the complicated emotions simmering between them. He couldn't let that go.

> JasperThePrivateDick: Of course. But don't forget to consider what you want for yourself, too. Trust me, as someone who's lost the woman he loved, if you still care about your ex, you shouldn't take a single day with him for granted. Even if things are messy and confusing, it's way better than being brokenhearted.

Nash held his breath, hoping he'd get through to her. Again, Haisley's reply was slow to come.

> RedHotSavvySleuth: Maybe you're right. I'll think about it. BTW, if you ever want to talk about your lost love, I'm a good ear. I won't pry, but you've been such a good listener, I'm happy to return the favor.

Nash's throat tightened. He couldn't go there, not even in their anonymous online bubble. The wounds were still too raw, and Haisley was no one's fool. She'd probably catch on before he was ready for the big reveal.

> JasperThePrivateDick: I appreciate the offer, but it's ancient history. Not nearly as interesting as the present. 😉 And it's getting late for this old fart, so I should sign off. But think about what I said, okay? Take it from someone who learned the hard way. Don't let fear and pride keep you from something real with your ex. Even if it's complicated.

> RedHotSavvySleuth: I'll try. Thanks for listening. Have a good night. 🖤

Nash exited the chat and powered down his laptop, his mind racing. Had he gotten through to Haisley? Planted a seed that would make her rethink keeping him at arm's length?

Knowing how stubborn she was, maybe not. Time would tell. But the truth was, he couldn't maintain his strictly professional charade for long, not when every cell in his body was screaming to haul her against him and kiss her until they were both senseless.

She was right about one thing, though. Complicated didn't even begin to cover their relationship these days. He hoped that playing Jasper didn't bite him in the ass, but he'd meant what he'd said. He didn't want to waste a single day with Haisley—even if it meant breaking every rule in the book to prove she still wanted him just as badly.

Late the next afternoon, Nash strode into Haisley's office, his heart doing that familiar little flip when she glanced up from her computer screen at him. Her eyes widened slightly, surprise and something else he couldn't decipher flickering across her face before she schooled her features into a neutral expression.

"Nash. What's up?"

He shrugged, aiming for a casual tone, even as his pulse kicked up a notch. "Thought I'd swing by and see if you were available to join me on a field trip to the mall."

Haisley arched a brow, leaning back in her chair. "Weren't you the one who demanded that I stay in the office, far from any potential danger?"

Nash bit back a smile. She never could resist pushing back, even against his protective instincts. "I did. And it pains me to admit that you were right about me being intimidating to teenagers. Abby wouldn't talk to me or Ethan last night. She clammed up tighter than a nun's—" He caught himself, clearing his throat when Angela, hovering nearby, raised her pierced, disapproving brow. Yeah, probably not an appropriate metaphor for the office. "You get the idea."

Somehow, Haisley managed to keep her expression neutral, but he saw her repress a grin. "So you agree that I might have better luck getting a sixteen-year-old to talk?"

"I know you will." The words came out with a soft certainty that made Haisley blink. "Will you come with me?"

She hesitated, worrying that plump bottom lip between her teeth. Nash itched to reach out and smooth the tiny furrow between her brows, but he kept his hands to himself—reluctantly.

"Why not?" She stood and grabbed her purse. "Just let me tell Mila where I'm headed in case Mr. Benedict asks."

Nash nodded, tamping down his irritation at the mention of her boss. The way she avoided the asshole, he'd bet the man had been giving her a hard time. He itched to march into Benedict's office and give the bastard a piece of his mind. But he reined in the impulse.

Haisley wouldn't appreciate him fighting the battles she was more than capable of handling herself.

No doubt she was sidestepping conversations with Mr. Benedict, not because she was afraid of him, but because she was worried she'd snap back and get herself fired. Haisley refused to take shit from anyone. That, along with her cleverness and loyalty, were some of the things he loved most about her.

They stopped by Mila's desk quickly, but she wasn't in her office. And her boss's door was closed, so Haisley sent a text to Mr. Benedict.

As they headed to the elevator in thick silence, Nash couldn't help stealing glances, drinking in the determined set of her jaw and the way the fluorescent lights lit up her fiery hair. Her ass looked damn fine in that skirt, too.

God, she was beautiful. She sucker-punched him every time he looked at her.

"You're staring," she murmured as they stepped into the empty elevator. "If I have food on my face, you need to tell me."

Nash laughed, leaning back against the wall. "Nothing like that. It's just been a while since I've seen you get involved in something you're passionate about. It looks good on you."

A pleased flush spread across her cheeks. "Flattery will get you nowhere."

"Just stating facts." He let his voice dip into that low, teasing register he knew drove her crazy, gratified when her breath hitched almost imperceptibly.

The elevator dinged, doors sliding open, and Haisley darted out into the lobby. Nash fell into step beside her as they headed for his truck.

Once they were on the road, he glanced over at her and caught her fiddling with the strap of her purse. A sure sign she was nervous. Or upset.

"Hey," he called softly, waiting until she met his gaze. "You okay? You seem a little off today."

Haisley shrugged, looking out the window again. "Just a lot on my mind. You know, with the case, not to mention Mr. Benedict being an absolute douche nozzle to work for. He hired me because I know social media in a way he doesn't, but he keeps trying to tell me how to do my job. It's annoying; that's all."

That wasn't all. Even after two years apart, Nash knew Haisley too well to believe that. Her skin was too thick for the bastard to crawl under it in a handful of days. Which left Nash to wonder... Was she actually upset because she still believed he'd considered her an easy hookup? Or confused because he'd stopped flirting?

She changed the subject. "How did the rest of the interviews go yesterday?"

"Mixed bag. I want to circle back with Bianca, one of the targets who escaped. She was at the mall with her ex-boyfriend. They got into a fight, and the asshole left her there. She called her mom and was waiting in the food court for her ride."

"And she went to the bathroom." Haisley sighed. "Then her bad night turned horrific."

Nash nodded. "At first, she thought her assailant was her boyfriend messing with her. Then she realized this guy was much bigger and stronger. Since she had just finished a self-defense class, she managed a few maneuvers and fled to the well-lit food court. She said ten seconds later, she looked back to scream at someone to grab him, but he'd already disappeared."

"Oh, god. How terrifying, but I'm glad she escaped."

"Me, too. Her mother has hardly let her out of her sight since that happened in September. Bianca has anxiety and nightmares now. She even insisted on being homeschooled because she's afraid to leave her house."

"I hope she broke up with the boyfriend, too."

Nash sent her a ghost of a smile. Haisley always advocated for herself. She never understood when other women didn't have her backbone, and he loved that about her. "She did. I asked. After that interview, I talked to another of the victims who escaped, Summit."

"That's her name? Poor thing. As another person with an unusual name, I feel for her. I've always said that I'll punch the next person who calls me Paisley, but I'm sure she gets called all kinds of crap."

"Probably. Hell, I've been called Hash, Mash, Lash, Bash, Stash..."

He laughed. "But Summit has multiple ways for people to abuse her name. Sydney, Sheila, Shelby—"

"Or synonyms like Mountain, Peak, and Pinnacle." Haisley rolled her eyes. "Since tons of people are inconsiderate and can't be bothered to learn someone's actual name, she probably gets all of the above. What was her mom thinking?"

"That she would be 'unique.'"

Haisley snorted. "That's overrated. Sorry to sidetrack you. So you and Ethan talked to Summit…"

"I did for quite a while. Garrison had to take care of something for the bosses. She broke down a couple of times. Her dad glowered at me and kept trying to end the interview, but she insisted on continuing. She told a story similar to Bianca's, except that Summit mentioned a janitor closing off the hall to the bathroom just before someone tried to nab her. Earlier in the day, I spoke with Mrs. Wright, mom of Kaylee, the girl abducted on Christmas Eve. She couldn't tell me much, but she thought she remembered seeing a male janitor, too. I want to ask Bianca about that. Maybe he's not involved, and it's just a coincidence that he cleaned the bathroom before Kaylee's disappearance and before Summit was nearly abducted. But maybe not."

"Good idea. It sounds like too much of a coincidence, if you ask me. Just to let you know, I followed up with Mr. Benedict about his involvement in the day-to-day operations of the mall. He said he's far too busy for that." Haisley rolled her eyes. "Yeah, too busy giving me a hard time. He claims he leaves all the 'little things' to the mall's general manager. Have you caught up with him?"

Nash shook his head. "He's back from vacation tomorrow. Apparently, he left four hours after Kaylee's abduction to spend Christmas away. Who does that?"

Haisley reared back. "I get that it was a holiday, but we're talking about a girl's life. Asshat."

"Exactly."

Silence fell between them, and Nash filled it, if for no other reason than to keep Haisley talking to him. "So what did you do last night, besides stop in and check on Madison? Ethan told me. That was nice of you."

"Poor thing looked green. She says she felt loads better, so I can't imagine how much worse she must have felt when it was bad."

"Do anything interesting after that?"

Haisley hesitated, and he could almost see her trying to decide whether to tell him about Jasper. Finally, she shook her head. "Surfed online. Watched some TV. Went to bed early."

Nash stifled his disappointment. She'd open up to him eventually. He was determined. But it would require patience. And he'd have to thaw the ice between them first. How he'd do that wasn't clear, but he'd improvise until he succeeded.

"What about you?" she asked. "After you were done with your interviews?"

Just a guess, but *masturbating to thoughts of you* wasn't the answer she wanted to hear.

He shrugged and avoided the subject of Jasper and CSI. "Ate while I flipped channels. Nothing special."

It would have been so much better if he could have cuddled up with Haisley before he stripped her down and spent half the night inside her. Even the thought had his cock hard and pressing uncomfortably against his zipper, as if it knew Haisley was close and wanted a hit of its favorite drug.

Down, boy. Down.

"Anything else about the case I should know? Any suspects?"

At this point, everyone remotely associated with the mall was a suspect, but between his brain and his gut, he was narrowing it down. "Not yet."

She bit her lip again. That was Haisley's thinking face, but watching her sink her teeth into that plump, soft lip always drove him a little insane. "I've been thinking about a conversation I had with, um...a friend recently. At this point, I'm convinced these abductions are an inside job. It would be easy to point the finger at the maintenance man since he seems super resistant to keeping that hallway lit, but I'm wondering if this is a group effort?"

"I'm thinking the same thing. I mean, it's not impossible that one guy is pulling this off alone, but realistically?"

"Right? He would have to get the victim out the door quietly and get her to a vehicle nearby. He can't very well be abducting someone and have a van idling at the curb, I wouldn't think. It's a no-parking zone, and the chances of the mall cops sweeping the parking lot should be high…"

"Not to mention that he'd have to drug or secure his victim before he could even drive away so she couldn't fight back or escape while he was focused on the road…"

"But if this is a money-making endeavor, maybe the person responsible isn't even doing the dirty work. He probably wouldn't be, right? He'd entrust his buddies or hire that out. Because how would thugs with no connections sell their 'product'?" she asked.

"There are ways, but it's much easier when you know shady people."

Haisley fell silent again, worrying that lip with her teeth.

"Out with it," Nash demanded. "What are you thinking?"

"I can't decide if Mr. Benedict is a good suspect because he has the ability to make things—good or bad—happen at the mall or because he's a prick. I mean, other than financially, he didn't seem personally distressed about the abductions. According to him, Kaylee Wright ruined Mila's Christmas, but he didn't say anything about the kidnapping impacting his. He even admitted to covering it up. According to him, he did it to avoid the bad press and financial implications…but what if that's a front for the truth? What if he's really covering it up to hide his involvement. Because I've got to be honest. I chatted up the accounting supervisor earlier today, and she said the mall was hugely in the red. The place opened just as the economy started tanking, and at this rate he won't make his money back for fifty years. Maybe…he decided to make his money off the mall in a different way."

She wasn't thinking anything that hadn't crossed his mind, but… "It's a good theory, but we don't have any proof. Hell, we hardly have any clues. But we've only been at this two days. We'll get there."

"We?" She raised a cool brow his way. "Isn't Ethan your partner?"

"According to Hunter Edgington, yes. Just like I'm not supposed to look into your boss without his authorization. But Ethan and I mostly work better when we operate separately and compare notes. He doesn't really like anyone disturbing his 'thought process.' I think what he really hates is anyone telling him his unorthodox methods are likely to piss someone off." He shrugged. "But you... I like that we can bounce our ideas off each other, you know?"

"So you only like my ideas?" She crossed her arms over her chest.

Nash knew Haisley in a snit when he saw it. And as much as he'd wanted to tell her how much he loved her pussy, her heart, and everything in between, she wasn't ready to hear that. He had to keep this professional, the way she'd insisted their interaction should be.

"You know better than that, baby." That was as much as he dared to say now.

Haisley sent him a snappy little stare but said nothing.

Finally, they reached the mall and pulled into the parking lot. "When we get inside, I'll introduce you to Abby, the girl who works at the pastry shop, then let you take the lead—"

"No offense, but you asked me to talk to her because I'm less intimidating. You breathing down her neck isn't going to accomplish that."

As she hopped out of his truck, he followed suit, locking it with the fob and barreling after her in the chilly twilight as she headed for the entrance. "I'm not leaving you alone, not in this mall."

Haisley rolled her eyes, but it was halfhearted. She knew he was right; she just hated to admit it. The woman had pride in spades.

As they walked toward the entrance, shoulders brushing with nearly every step, Nash made a silent vow. He would find a way to make Haisley feel special and show her that what they had was worth fighting for. Even if it meant taking things slow, building that trust brick by painstaking brick.

She was more than worth the effort.

"Fine. But you need to stay back enough to let her breathe. And no glowering."

"I don't glower," he insisted, pulling the door open for Haisley.

"Oh, please. You think people just get out of your way because you're tall and they're afraid you're going to step on them? Really? It's your don't-mess-with-me glare. Shelve that. She's a girl. I'll show you how this interview should be done."

CHAPTER TWELVE

The mall was quiet for a Wednesday night. The unseasonable cold meant the place was even less crowded than usual. Abby stood alone behind the counter at the pastry shop, looking both bored and nervous.

"Stay behind me." Haisley raised a hand so he'd back off. "I got this."

He grabbed her by the wrist. "Wait."

"What?"

God, he was such a sucker for this woman. Even her impatience was adorable. "I know you've got this. I just wanted to say I'm glad you're here. We make a good team. Always have."

Something raw and vulnerable flickered in her eyes before she blinked it away. "Maybe. Now let's get the job done."

Haisley hadn't given him much…but she'd exposed a little crack in her seemingly impenetrable armor. It was a start.

As she faced the teenager, she pasted on a soft smile and approached. "Abby?"

"Um…yeah." The teenager cut a skittish stare over Haisley's shoulder at him.

Since Nash couldn't make himself smaller, he stepped back, parking himself at the nearby bistro table to give Abby plenty of space for comfort and Haisley room to work.

"Hi. I'm Haisley Rowe. I work with the man who interviewed you last night, Mr. Scott. Do you have a minute to talk with me?"

Abby sent a questioning gaze to her manager, who lurked a few feet behind. Then the girl flashed another cautious stare Nash's way.

"It's up to you," her manager said, but the woman's tone encouraged her to say yes.

"Absolutely," Haisley seconded. "I know you're scared, and we're only here to help. If you're worried about backlash—"

"A little." Abby fidgeted. "But terrible things are happening to girls my age. I talked to my mom, and I-I really thought about it. I can't sit back and let it happen just because I want to protect myself." The girl took off her hat and apron and shelved them under the counter, then turned back to her manager. "I won't be long."

"Take your time. This is important. It's a slow evening anyway."

Abby nodded, then raised the counter between her and the rest of the food court and emerged before following Haisley to the table beside his. Bless her for understanding that he needed to hear whatever Abby said rather than getting the information secondhand. And she was also smart enough to put Abby as far from him as possible to set the girl at ease.

Nash sent Abby the kindest smile he knew how. "Hi, Abby."

"Hi, Mr. Scott."

"Just Nash, okay? I want you to relax. You're with people who will do anything to protect you." She nodded nervously, and he gave the girl props for her courage. "Haisley is going to ask you questions. Nothing hard. I'm happy to help or clarify if you need me to, but I promise you're in the best hands. She's great."

Haisley flashed him a surprised glance as she stripped off her coat and hung it on the back of her chair before giving Abby her full attention. "Thanks. I appreciate you taking the time to talk to me. I know you've been asked a lot of questions."

"Not really. The detective who spoke to me only asked if I saw any part of the two most recent disappearances. I didn't work here for any of the others. But I wasn't scheduled for a shift during the abduction last September because school had just started. I didn't see anything on Christmas Eve. It was too crowded. Once Officer Haskins heard that, he was done with me."

Haisley's face tightened. For a moment, she looked as annoyed as he felt, but she did a great job of smoothing her expression and giving Abby an encouraging nod. "I'm guessing Nash asked you a lot more questions."

"And the guy he was with, yeah. Ethan? Is he here?" she asked softly, a little blush staining her cheeks.

Nash reared back. Holy shit. Maybe Abby hadn't been intimidated by him as much as she'd been tongue-tied around pretty-boy Ethan. He hadn't seen that coming…

"He's working another angle of the case."

"Oh." She looked a little disappointed.

He and Haisley exchanged a glance. Clearly, this development surprised her, too.

Thankfully, she didn't let that derail her. "Do you remember seeing anything odd recently? Or potentially dangerous?"

"A-a few things. Maybe. I've complained more than once that the janitor is creepy. I guess it's his job to lurk around the bathrooms and clean them. I don't look on the other side of the food court where the men's room is, but he doesn't spend as much time there as he does slinking around the women's room. I know that doesn't make him actually guilty of anything, but I'm putting it out there."

"You're doing great. Every detail helps. We just want to hear whatever you've noticed that caught your eye. Has he done anything you would consider threatening or over the line?"

"Not specifically. He just stares a lot." She shivered. "Like I said, he's creepy."

Abby was right. The janitor's behavior sounded shady, but that didn't make him guilty. On the other hand, that didn't mean he wasn't a person of interest since he'd come up in multiple interviews. Nash had intended to sit down with him anyway, but now he'd grill the dude.

"I know it can be tough and scary to work around someone who hits your ick button," Haisley empathized, making the girl feel heard and validated.

"Oh, my god. Exactly! He just gives me the willies, and I can't even…"

"I get it. But nothing specific that made you think he might be involved with the kidnappings?"

Abby shrugged. "I just feel like he watches all the girls at the mall, especially the pretty ones. He doesn't actually say anything, but he leers. It's gross."

Haisley sent her a sympathetic smile. "Are you ever asked to take out the trash down that hall and through the door to the bins out back?"

"Not anymore. My manager makes the guys do that. Or it stacks up until she can do it. But all the girls around my age know better."

"When you use that bathroom yourself, have you noticed anyone or anything else that made you anxious or uncomfortable?"

Abby shifted her gaze, then glanced toward the hallway in question. "When I work evening shifts, I try to hold it. It's a long four hours, but I can usually make it. Weekends are a full shift, though. I wait to use my lunch hour to walk to another bathroom, but I can't always make it, especially if it's…you know, that time of the month."

She whispered the words so softly, Nash barely heard. Poor thing seemed embarrassed about mentioning her period in front of a man. She had no way of knowing that, growing up, he had three sisters with whom he and his four other brothers shared a single bathroom. He lacked delicate sensibilities when it came to menstrual cycles. They were merely a fact of life.

"I know exactly what you mean," Haisley assured. "Go on."

"Well…"

Nash couldn't tear his gaze away from Haisley's profile as she listened to Abby. The determined set of her jaw and the keen intelligence sparking in her eyes as she absorbed every word mesmerized him.

God, she was incredible. A force of nature in her own right, with a knack for reading people and getting them to open up that left him in awe. He'd always known she was whip-smart and tenacious, but seeing her effortlessly accomplish what he hadn't been able to made his heart swell with fierce pride and admiration.

And a bone-deep, unshakable love that felt like a battering ram to the chest.

"The night not too long ago, when one of the girls got away? I was going to run to my car because I'd left my phone in my glovebox. It wasn't quite dark yet, so I thought it might be safe, and my mom was probably getting frantic that I hadn't checked in. But when I opened the door to sneak out to the parking lot, I spotted a brown van and a guy in a dark skull cap hanging around. He bolted the second he saw me."

Nash leaned in to bark out a follow-up. Haisley shot him an emphatic glare, so he bit his tongue. He wasn't used to downshifting, much less taking a back seat, but she was making strides with Abby. He just had to let her do her thing.

With an almost imperceptible nod, he leaned back in his chair and ceded the interview to her.

She flashed him a grateful smile, then turned back to Abby. "Bolted? He got in the van and left?"

"Yeah. Tore away from the curb, burning rubber and everything. I ran back into the food court. I was so freaking scared, I trembled for the next hour."

"I'm sure. I would have been afraid, too. Did you get a good look at the guy?"

"It was starting to get dark out there, but I saw enough."

"Had you seen him before?"

Abby thought about it, then shook her head. "Not that I remember. I mean, I see a lot of faces here, so if he was milling around the mall, I didn't notice him. He wasn't super tall, like him." She glanced Nash's way. "Or even particularly memorable. He seemed…average. But, you know, on the disturbing side. Besides the dark skull cap, he had brown facial hair and brown eyes. Um…his complexion wasn't dark or light. Maybe in the middle? That's harder because it was shadowy out there."

"Any identifying characteristics?"

"His nose was crooked, like it had been broken at some point. He had this blue teardrop tattoo under his eye." She pointed. "It was attached to something...tribal looking, but most of it was covered by his skull cap. And more tattoos on his knuckles, but I couldn't make them out."

Nash jerked upright and exchanged a glance with Haisley. Sure, that teardrop might mean the guy had lost someone, but it was also a common tattoo for gang members or those who had served time. Then again, attached to something tribal, the ink could mean something else altogether. "Could you describe him if we brought in a sketch artist?"

"Yeah. I have a good memory. I suck at names, but I remember faces."

Nash reached for his phone, happy to help and have some purpose in this conversation. "I'm on it."

As he texted Hunter Edgington, he heard Haisley continue with questions. He was so damn proud of the progress she was making. This was their first possible break in the case.

"Fantastic. Did you get the make and model of the van? Did it say anything on the side, like the name of a business? Did you get a license plate?"

"It was a Chevy, but not like a minivan. It was more old school, like something out of the seventies."

"A conversion van?"

"Yeah. There was nothing on the side. More than that?" Abby shrugged. "Sorry. I was too rattled to look at the license plate, but I did notice the front right hubcap was missing. The whole thing looked dingy. Tinted windows and a dented chrome bumper."

"What shade of brown? Light, like a tan color or—"

"No. Darker, like a coffee brown. That's all I remember."

"That's a lot, and it's incredibly helpful. Have you told anyone else?"

"Just my mom. I was too scared to tell anyone else."

"Do you remember anything else about that incident? Did you see anyone else outside? Or in the hallway when you came back in?"

She paused, then frowned. "I didn't think about it then because I hadn't been working when anyone was abducted, but the janitor was hanging around the women's bathroom. When I came back in those doors, he had the hall blocked off, and he looked…"

"Annoyed?"

"Startled. I didn't know what was up with him, but I didn't stick around to find out."

That was the third mention of the fucking janitor. Nash made a mental note to move him to the top of the interview list. Even if the creep wasn't involved, even if he was just doing his job, he must have seen something at some point.

The glance Haisley sent him suggested the same thing. He nodded, letting her know they were on the same page.

Damn, she was good at this. He already respected her intelligence, but tonight had taken it up another notch.

"You absolutely did the right thing, hustling back to safety," Haisley assured the girl. "Anything else you remember?"

Abby paused again. "Not that I can think of. Sorry."

"No, you've done great. You've helped more than you know. Do you have your phone handy? I want to give you my number in case you think of anything else."

Abby reached in her pocket, unlocked the device, and handed it to Haisley. "Cool."

Haisley tapped in her number as a new contact and saved it, then texted herself from Abby's device. "Got it. I'll pass your the info on to Nash and Ethan, too, okay?"

Good call. Her mother was probably in protective mode, and who could blame her? Given that, if a grown-ass man gave her underage daughter his phone number, she might not take it kindly.

Abby nodded. "Yeah."

Finally, Nash leaned in. "You've been a big help. We appreciate it."

The girl looked relieved. "I wanted to do whatever I could."

"Have you thought about quitting your job until this is resolved?"

Abby winced. "My mom wants me to, but I'm saving for college. I need the money. Otherwise, I can't go."

She was in a tough place, and Nash understood. He'd grown up the dirt-poor kid of a coal miner. There hadn't been money for more than the necessities when he was a kid, and he'd worn nothing but Trees's hand-me-downs until he was an adult. "If I put out some feelers for a different job that has similar hours and pays at least as much, would you consider it?"

Haisley snapped her stare to him, clearly surprised. By his offer? That he cared what happened to the girl? God, did she think he was the kind of asshole who didn't give a shit about anyone but himself?

"Y-you would do that?" Abby breathed.

He purposefully softened his voice. "Sure. I can't promise anything, but this world is scary, and you shouldn't have to feel unsafe where you work."

Abby glanced over her shoulder to her waiting manager. When she turned back, her expression looked guilty as hell. "I hate to leave Ginger. She's been really good to me, almost like a second mom."

"Then she should want the best for you. I think she'll understand," Haisley said, backing him up.

"Yeah. Then, um…if you hear of something and I'd qualify, I'd appreciate it."

They wrapped up the interview and stood so Haisley could don her coat. Nash insisted on watching Abby until she made it back to her unit and was ensconced safely behind the counter.

As they headed for the exit, Haisley turned to him with a triumphant grin. "I think that was a success. We have a solid lead to chase down."

"Thanks to you," he said, unable to keep the note of pride from his voice. "I couldn't get her to even look me in the eye yesterday. But you? You were amazing."

"Thanks." She gave him a faint grin. "I've had a little experience. Well, it was a simulation with an online crime-solving group, but the others involved told me I did okay. It was good experience to do the real thing in person."

"You've got a knack for it."

But he wasn't surprised. Haisley wasn't merely amazing. She was the kind of woman who would keep him on his toes, challenge him in all the best ways. And he wanted nothing more than to support her and stand by her side in every sense of the word.

A pretty flush stole across her cheeks at the praise, but she shrugged it off. "I just approached her a little differently, and you did a really good thing, offering to help her find a safer job. Think you can pull that off?"

"No promises, but I know some people. I can make some calls."

"I love that you'd do that." She smiled as he opened the door to the parking lot. "And you're right. We make a good team."

Her words were like a caress to his heart, igniting a fierce spark of hope in his chest.

God, he wished she'd tell him why she'd left two years ago... Or he needed to work up the guts to ask. If she'd be honest, they could work through anything. He was convinced of that, just like he knew they were meant to be together.

For now, he bit back the words and helped her into his truck. The time wasn't right. He hadn't regained her trust. They were in the middle of a dangerous investigation and emotions were running high, fueled by worry and adrenaline. But she'd moved back, and that bought him time. She'd find out soon enough that he wouldn't give up until she was his again.

"We do. In every way." He sat beside her and let the words hang in the charged silence, heavy with barely restrained desire.

Haisley's breath hitched as he started the engine, her pupils flaring wide as she stared back at him. He felt caught in the magnetic sway that pulled them inexorably closer.

But then she blinked away and cleared her throat. "We should start running down this information, see if we can locate that van. Oh, and revise the list of people who need interviews and the questions we should ask."

"You're right. Want to do that over pizza and beers?"

"I-I...don't think it's a good idea."

Nash tamped down a flare of frustration. But even if he couldn't say the things burning the tip of his tongue, he could show Haisley that he was all in. That he believed in her, understood her, supported her, and loved her with every fiber of his being. "Then we'll start again tomorrow. I'll track down the janitor, and together, we'll solve these abductions."

And as he drove her to her car and secretly followed her home to make sure she got inside her place safely, he hoped that maybe, if they kept chipping away at this case together…she'd truly believe in them again, too.

CHAPTER THIRTEEN

On Thursday morning, Haisley made her way to her desk, only to find a steaming cup of coffee in an insulated mug and a blueberry muffin on her desk. She glanced around the big, open office space, but other than a few of the accounting folks, she saw no one who might have left her breakfast. She lifted the delicious-looking muffin, complete with streusel, and nearly moaned. This had to be from her favorite bakery—the one that had contributed to her carrying an extra ten pounds when she'd lived here before.

Then she saw a note under the pastry.

I came by early, hoping to catch you. Sorry I couldn't stay. I'm heading out to meet Ethan at the mall to interview the janitor and some other food court employees. This afternoon, I'll be talking to the final target who escaped. Ethan has been focusing on the mall manager and says he has a new development. I'm hoping you're able to make some progress on your end, especially in talking to Benedict.

I know you used to enjoy these muffins. Have a good day.

-N

Against her better judgment, Haisley was touched. Leaving her coffee and her favorite muffin was sweet. Considerate. Almost...boyfriend-like. Not something a mere hookup would do. Not strictly professional but not pushy or flirty, either.

Damn it, that man confused her, but she couldn't stop thinking about him. What was he up to?

Being with him the last couple of days had felt...different. He acted as if he liked her as a person. Respected her. Cared about her opinion, even. He hadn't tried to push her into bed again or even kiss her. Her head told her that was a good thing. Her heart wasn't sure. And her body was calling her twenty kinds of stupid because it only wanted Nash.

Maybe that's why the dam of feeling she'd been desperately trying to contain behind her walls had begun to break free. Somehow, Nash had worked his way under her skin again and seeped into the carefully guarded corners of her heart. With every heated look, every teasingly suggestive remark, and every compliment that rolled off his tongue, he'd chipped away at her resistance.

Two years ago, she'd sputtered a halfhearted BS excuse, cut off all contact, and fled halfway across the country. She'd felt horrible that she'd lied to him, but she'd spared him the worst of the pain, right? Yes. And she'd stayed far away until she'd convinced herself she was over him. But nothing had loosened Nash's death-grip on her heart.

Now, Haisley had to admit that she was falling for him all over again. Maybe it was time to face the fact she was always going to be in love with him.

Where did that leave her?

The prospect of confiding in him was utterly terrifying. If she told him the truth, would she lose him again? Maybe. Probably. But if she didn't...wouldn't she lose him again anyway? How could their relationship deepen if she wasn't honest?

Besides, not coming clean also meant resigning herself to this frustrating limbo of unresolved feelings and unfulfilled yearning. She'd done that with him once. Did she truly want to do it again?

Haisley didn't have answers, just a jumbled mix of hopes, fears, and aching needs making endless waves of confusion.

The only thing she knew for certain was that she needed to figure out how to balance her growing feelings with the job at hand. Neither of them could afford distraction when innocent lives were at stake. And Nash inevitably turned her thoughts to mush simply by smoldering at her from across a room.

The rest of the day passed without any peep from him except a frustratingly impersonal text message about needing more time with potential witnesses and Ethan's lead blowing up, but he'd fill her in later.

Later turned into complete radio silence for over twenty-four hours, leaving Haisley feeling unmoored and unsettlingly dismayed. Clearly, she was in deeper than she'd thought if his one-day absence left her feeling this unbalanced.

Finally, he waltzed into her office on Friday afternoon with a cocky grin that both annoyed and relieved her. She scrambled to tamp down the flutter of relief and giddiness that spread through her at simply laying eyes on him again.

Of course, her facade shattered the second Nash gave her a nakedly admiring once-over. He dumped his messenger bag on her desk and trashed his empty energy drink with a wink. "Miss me?"

Way too much. But she couldn't blurt that, especially in the office with prying eyes and ears all around. Not when lives were at stake. Their twisted whatever-this-was had to take a back seat.

She scoffed. "You wish."

His grin widened, and he bent close, under the guise of pulling something from his tote. "Liar. You forget how well I know you."

Haisley looked down as a flush swept up her face. No, she didn't forget. She could never forget.

"Did you make progress on the case?" She pretended to schlep papers across her desk.

"Oh, yeah. Sorry it's been a hot minute since I checked in and updated you. We're definitely getting somewhere." He leaned even closer. "But I missed your...skills in action."

Her heart rate surged. Did he mean that as suggestively as it sounded? "Oh?"

"Yep. More than you know," he murmured in her ear before he pulled a nearby chair close to hers and sank into it, suddenly business as usual.

Haisley tried to deal with the sudden whiplash. Of course they needed to focus on solving this case, but she'd be lying if she said a reckless part of her didn't love the idea of unleashing her "skills" for Nash at every intoxicating step. "What did I miss in the investigation?"

"Let's take this somewhere...private."

At his insinuation, her pulse leapt. An ache settled between her legs, insistent and throbbing. It had been so long since he'd touched her—since anyone had. Her trusty battery-operated boyfriend wasn't doing it. Her picky pussy only wanted Nash.

But she didn't dare invite him closer. As weak as she felt, she'd drop her clothes for him in thirty seconds or less. "The conference room? I don't think anyone is using it."

He grabbed his things. "Lead the way."

She plucked up a few file folders, along with her laptop, and guided him to the executive wing, then inside the small room at the opposite end of the hallway from Mr. Benedict's office. Together, they sat at the wood laminate table.

As she spread her stuff out, Nash texted someone, then tucked away his phone. "Where were we? Oh, the mall's general manager. He suddenly resigned yesterday. Benjamin..." He dug through his papers.

"Yuslav," she provided. "He just quit?"

"Ten minutes before we were set to meet. He apparently tendered his resignation to Mr. Benedict, giving no notice, and hauled ass off the premises. At least according to what the folks in the mall offices told Ethan."

She winced. "Well, that explains why Mr. Benedict was in such a shitty mood yesterday and why he was shouting at Mila to 'do something' ASAP. The poor woman was nearly in tears and started calling everyone she knew…"

"Yep. The timing is awfully shady. Especially since, rumor is, he didn't leave a forwarding address for his final check."

"Seriously? I'll see what I can find out. At the very least, his personnel records should have some contact information."

"That would be great. Unless he left home like he did his job, I'd like to chat with him. And that's one interview I don't want you coming along for. I've never met the guy, but based on what I've heard, I have a bad feeling."

"What about the janitor? How was his interview?"

"He was mysteriously sick. Just couldn't make it in today. He didn't know when he'd be well enough to talk. I offered to ask my questions over the phone, even though I prefer in-person sit-downs so I can read body language. But he told his boss that he'd lost his voice, so it would be a while before he was available."

"Well, that's awfully convenient."

"Absolutely. The third target who escaped, Caitlyn Gale, was really helpful. She described her incident. It was close to closing, and she decided to hit the restroom after meeting a girlfriend for an evening of shopping and some dinner at the food court. The friend had just left, and she made a pit stop before heading to her car."

"I'll bet she wishes she hadn't."

Nash nodded. "She says she still has nightmares, and she's in therapy. But she also added some very interesting details no one else provided. She's convinced there are multiple people involved because someone grabbed her from behind, the way the others described, but she claims another man held the door open for him as he dragged her out."

Shock seared Haisley. "We've suspected it was an organized ring, but I didn't think we'd get confirmation that quickly. Did she tell the police?"

"When Detective Haskins found out she had only been dragged as far as the curb before she managed to escape and that she couldn't describe her assailant, he declined to interview her. Said she didn't have any information he'd need." Nash shot her a cynical stare.

"Is this guy lazy or crooked?"

"That's my question. Could be either. Or both. But we'll put a pin in that and come back later."

"How did Caitlyn get away?"

"Clear thinking under pressure and luck. Before the guy could take her purse, she yanked a can of pepper spray from inside and shot both him and the guy holding the door. While they were howling, she darted back inside and found one of the security guards, who waited with her while the police showed up. Of course, by the time they arrived, the assailants were long gone. So was any evidence of the scuffle."

"Did Caitlyn mention seeing the janitor that night?"

"She did. When she came out of the bathroom, the hallway was roped off to traffic from the stragglers in the food court. As soon as she walked out, he disappeared inside the ladies' room, leaving her alone in the hall."

"So the janitor couldn't have seen anything?" Haisley frowned. "But does that mean he didn't know anything?"

"Great question. Since we haven't talked to him, I don't know, but my assumption is he must have some idea what's going on. How much is the question. Him disappearing into the women's room gives him plausible deniability, but with the frequency of women sighting him just before someone grabs them from behind? I'm not buying it."

"I'm not sure I do, either. In fact, it seems to me that he could have been the one to clean up after Caitlyn's failed abduction. Who else could it be?"

"Right. It was almost closing time, and not that many other people were around. It's possible someone else was waiting to mop up, but Caitlyn didn't remember seeing another mall employee in the area."

"So what are our next steps?"

"Is Benedict here?"

Haisley sent him a reluctant nod. "He's been holed up in his office all afternoon. But something pissed him off earlier today, because I've heard him shouting way more than usual. I can't tell what he's saying, even when I tried to loiter outside his office. But whatever's going on, he's furious."

"I only know of him what I can glean from a few brief interactions. What does your gut say?"

"You mean, is he involved? We talked about this once, but I'm thinking it's a strong maybe. I'm a little worried I'm biased because he's such a dick to work for, but logically, I can't rule out him being involved."

"I'm wondering if he's knee-deep in it, too."

What a crazy, tangled mess. "Where do we go from here?"

"We're only seeing part of the picture. Yesterday, Ethan said he snagged a new lead and wanted to follow— Hey!"

Haisley looked up to find Ethan Garrison in the doorway with mussed dark hair, a five o'clock shadow, and ink strategically placed to drive women wild. Oddly, she wasn't affected, but she knew that everywhere he went, women flocked to him.

"Hey." Ethan entered and shut the door behind him, then settled into the seat next to her, bumping her shoulder. "Hey, beautiful."

"Back the fuck off," Nash growled, his posture threatening to come across the table.

Was he jealous? Of Ethan? He didn't need to be, but if he was…

Hiding a grin, she bumped his shoulder back. "Hey, yourself. What's up?"

He looked down at his lap, then back up with a sly grin. "You wanna see?"

Nash slammed his fist on the table. "This is a fucking office building, and we're here to do a job. Haisley asked for professionalism, and we're going to give it to her or I'll smash in your fucking face."

Whoa. He wasn't even trying to hide his pissed-off. Maybe she should downshift on the fake flirting.

"Sure you will," Ethan tossed back with a sparkle in his eye. "But if you want professional, beautiful, I got you. Besides, we have a lot to cover."

"Tell us," she insisted, glad he'd backed down.

"Well, I had a gym buddy who's also a Lafayette PD officer. He was trickling information my way...until he suddenly clammed up. Apparently top brass threatened anyone who leaked a word. So that's interesting and noteworthy."

Yes, and probably Mr. Benedict's doing somehow. He had money, and he had influence. He'd proven he had no trouble using it to protect his interests.

"Damn it," Nash muttered.

"Exactly, so I bailed to Plan B. I started chatting up the mall manager's assistant yesterday. Well, former mall manager. Cute little thing named Julia. I flirted, and she wasn't paying attention when I slipped her boss's office key off her desk and into my pocket."

"How did she miss that?" Haisley couldn't picture a scenario in which the assistant had been flirting so hard that she'd completely failed to notice Ethan swiping something important.

Garrison grinned. "She was too busy screaming into my shirt because I had my hand in her little black panties."

Haisley's jaw dropped. "You got her off at her desk?"

Ethan's grin widened. "Don't look shocked. It worked, didn't it?"

She rolled her eyes. "You're worse than a fukboi."

"I prefer man whore, thank you." He winked. "Afterward, I got her digits and pretended to leave. Then I watched her head to lunch with a loopy smile on her face, and I slinked back into the former mall manager's office. It had mostly been cleaned out, which he must have done overnight, because I swung by late on Tuesday and tried to ask him a few pointed questions. He was suddenly too busy—seemingly doing nothing more important than picking his nose—to talk to me. His office was a fucking catastrophe when he had security escort me out for 'harassing' him. Today? The place was virtually empty. His laptop was still on his desk with an order for IT to wipe it clean, so I absconded with it."

"Anyone see you?" Nash asked.

"Nope. There are no cameras in the office. Julia told me in confidence just before her big O, and I double-checked for myself." He pulled the computer from a crossbody briefcase hanging off his shoulder and plopped it on the table. "I called your brother as soon as I got it. It took us until three a.m. to finagle past the asshole's login. Most of the files on there were boring as fuck, day-to-day mall business. But he had a whole section on his hard drive partitioned off from the automatic backups. Every fucking file is encrypted. Trees has been working on them all day. When he texted to say he'd gotten into that part of the drive and opened the files, I picked it up and headed over here."

"Did my brother say what was in the encrypted files?"

"No. He said he was fucking tired after being up all night and half the day, so he was going to bed. Laila shooed me out. She's so protective of her man." Ethan laughed.

"He's crazy protective of her," Nash put in.

Haisley couldn't argue. She'd seen that in action. "So you have no idea what Yuslav was hiding?"

"Nope. Let's find out together. I'm really hoping it's not his personal porn collection. He was the human equivalent of a pimple on a leper's ass, and I really don't want to think about his…proclivities."

She shuddered. "Let's hope he was hiding something more useful."

A collective hush settled across the room as Ethan lifted the lid on the laptop, entered the password Trees had hacked for him, then started fishing around the hard drive. She and Nash huddled closer and watched him methodically search the laptop.

At first, nothing made sense. Folders had nonsensical names, but all followed a pattern of a six-digit number, followed by a single letter. Some of those were empty. Some of them had sketchy documents full of more combinations of letters and numbers that Haisley didn't understand.

"Does any of this mean anything to you guys?"

Nash and Ethan exchanged a solemn glance, but neither responded. Instead, Ethan's cocky disposition morphed into hard steel. And Nash tensed, looking both dangerous and so protective, she nearly scooted away from him.

"I need the list of victims." Ethan held out his hand.

Nash rifled through his bag until he pulled out a notebook and flipped it to a page full of his chicken scratchings. "They're listed here, in chronological order, including the ones who got away."

Ethan grabbed the notebook and slapped it on the table next to the laptop, glancing back and forth between the page and the screen. "Fuck."

"It matches?"

Ethan nodded. "Exactly."

"What?" Haisley felt like they were talking over her head, and it was pissing her off. "What matches?"

Ethan dragged her closer for a better view of the screen. "Each of these six-digit numbers corresponds to a date—the one in which the victim was abducted. The letter corresponds to her first initial. So see this? Twelve, twenty-four, and two digits for the year, followed by a K. That's Kaylee, who disappeared on Christmas Eve." He clicked on her file, only to find another assortment of numbers and letters.

"Shit," Nash muttered. "This spells out everything about the girl abducted. H must be height. The fifty-two must mean she's five foot-two. The W corresponds to weight. She weighs one twenty-two. The next numbers… B? W? H? I don't know. We did weight and height, so what would another W or H mean?"

Haisley glanced at the numbers herself and it hit her. "Bust, waist, and hips. They're measurements."

Ethan nodded. "So the other stats just below? Another H and an E, next to abbreviations for colors, must be—"

"Hair and eye color," Nash cut in. "This lists Kaylee as having brown hair and eyes…and that corresponds to the information her mother provided. Son of a bitch." He scowled. "But what's the V for? There's a Y next to that."

Haisley knew and it made her sick. "If they're selling these girls for sex, I'm sure they're finding out whether or not she's a virgin."

"That's disgusting," Ethan growled.

"These fucking bastards don't deserve to live." And Nash looked ready to kill each and every one of them himself.

A few minutes later, they had verified that all the victims had a file folder with a document outlining her stats. Those who had been missing longer had other details, but interpreting their meaning wasn't easy.

"What do you suppose the B stands for on this file?" Haisley pointed to the file they found on the first victim, Taylor. She worried like hell what the "yes" after it meant.

Both men shrugged. They might not know the answer, but their grim expressions told her it was probably bad.

"And what is this weird combination of stuff below? They both have decimal numbers, they're separated by a comma, and the last number is negative. Is that…longitude and latitude?"

"It is." Nash was already pounding away on his phone. Then he looked at Ethan with a shake of his head.

"An island. Am I right?" Ethan asked.

"Tiny. Private. In the middle of the Atlantic, sandwiched between the west of Cuba's southern tip and the most westerly Cayman Island."

"Fuck."

"Is that where they're taking those girls?" Haisley asked in dawning horror. It was terrible enough for these victims to be ripped from their homes, but to be transported out of the country to a foreign land with no government reach, no help in sight…

"This one at least," Ethan answered. "But look, victim two, Collette, has all the same information after her abduction date and her initial. Except…wait. There's another seven-digit code beneath the B we can't figure out and the location."

"What the fuck could that mean? Damn it," Nash grumbled.

"I don't know. Where does that leave us?" Haisley asked.

"Still searching," Ethan admitted. "Sometimes cases are one step forward and two steps back. We just keep plugging away."

"And hope for a break." Nash sighed.

"What he said." Ethan's eyes were fixed on the computer screen as he clicked away. Suddenly, he sat up straighter. "Anyone ever heard of a business called Rugs Direct Unlimited?"

"Nope." Nash shrugged. "Should I?"

Haisley shook her head. "I've never heard of it, either."

Ethan scowled at the monitor. "I found an advertisement of sorts. There's a picture of a pretty typical area rug stretched across a hardwood floor. The ad copy reads: *Exclusive, one-of-a-kind decor. Lay them right the first time, and they'll be yours forever.* They're based out of Cuba."

Nash lifted a brow. "Want to bet their 'headquarters' is on a small island between the mainland and the Caymans?"

"Oh, god." Haisley slapped her hand across her mouth. "They don't mean rugs. They're talking about…"

"Women," Nash confirmed.

She was going to be sick. "Is this how they're finding…buyers for these girls? Through a fake rug business?"

"That's my guess. Let me see if I can find a website." A few clicks later, Ethan swore. "It's prompting me for a password."

"So anyone with the right credentials can just…shop for a sex slave?" Haisley pressed a hand to her chest. "That's…"

"Disgusting? Repulsive? Terrible?"

Even imagining the horror these women must be enduring was hard. "All of it. And nothing on the computer might help us get into that site and rescue those girls?"

"I need more time. Nothing is jumping out at me right now, but I'm going to head home and keep looking." He raised a brow at Nash. "You staying?"

Nash looked between her and Ethan. Half of her hoped Nash remained. She missed him when he wasn't around. And this investigation was taking a dark, creepy turn. On the other hand, despite their spontaneous New Year's Eve kiss and her blossoming feelings, she and Nash were no longer an item. Being this close to him for too long would only land her in trouble.

"Nah, I'll go with you. We'll look through this together." Nash gathered his things as Ethan did and stood. "I'll catch up with you when I have something, Rowe. Text me if you stumble across any clues or talk to Benedict, okay?"

Everything on his face said he could take or leave her, that he didn't need or want her anymore. It hurt like hell, but what had she expected, especially after she'd told him to back off? When tequila wasn't doing his talking and he wasn't flirting for the hell of it, she was just another of his former flings. She didn't mean anything to him.

"Sure. See you next week." She hustled out of the conference room and into the women's bathroom before hot, unwanted tears fell.

CHAPTER FOURTEEN

The French bistro was buzzing with the Friday-night crowd when Haisley arrived the following evening. She scanned the upscale space full of dark wood, mirrors, white subway tile, and Louis XIV touches that gave the restaurant a Parisian feel until her gaze landed on Gracelyn, who practically glowed as she read a menu at the corner table.

"Hey, you." Haisley sat and pulled her friend into a hug. "Sorry I'm late. I got held up at the office."

Waiting to hear from Nash again about the case, hoping he'd wander in before quitting time. But he'd been a no-call, no-show.

What was he doing tonight? Haisley wasn't sure she wanted to know. Instead, she pasted on a smile and did her best to be present with her friend, who looked like she had big news to spill.

"No worries." Gracelyn smiled. "I just got here myself. Busy day."

The petite brunette looked rosy, sated, and sublimely happy. Haisley had a suspicion Gracelyn's job wasn't the only thing keeping her occupied. "And what about your nights? Looks like you met someone special."

Gracelyn's blush deepened. "Those are busy, too…if you know what I mean. I've been seeing Kane Preston since New Year's Eve."

Haisley's jaw almost dropped. He was the last person she would have thought her friend would go for. "Wait. Kane Preston, the loner with the beard who works with Nash and Ethan and—"

"Yes. We got together on New Year's Eve, after almost everyone else left. We've been inseparable since. He's…everything I never thought I'd want in a guy, but he's amazing."

Haisley's chest squeezed with longing as memories of those first giddy, lust-fueled days with Nash resurfaced. She couldn't help but remember all the ways they'd indulged their hunger for each other while they'd laughed and talked…and she'd fallen ridiculously hard. Then one day, everything had become complicated, and her life had turned upside down.

Gracelyn waved a hand in front of her face. "Hey, you okay? Where'd you go just now?"

"Sorry." Haisley forced a tight smile. "Wow, I'm…shocked. I don't know Kane well, but he seems like a decent guy."

"He really is. You know I've always been attracted to cerebral men, right?"

"You mean nerds."

"Smart individuals," Gracelyn corrected with a grin. "But Kane is not only brilliant, he also happens to be hot, muscled, tatted, amazing in bed… He's, like, the perfect package."

"Well, if you're happy, I'm happy for you."

Gracelyn frowned. "I know that expression. You have reservations. You're worried I'm getting in too deep too fast."

Sometimes Haisley was startled by how well her friends knew her.

"If I'm being honest, yeah." She grabbed the water a waiter set in front of her. Once the fifty-something man said he'd be back to take their order, she focused again on Gracelyn. "Look, I want you to be happy. You deserve the best guy out there."

"But?"

"But…it can be messy to get tangled up with one of these operatives. You should guard your heart until you know where you stand."

"Like you did? How did that end up for you?" Gracelyn shook her head. "I don't want to play games. Kane and I haven't talked future or made any promises, but I want to be upfront about how I'm feeling.

How will I ever know if it's mutual unless one of us puts ourselves out there?"

Haisley opened her mouth to argue, then snapped it shut. Was that her problem with Nash, too much between them unspoken? Feelings seemed like a giant, room-swallowing elephant they both ignored. Or maybe that was just her. Maybe she was projecting her emotions onto him. Maybe he didn't feel a damn thing. She was too chicken to find out.

Gracelyn's expression softened as she sighed. "I know you. I know what happened. I know you got hurt, just like I know you still love him."

"I don't want to get into this."

"Too bad. You need to. Did you ever tell him why you left?"

Haisley winced. "No."

"How is anything supposed to work out if you don't level with him?"

"He gave up on me, Gracie. Whatever he felt is gone."

"It didn't look like that on New Year's Eve."

"That was tequila, and things have changed. What would be the point of telling him I love him now, when he's so clearly moved on?"

"Because that's *not* clear. And you need to get this off your chest. Put the ball in his court. Make him think."

"Charli did that once upon a time with Daniel, and look how that isn't working out."

"Apples to oranges. Nash is hardly Daniel."

"Thank god."

"You never thought he was good enough for Charli."

"Because he's not. Rat bastard."

"What I'm trying to say is, we're all different people in different situations. Just because it might not work out for them doesn't mean it can't for me. Or for you…"

Haisley shifted in her seat, hot discomfort prickling her skin. She was being a coward; she knew that. Was it possible that, all this time, Nash had been harboring feelings, too? That he'd been reluctant to tell her and risk his heart?

The thought tilted her world on its axis. Her head spun.

"But even if Nash has moved on—which I don't think he has—wouldn't you rather know instead of angsting about it?"

"You…might be onto something. I have to think. But this conversation isn't about me. Tell me all about Kane. What's going on?"

"Besides the fact he makes me laugh and he's upped my orgasm quotient by about a million?" Gracelyn flashed her a lopsided smile, complete with dimples.

By the time they left the bistro, Haisley was cautiously optimistic for her friend. But when it came to Nash, she was still reeling. What if she was missing out on something deeper with him, something that could make her profoundly happy, all because she was too afraid to risk her heart again?

As she pulled away from the restaurant to head home, her phone rang. Seeing Nash's name on her display made her heart leap and race. Did he want to see her tonight?

"Hey." She tried to sound casual, not like she was freaking out. Not like she was eager to lay eyes—and anything else she could—on him. Definitely not like she was on the verge of blurting *I love you.* "What's up?"

"Did you get the chance to talk to Benedict this afternoon?"

So he didn't want to see her. Yes, she'd asked for professionalism… but she still felt let down.

"No. He was in another shitty mood. About four, he tore out of his office, marched down the hall, and yelled at Mila. Then he screamed some more at a few of the accounting folks. He kept tearing through the office like a tornado before he unloaded his temper on me about negative press from some independent journalist on YouTube before he slammed out of the office. Mila crept out a few minutes later, looking shaken, and left, too. I doubt she went home." At least Haisley wouldn't have if she'd been Benedict's wife.

"Any chance anyone is still at the office?"

"There's always a chance, but I doubt it. Most of those people… When five o'clock rolls around, they blaze a path to the parking lot. What's going on?"

"I need to search your boss's office."

"Tonight?"

"I don't think this can wait. Ethan intercepted a new communication on the laptop he swiped. Apparently, someone wasn't aware that Yuslav quit his job because they sent him an urgent message. It's encoded, but between Ethan and my brother, they figured out the cipher. Whoever reached out says they have another buyer, and they need fresh product—fast. The request was for someone younger than usual."

"Younger than sixteen?" That made Haisley sick. "Ugh. You're right; we can't waste a moment."

"My bosses will be pissed that I'm going behind their backs, but I have to take the investigation where it leads me. I'll fill them in once I'm sure this is the right path, but I think we have to give Benedict a hard look."

"He's looking awfully suspicious."

"It's possible he's guilty. Plausible, even. You said yourself this is an inside job. He personally hired Yuslav to manage the mall. His sudden resignation seems to have pissed your boss way the hell off and sent him scrambling to find a replacement."

"But we have to acknowledge that he could be scrambling simply because replacing any employee with mall-management experience will be difficult, not to mention time-consuming and costly." She wasn't defending Benedict as much as she was playing devil's advocate.

"True, but he could also be worried that his partner in crime got exposed and is now hanging in the wind with his dick flapping around."

"You're right. So…let's try to figure out what's up with my boss."

"There's no 'we.' You're not going."

Is that what he thought? "How are you going to get into the office without me?"

"You're going to give me your key."

"And send you to rifle through Benedict's things alone? That's what you think?"

"I'm not bringing you, Haisley. That's final. This could be dangerous."

"Life is dangerous. I could be hit by a bus tomorrow."

"There aren't that many buses in Lafayette," he pointed out.

"You know what I mean. Besides, if we're caught, I'm your get-out-of-jail-free card. I can say that I needed something I'd left in the office, but I was too afraid to come alone after dark... If you're caught without me, no one will ask questions. They'll just haul you off to jail."

"I won't get caught."

"You don't know that. Besides, I've been in Benedict's lair a few times. I have a sense of his organization system and where he might hide things. It will take me less time to find anything implicating, which means less time to get caught. You're taking me with you."

Nash sighed in defeat. "You're a pain in my ass, Rowe."

"Does logic hurt your posterior, Scott?"

"No. But you clearly need yours spanked red."

Haisley clenched, memories of all the pleasurable times he'd warmed her cheeks with his bare palm—slowly, steadily, inexorably heating her up and making her drip with need for him. But that was a long time ago. "Don't change the subject."

"I'm trying to keep you safe."

"I didn't ask you to. We're supposed to be working together. Benedict said so. Should I meet you there?"

"Fuck," he muttered. "No. I don't want your car captured on the lot's cameras. I don't want him having any way to connect you in case he realizes someone searched his office."

Yeah, she'd rather not be harangued by her asshole of a boss, either. "So what's the plan?"

"Oh, you're going to let me come up with that part?"

"If you're dispensing sarcasm, that's lame. You better bring your A-game, because I'm damn good at it."

"Vixen." He sighed. "I'll pick you up in twenty. Wear head-to-toe black."

"So I blend in better when all the lights are off?"

"And because you look hot in black. Bye."

Haisley tried not to smile. "I've moved since I had that apartment way back when. Don't you need my address, hotshot?"

Nash laughed. "No."

Dead air told her he'd ended their call. That sexy bastard had already figured out where she lived? Because he'd been curious? Because he was a control freak? Or…because she mattered to him?

The unanswered questions spun in her brain as she tossed on some dark yoga pants, a black turtleneck, and matching tennis shoes. She shoved her hair into a messy bun and tucked it under a black cap she'd bought on a ski trip to Colorado a few winters past.

Ten minutes later, Nash pulled up on his motorcycle and tossed her a helmet. Wordlessly, she climbed on behind him and wrapped her arms around his waist.

As he took off into the darkening night, she resisted the urge to lay her cheek on the wide, muscled expanse of his back. She hadn't touched Nash since New Year's Eve. She hadn't cooled down since then, either. Being this close to him thickened her desire and sent her self-control reeling.

Ten minutes later, he parked in the lot of a twenty-four-hour greasy spoon down the street from her office and helped her off before locking away their helmets. "Let's go."

"How are we approaching? There are only two doors in and out of the building and—"

"There are three. We're using the service entrance. I scoped it out the first day, looking for the building's weaknesses and escape points. Once we've gone up the freight elevator, you can get us inside your office door. Thank god this is an historic building, and no one wanted to sully tradition by installing electronic card readers that would leave a digital trail of your visit."

Haisley pulled her keyring from her pocket. "Lead the way."

As they neared the building, he lifted his finger to his lips to indicate silence, then guided her toward a side entrance she'd never noticed. Then again, she'd never been to the building's loading dock.

Outside, an elderly black man waited under a dim light, flipping a coin in a rickety old chair.

"Hey, Zeph," Nash called.

The older man rose. "Door's open, like you asked."

"You're a hero." Nash slid him fifty bucks. "As promised."

"Just doing my bit. Hope you find what you're looking for. You've got an hour. Then I have to lock up."

"We'll be out of here in half that." Nash clapped his shoulder. "You have my number if you see anyone coming."

"I do, and I'm watching." The old man nodded her way. "Miss."

She smiled. "Thanks. We appreciate you."

He tipped his cap to her as they slid inside the building and headed through the section that had been cordoned off as a warehouse. Through another door, one she'd bet was usually locked after hours, Nash emerged into the building's main lobby. He plastered himself against the wall, then settled his arm in front of her to press her flat, too. "Cameras are here and here." He pointed with a whisper. "We're in a dead zone. Zeph has a friend in security who's going to reboot the system, including the cameras. It should take two minutes. We'll have to be on the elevator by then."

"Got it."

He reached into his coat pocket and pulled out a pair of leather gloves. He handed her a purple latex pair, like she'd seen in a doctor's office. "Put those on and listen to me. No matter what happens, you follow my instructions. Do you understand? If I tell you to hide, you hide. If I tell you to run, you run. No questions asked."

"Nash..."

"Nope. Agree now or I'm taking your office key and sending you outside to spend an hour with Zeph. Your choice."

She loved how protective he was, and she even had an appreciation for his bossy side. Not that she would tell him. Who knew if he was cautious because she mattered to him...or because he didn't want to clean up her blood and guts?

She rolled her eyes. "Do I need your permission to breathe, too?"

"This is no joke."

"Yes, your highness."

"Keep with the attitude, and I'll—"

Nash's phone buzzed in the otherwise silent lobby. He read it, then scanned the room.

"You'll what?"

"Later." He gestured her to follow. "We're on the clock. Let's go."

He hailed the elevator. Together, they crashed inside it with just under a minute to spare. Thankfully, the people helping Nash had not only killed the cameras in the lobby, they'd cut off the lights inside the car, too.

God, she loved to see him at work. He was methodical, thorough, and seemingly thought of everything. It was surprisingly sexy. Maybe because that was the way he functioned in bed, too.

When they reached the floor of Benedict Land Development's office, she inserted the key and let them in.

Surprisingly, the floor wasn't totally dark. More than a few computers were rolling through their screen-saver sequences while ambient lights shone from the faux industrial ceiling. Neither of them bothered with more than a glance at her desk. Instead, they tiptoed down the hall, past the executive suites.

Mila's door was closed and locked. Haisley wondered if she'd gone home to the man who had yelled at her or if she'd decided she'd had enough and found someplace else to spend her weekend. If Haisley knew the woman better, she would have reached out and offered her a spare bedroom as a kindness to someone going through a rough patch...but Mila might find that weird. Besides, her boss wouldn't appreciate her trying to come between him and his wife.

At the end of the hall, she stopped and whispered, "You know I don't have a key to the boss's office, right?"

Nash nodded. "I would have been shocked if you did. But this door I can handle."

He withdrew something from his pocket, stuck it in the lock, and started jimmying it. In less than thirty seconds, he was pushing the door wide open and, gun in hand, sweeping the office. "Clear. Come in."

She did, carefully closing the door behind her. "Do we dare turn on the lights?"

Nash shook his head. "He doesn't have cameras installed anywhere on this floor. I looked. But I don't know if he has any other sensors, and I wouldn't want to tip off the janitorial staff if they happen to see something. Hold this."

When he handed her a flashlight, she took it with a scowl. "And do what?"

"Tell me where you think we should start looking."

For the next ten minutes, they searched his desk drawers, his filing cabinet, and a credenza in which he kept various plaques and trophies he'd collected over the years. Nothing jumped out at Haisley as being suspicious. "It's hard to find something when you don't know what you're looking for."

Nash nodded. "There's a reason his door is always closed, and he locks it the minute he leaves. It's possible he's merely private, but…"

"He could be hiding something, too. If he's involved, what would he keep here?"

"If he was smart, nothing. But Benedict clearly thinks he's better than everyone else, so it wouldn't surprise me if his cockiness makes him sloppy. We're looking for ledgers, receipts, notes…anything that would tie him to Yuslav beyond the employee-employer relationship."

"I have an idea." Haisley didn't wait for Nash to follow her to the back of the room since she had the flashlight.

"Tell me."

"When I tried to talk to Benedict earlier this afternoon, I knocked on his door and poked my head in. I noticed him fiddling with something on these bookshelves." She gestured to the massive, wall-to-wall unit behind his desk. "Here on the right."

She fished around and found a humidor. When she lifted it from the shelf and shined the light on it, she found it padlocked. "Damn it. He was either looking in or putting something into this… Everything happened so fast, but—"

"Hand it to me."

She did, watching as he set the fancy wooden box on her boss's pretentiously large desk. "What are you going to do?"

He pulled another pick out of the little kit in his pocket. "It would be easier to just break the lock, but he'd know someone was onto him. So picking this sucker it is."

"Won't it take a while to— Okay, that was fast," she murmured as he lifted the lid. When she flashed the light on the interior, she was surprised as hell. "That's not a cigar."

"Nope." He lifted the Glock out of the humidor and checked it out. "Loaded. He's ready for action."

That terrified her. "Does he intend to defend himself or go postal on the office?"

"Or something else entirely. And what do we have here? His passport, valid and in his name, along with a wad of cash—at least ten grand in hundred dollar bills."

"Is that, like, his go-stash?"

"Or a nefarious, hiding-shit-from-his-wife stash. Maybe this will give us the answer." Nash pulled a phone from the box's interior.

Haisley frowned. "That's not his usual phone."

"Your boss having a burner phone doesn't automatically make him guilty...but it looks suspicious as fuck." Nash tapped a button, and the screen flickered to life, prompting him for a passcode. "Damn it. Any ideas?"

"Mila's birthday?" She rattled off the date.

Nash tried the numbers. "Nope. We don't have time to stand here and guess. And I don't want to lock us out of the device. I'm taking this with me. My brother will get it pried open easy."

"Are you insane? What if Benedict comes back for it before Monday?"

"You got a better idea?"

She didn't. "If you get it back to me by Sunday night, I'll come in early Monday morning and try to sneak it in before he arrives."

He shook his head and shoved the device in his pocket. "We'll have to lock Benedict's office door behind us, and you won't be able to get in without me. I'll take care of it. What else is in here?"

Did he really think she was going to let that slide? "You're cutting me out."

"I'm keeping you out of the danger as much as possible."

"But—"

"I already didn't want you here, where you might be implicated if something goes south. But I'm not involving you any deeper. You're going to be a good girl and give me your office key so I can repeat this tomorrow—alone."

"The hell I am."

He turned to her, the kind of displeasure all over his face that used to make her shiver. "What is it you don't understand? I'm trying to protect you."

"I didn't ask you to. And if you get caught with my key, I'm out of a job. So stop shoving me out of the way."

"What? I respect you too much for that. Baby, you're smart, and you keep me on my toes. If it weren't for the bad guys and all the women disappearing, if we were holed up in a war room trying to solve this shit, there are few people I'd rather have helping me than you. But you understand that being fired for helping me is way better than what will happen if you're caught by the bad guys? You'll be dead—or worse. This is my *job*. No. Fuck it. That's not the only reason. I didn't have you in my life for two goddamn years. Do you think I'm going to risk you when I've only had you back for a handful of days?"

Haisley gaped, her heart suddenly chugging. Did Nash mean that the way it sounded? Romantically? Like he'd never gotten over her? "Nash, I—"

"Shh." The sound was soft, but he zipped a hard palm between them. He whipped his phone from his pocket, his face tightening as he scanned the illuminated screen, then cursed under his breath as he arranged everything but Benedict's hidden phone back into the humidor. "Put the box back. Someone's coming."

CHAPTER FIFTEEN

Goddamn it.

SIG in hand, Nash watched in his peripheral vision as Haisley set the locked humidor back on the shelf with shaking hands, then spun to face him.

But Zeph's text had made one thing clear: company was coming. The sound of footsteps treading down the hall—straight toward them—made that all too real.

How the fuck were they going to get out of this without being spotted? Or worse?

Haisley's eyes widened as she held up her hands, silently asking what to do. Good question. The room's lone window was a four-story drop straight down to concrete, so that was a no-go. Benedict's office only had one other escape, and whoever was walking down the hall was blocking their path and heading straight for them.

Fighting their way out wasn't optimal, and Nash didn't want to do anything that might risk Haisley. But he wasn't sure he had a choice. He'd do whatever necessary to make sure she made it out alive and unscathed, even if that meant killing the intruder or sacrificing his own life.

Jesus, he really should tell this woman he was in love with her. Now simply wasn't the time.

The footsteps were nearly on them, and time was ticking down. He grabbed Haisley's arm and dragged her to the dark corner behind the door.

With his heart thundering, he readied himself for combat. The hinges holding the heavy slab creaked, and the door opened, sandwiching them between the portal and the wall. Nash peeked around the obstruction and spotted a lone figure entering and thankfully eschewing the lights.

The person making their way across the shadowy room was petite and female. She sniffed once, then again. Allergies? Illness? Or…

She reached for the humidor and found it locked. Then she broke down in sobs, leaning against the bookcase. "G-George…"

Was that…Benedict's wife? What the hell was going on with her?

Behind Nash, Haisley poked his ribs.

He risked a glance over his shoulder.

Mila, she mouthed.

Holding in a curse, he nodded, then tucked himself behind the door again, using his big body to shield Haisley. A few minutes passed before Mila Benedict sniffled one last time, lifted her chin, and made her way out of her husband's office, softly shutting the door behind her. Moments later, he heard her enter the office just down the hall. She closed the door. Nash nearly sagged with relief.

"We've got to get out of here," he whispered. "I have the burner phone. Let's go."

She grabbed his sleeve. "Maybe you should go, and I should tell Mila that I left something here and—"

"No. I don't want anyone knowing you were here tonight."

"But—"

"Baby, I'm not risking you. Let's go." He took her by the hand and used his other to slowly open Benedict's door before locking it behind them.

Together, they tiptoed down the hall, treading ever so slowly past Mila's office. Light seeped under the door, and he heard more sobbing.

Haisley squeezed his hand, and he felt her tremble as they crept toward the elevator—and escape. He hated like hell that she was scared. He should have fucking insisted that he go without her, but a tricky deadbolt secured the main office door. He could have gotten past it...but it would have taken precious time. And he'd been stupidly swayed by how insistently she'd lobbied to come along. Their banter had felt...normal, like the old days. He hadn't wanted to cut her off.

And now she might pay the price for his weakness.

Finally, they cleared the hall and sprinted on tiptoes across the hardwoods of the main office, then around the reception area. Cursing the fact the emergency stairwell dumped out directly onto the most surveilled half of the lobby, he hit the elevator button.

"We made it," she whispered, breathing hard.

"Almost." He was relieved as fuck when the elevator showed up quickly.

The ding of its arrival chimed way louder than he remembered. His heart thrashed in his chest. Goddamn, that sound might as well have been a fucking blow horn. Could Mila hear that, cocooned down the hallway in her nine-to-five sanctuary?

While he worried, the elevator doors seemed to take forever to open. For fuck's sake, molasses in January moved faster. Snails could race more quickly. They needed to get the hell out of here.

And inside the car, the goddamn lights were on bright.

"Who's there?" Mila suddenly called in a shaking voice across the big, open space.

Beside him, Haisley gasped, then tried to bite back the sound.

Heart lurching, he yanked her down until she crouched next to him behind the reception desk. Then he pointed to the elevator doors.

She nodded.

But Mila kept coming. "I heard you. I have a gun I'm not afraid to use. And I'm calling the police."

He hated to move or for Haisley to potentially be seen, but the elevator doors that had taken forever to open were already starting to close.

"Go," he hissed, shoving her forward and blocking her with his body.

She hauled ass, doing some cross between a scramble and a knee-walk. He followed close behind. Once they were inside, he plastered her against the wall near the panel and dropped his chin as he pushed the button for the lobby. "Hide your face."

She buried it in his chest as he heard Mila's footsteps barreling toward them. He shoved his face in the corner of the elevator car, holding his breath and palming his SIG. He felt Haisley's heart thudding against his, and everything inside him crawled out of his skin to protect her. He didn't want an altercation, especially with her life on the line.

Fuck, fuck, fuck.

Finally, the doors slid shut just before Mila reached them. He heard her cursing, then more talking, which he presumed was her calling 911, before a whoosh sent them down to the lobby. He had zero idea what waited for them. Had Zeph been found? Was that why the lights in this metal box were on?

Just as they descended, Zeph texted again.

> Sorry about the lights. Lobby is dark. Get the hell out.

The man didn't have to tell him twice. The instant the elevator dinged and the doors slid open, he hustled Haisley into the shadowed lobby, hugging the wall again to avoid the potential cameras until they found their way to the warehouse area.

Zeph was waiting as soon as they slipped through the door. "Glad you're out in one piece. Security says the cops are on their way."

He handed the older man another fifty. "You've been gold."

"I didn't think the boss lady was going to show up."

"That makes two of us. Any idea why she's here?"

"Nope. She just went in. I let you know as quickly as I could."

"Appreciate it."

Zeph nodded and handed back the money. "Keep this. I just hope you find whoever took those girls. Go!"

Nash wanted to argue, but sirens started wailing in the distance, so they dashed around the building and across the street, running full sprint until they ducked behind the old brick buildings erected in the downtown area's heyday, then huffed-and-puffed their way to his motorcycle.

He willed his adrenaline to take a back seat to urgency and unlocked his saddlebags before tossing a helmet her way. "Put it on."

Thankfully, he didn't have to ask her twice or give her any other instruction. He hopped on as he secured his chin strap, then revved the engine. Haisley was already behind him, clutching his middle tight. He was ridiculously grateful not just because she kept him warmer in the winter chill, but her body temperature and grip assured him she was okay and with him. Her exhalations on his back as he eased out of the parking lot and onto the street before flipping on his headlight reminded him that she was alive and vital.

He'd risked her too much.

His head spun as he raced through the dark, nearly empty streets. Her place was closer than his. And he'd rather have her in his space where he could watch over her. Protect her. But she'd only balk if he took her to his home. And fighting wasn't what he wanted to do with her.

Fear, adrenaline, and need all pounded through his veins, scorching his insides. His cock was hard as concrete and throbbed for action. He had to calm the fuck down. But that wasn't going to happen until he got alone and took himself in hand. Haisley wanted "professional" from him, and he couldn't trust himself around her until he bled off this surge of excess energy.

They reached her place without incident. He parked on her side yard and killed the engine. "Inside."

"You okay?" she asked as she peeled off her helmet.

"Fine," he lied as he stashed their brain buckets. It was taking every fucking ounce of his restraint not to push her against the wall and seize her soft mouth while he tore away her yoga pants, then plowed into her sweet cunt.

Her scowl clearly said she didn't believe him. "If you say so. I got it from here. Let me know about the phone once you get it—"

"No." He grabbed her by the arm and hauled her to her front door. "I'm going to go in and make sure that you're alone and it's safe. Then

I'll leave you. Don't tell a soul you left your place tonight and don't open the door for anyone."

"What do you think could—"

"Happen?" He gestured impatiently until she unlocked the door. "Anything. The police could come. Mila and her gun could pay you a visit. Whoever's behind the abductions might know we're onto them."

She let them in the front door, then pressed a hand to her chest. "Maybe you should stay."

Was she trying to kill him? Or tempt him beyond what he could endure? "That's a bad idea."

"Wouldn't I be safer with you?"

Jesus, did she not understand that he was hanging on by a thread? That his self-control was slipping, and the longer he stood near her, smelling the remnants of her fear tinged with her female musk, the more likely he'd lose his goddamn mind? "From a life-or-death perspective, yes."

"Is there another perspective that would make me unsafe near you?"

"You ever spent time with anyone directly after a combat mission?" If she had, it wasn't him. He'd always been careful not to bring his battle hangover to their bed because he'd never wanted to scare her.

"No. I don't—"

"Understand?" He walked at her, his stare fierce. She backed away. Making herself his prey was the worst thing she could do now. His hunting instincts activated, adding to the electric fire ripping through his system. "I'm about two seconds from stripping you, penetrating you, and not letting you up until we're both exhausted and sated."

She gasped, her rosy lips parted, her big blue eyes searching him. She licked her lips as she retreated another step. Her back hit the wall. "Nash?"

"Let me check the fucking house. Then I'll go." Doing his best to ignore his screaming need to touch her, he pulled the SIG from his holster and scanned the dark foyer.

Behind him, she shut the front door and locked it. "Stay with me."

There was no fucking way he'd heard that right.

He whirled on her. The question must have been all over his face, but she nodded silently in answer.

Oh, holy fucking shit. Was she serious?

"If I do, I'm going to fuck you, Haisley. Hard. Ruthlessly. Repeatedly. I'll be an animal without mercy because I want you so fucking bad, and everything primal in me needs to be reassured that you're alive. So think about what you're saying. I'm going to sweep the house, and I expect you'll have come to your senses by the time I get back."

Nash dragged in a ragged breath and did his level best to ignore a stunned Haisley as he crept through her house, flipping on lights and checking behind doors and in closets, proclaiming each room clear as he worked his way through the bungalow.

When he reached her bedroom, her scent pooled so strongly here that it nearly brought him to his knees. He swallowed back a snarl. Why did this woman alone make him so fucking feral?

After a quick check of her messy-as-usual bathroom, he swallowed back another lust bomb and charged into the hallway, far enough away from her scent that he could breathe without seething and craving her. He backed against the wall and dragged in rough breaths, trying to regain control of himself before he fell off the fucking cliff.

After a handful of deep inhalations, he was no longer pinging off the walls. Oh, his skin still felt electric and his blood still burned, but he'd bought himself about sixty seconds of sanity—hopefully long enough to run out the door and make sure she locked it behind him before he jumped on his bike and hauled ass through the frigid night back home. He could take this drugging need out on his hand. Tomorrow, he'd call her and apologize.

For a lot of things.

Tucking away his SIG, he dragged in one last breath and did a death-march down the hall. The last thing he wanted to do was leave her, but it was for her own good.

"You're clear. There's no one inside, and I—" He stopped short when he looked up.

And he almost lost his fucking wits.

Her skin gleaming like a pearl, Haisley stood in the foyer, every inch of her naked. "Nash? Don't go."

CHAPTER SIXTEEN

Haisley hoped like hell she wasn't making a mistake.

"Say something," she breathed.

Even in the shadows, she saw him swallow hard. His breathing turned rough. "You don't know what you're inviting."

"I do." She bit her lip, wishing he would just step closer, take over, give her some indication that she hadn't totally embarrassed herself. "And I want it."

"Baby, if you don't put some clothes on in the next five seconds, I will fuck you hard until you cry for mercy. Spoiler alert: I won't have any. You will wake up tomorrow sore, covered in bite marks and bruises from my fingers, marked in every way possible. You'll be dripping of me. You'll be smelling like me. You'll be pushing at me to get off you. I won't budge." Fists clenched like he was fighting his baser instincts, he stepped back. "Last chance."

His words only made her heart flip and her womb clench. "I don't need it. I'm saying yes."

"Feel how fucking hard I am for you." He grabbed her wrist and pressed her palm to his cock.

She gasped at the pure steel under her fingers, thick and long, engorged and enflamed. She curled her fingers around his stiff length and roughly stroked him through his jeans, relishing the feel of him in her palm again after two long years. Haisley drank him in, nearly going weak in the knees. "Nash…"

He tossed his head back with a groan. "Jesus, I want you. You're a fucking fever I never recovered from."

Nash staggered closer, pressing her against the wall with his big body, giving off a heat so overwhelming, she felt faint. Instinctively, she looked up at him, watching him with wide eyes and shallow breaths until he gripped her hips and bent, pressing his forehead to hers. His harsh exhalations bathed her face.

"I'm burning for you, too." Now wasn't the time to divulge secrets between them, but in that moment, she needed him. "I never stopped."

He looked down into her eyes, a furrow settling between his dark brows as he silently asked why the hell she'd left. His breathing picked up. Against her pussy, his cock got impossibly harder. "Baby…"

Haisley didn't want to talk. "Kiss me."

Nash tangled his fingers in her hair and pulled with a growl. "Give me your goddamn mouth."

"Yes, Sir." The words slipped out before she rose on her toes and offered him her lips, curling her fingers into his shirt and holding her breath as her heart threatened to burst from her chest.

He was on her in an instant, rough hands pulling her body against his stiff denim and stiffer cock while he covered her mouth and sank in with his plunging tongue, dominating her with one sweep.

She whimpered against him. God, she'd missed him. So many times in the last two years she'd tried to convince herself that the desire between them hadn't been that hot, that their connection hadn't been that deep. The second his lips seized hers, Haisley knew she'd been lying to herself. The desire was stronger, eviscerating what little self-control she had.

A wave of dizziness assailed her. Her knees wobbled, threatening to give out, as she lost herself in him, because she believed that he—and he alone—would keep her sated and safe.

He tasted like testosterone, danger, ruthless hunger…and the sweetest memories. She'd grown up hating fairy tales because even as a child, she'd been too cynical to believe in everlasting love. Her father had skipped out on her as a newborn. Her mother had been devoted to her...but she'd ultimately chosen the danger of speeding a hundred miles an hour in her boyfriend's sports car over her young daughter. And her aunt had never done more than seen to her food, clothing, and shelter. By high school, guys had seen her as a challenge, a conquest to brag about to the other like-minded douches. In college, she'd taken control and slept with hot frat boys and football players, having zero expectations beyond her own gratification. She'd resigned herself to believing that's all "love" was...

Until Nash.

Touching him again was like basking in golden sunlight after two years in freezing rain. Haisley clung to him, wanting the moment to last forever. They couldn't go back in time and fix the rough patches and half-truths between them. She was too afraid to zip forward, to the moment when their passion was spent and Nash would, no doubt, want to talk. But now was sublime. Now was everything. She intended to lose herself here, where she felt safe, happy, adored, and protected in a way no man had ever made her feel.

Suddenly, he wrenched from her. Haisley opened her mouth to protest. He couldn't leave her. She'd burn alive.

But instead of retreating or putting professional distance between them, he cradled her breast and dipped his head, panting as he plucked her nipple in his inferno of a mouth. He pulled hard on the tip, sucking until she hissed in pleasure. God, she could feel his tongue tugging on every nerve ending between there and her clit, now throbbing for his attention.

As if he could read her mind, he shoved his hand between her legs, roughly covering her mound and delving his fingers between her folds where she needed his touch most. "You're so fucking wet, baby. So juicy. I swear I've thought of nothing but you since New Year's Eve. I can't stop."

He poured his words, sweet like melted sugar, all over her. She craved more. "Don't stop."

"Never," he vowed against her skin, his lips burning a trail up to her ear. "Do you hear me? I'm feeling this sweet pussy because it's mine. It's always been mine."

"Yes."

"It's always going to be mine. Is that clear?"

"Yes."

"Haisley..." he growled in warning. "You know what I am to you."

"Sir. Yes." She nodded helplessly. "Sir."

"Good." He nipped at her lobe as his fingers swirled insistently over her swollen clit. "You're close, aren't you?"

Close? She was on the edge, ready to come out of her skin, scream his name, and surrender everything in her heart to him again.

So, so dangerous...and in that moment she couldn't care that they were on a collision course and the truth might ruin them forever. This —his possession, their passion, her devotion—might also save them, right?

"Baby?" he prodded.

"I need to come," she whined. That was beyond honest.

"On my cock. I want to feel exactly how hard you come for me, so you're only going to do it on my cock tonight."

Haisley couldn't think of anything she wanted more. "Yes, Sir."

"Good girl." Nash rewarded her by shoving a pair of wide fingers inside her and filling her pussy that felt so very empty without him. "Where's your bedroom?"

"Upstairs, on the right," she gasped. "I don't know if I can hold out."

With his free hand, he pinched her nipple as he twisted his fingers deeper inside her, rubbing her G-spot. "I'm not inside you yet. So you'll wait."

As if to enforce his will, he withdrew his digits and swept her into his arms, then began taking the stairs two at a time.

"Nash..." She wanted to weep at the loss of his touch.

He said nothing, just dashed single-mindedly for her bed, kicking the door open to her room, then tossing her onto the mattress. As she bounced, he pinned her down with one hand and ripped his fly open with the other. "Is there any reason I should stop? That I can't fuck you bare?"

"No." She was on the Pill.

He grunted like that pleased him...but the implications of her still being on birth control didn't. Wouldn't he be shocked to know that she hadn't been interested enough in anyone since him to bother having sex? It was no surprise to her that he still didn't want kids. He never had.

"You haven't let anyone else…without a condom?" he asked, then finished his question with a curse.

"No. No one."

"I always glove up, but you…" He cupped her face in his hands. "I don't want anything between us, baby. Not ever again."

Haisley knew he hadn't been a monk in her absence. Of course not. She'd left him with almost no explanation and only the barest of goodbyes. When she'd first returned to Lafayette, Madison and Charli had both warned her that he fucked around a lot. She'd be lying if she said that knowing he'd wanted other women enough to take them to bed and share his body hadn't hurt. But even that pain wasn't so cutting that she could find the will to refuse him. "I don't, either."

"Thank fuck." He tore his shirt off and flung it across the room, then shoved his pants to his knees before kicking them away. "Spread your legs and look at me."

Breathless, she obeyed.

God, this was happening. Really happening.

Haisley lost herself in the dark possession gleaming from his eyes as he gripped her hips so tight it almost hurt. Almost…but his fingers digging into her flesh were like a drug. They would leave bruises; he knew her body well enough to know that. Just like she knew he'd always enjoyed leaving his mark somewhere on her, as if he'd been compelled to show the world that she belonged to him.

Thank god nothing had changed.

She raised her hips to him. "Fuck me."

Poised on top of her, Nash shook his head. "Just fucking won't satisfy me with you. I've waited too long, and I've wanted you too much. You, I'm going to own. By the time I'm done, there won't be a part of you that doesn't feel melded to me. Still saying yes?"

His words arced thrill through her body. Anticipation suspended her in breathless limbo, leaving her weightless and desperate and anticipating every exquisite moment they shared. "Yes, Sir."

She'd barely whispered her reply before he slammed his lips over hers and began pushing his way inside—his tongue into her mouth, his cock inside her pussy—his very being fusing her heart to his. Sensations swelled. Euphoria and dizzying need swept through her while he pushed his fat crest into her swollen cunt—rhythmic, insistent, demanding. He pierced her clenched tightness and slid down, deeper, filling her more and more until she stretched to accommodate every inch of him with a burn and sting that drove her pleasure sky-high.

Moaning in delicious torment, Haisley gripped the hard steel of his broad shoulders as he slammed into her, flattening her to the mattress.

"Take the rest of me," he growled. "Bend your knees. Tilt up. Surrender."

Accommodating all of him was always a challenge. Still, Haisley complied without hesitation. He rewarded her with more inches and more pleasure.

God, yes. This was everything she'd missed. His insistence. His intensity. His command of her body and soul.

Finally, Nash bottomed out inside her. He stilled for a moment, his forehead pressed to hers, their ragged breaths mingling in the space between them.

"You're real. This is real."

She knew exactly how he felt. "Yes. Yes…"

"And it's so fucking good." The pained moan tore from his throat.

Then he began moving again, and Haisley lost herself in the rhythm of their bodies coming together. Nash's hands seemed to be everywhere at once—gripping her thighs, palming her breasts, cupping her face with surprising tenderness.

Haisley met him thrust for thrust, pouring every ounce of her unspoken love into their connection. She traced the strong lines of his back, relishing the flex of his muscles beneath her fingertips. She dug her nails into his shoulders as the pleasure built, marking him.

As if he was determined to return the favor, he bent to her, sinking his teeth into the sensitive flesh between her neck and her shoulder, biting down just hard enough to make her swoon. He sucked, dragging her flesh into his mouth as his tongue laved her like a favorite candy. It would leave a mark, and the fact he couldn't stop himself, that he wanted the world to know that he'd taken her, sent her tumbling toward a bliss she hadn't known in way too long.

While he repeated the process on the bare cap of her shoulder, he thrust into her insistently, pounding at her slow and deep as if he couldn't merge with her enough, as if he wanted their two bodies to become one. Desire made her head swim as she twisted and angled her hips to welcome everything he gave her.

And he knew her so, so well, dragging the head of his cock over her G-spot and reawakening her need with a flurry of tingles until she was biting her lip, clawing his back, and crying out in desperation. "Nash!"

"Yes, baby. My cock is inside you. Anytime I'm filling you tonight, you come. Over and over. Show me how much you want this."

"Yes!" she warbled mindlessly, spiraling higher.

"Prove this pussy is mine," he snarled in her ear, banging her with another bed-rattling thrust.

"Yes. Yes..." she panted. "It is. It's yours."

He crashed into her again, again, tightening the ache only he could sate. "Tell me that you're mine."

Haisley hoped she didn't regret this, but she couldn't hold back. "I am. I'm yours. I always have been."

"That's fucking right. Come."

In his arms, she gathered and swelled, then exploded in a crescendo of sensation and need. She clung to him as the world blurred, leaving only Nash as her reality. With every demanding stroke, he drove her up and higher, far beyond a place where things like breaths, time, or the past mattered.

She soared, peaked, and floated, saturated by pure bliss. Other than pleasure, she only knew Nash—his scent, his perspiration, his thrusts deep inside her as he forced her to ride the high of her orgasm while his gritted teeth and harsh fingers told her the effort to hold out cost him dearly.

She coasted the downhill slope of her climax with a replete sigh, but Nash was nowhere near done.

With a low growl that sent shivers down her spine, he pulled free from her clasping pussy. His teeth grazed her collarbone, nipping and soothing in turn. Haisley's fingers tangled in his hair, holding him close, silently begging him not to leave her.

Nash gripped her hips, the hard planes of his body pressing into her soft curves as he began blazing a trail of kisses down her body, worshiping every inch of her with lips, tongue, and teeth.

Haisley's heart thrashed and trembled as he shimmied down to cup her breasts and take them, one after the other, into his mouth. She reeled at the pinch of his fingers, the scrape of his teeth, his groans that vibrated through her body.

This was everything she'd dreamed of for the past two years, yet so much more intense than she'd recalled. She probably didn't deserve this pleasure from him. The weight of her secret pressed at the edges of her consciousness, but she pushed it away. Right now, there was only Nash, only this moment. She needed him in a way she never let herself need anyone.

His mouth encompassed her nipple again, and Haisley cried out, back arching off the bed. Nash's hand splayed across her ribcage, holding her in place as he alternately lavished attention on her swollen tips. His touch was reverent yet animalistic and possessive, making sure she felt both adored and owned.

"Please," she whimpered, needing more. Needing what he silently promised as he worked his way down her body, his lips brushing across her abdomen, his tongue flirting with her navel, before his teeth made an impression on her hip bone. She hissed at the sting, reveling in his insistence as he wriggled down her bed. He laved and nipped her inner thighs before he inhaled her, eyes closed as if he'd been anticipating this moment forever.

Then Nash lifted his head, his eyes dark with desire and some emotion that made Haisley's heart race. Without breaking eye contact, he slowly lowered his head, his intent more than clear.

Haisley's breath caught at the first swipe of Nash's tongue against her clit. The jolt of desire jetted tingles to her toes as the ache began pooling between her legs again, as if she hadn't come mere minutes ago. He did it again, lingering over her most sensitive spot. She keened. Her hands fisted her sheets as he devoured her with single-minded focus, worshipping her pussy and drawing out every gasp and moan.

As the pressure and pleasure built, Haisley tossed her head back, helpless in the face of his overwhelming need. How had she survived two years without this man? Without his touch, his taste, the way he made her feel utterly cherished and desired?

He was unstoppable as he drove her up again, until she gasped and clawed and begged him for relief. Just one more lash of his tongue, and her world would explode in a bright, white-hot crescendo somehow even stronger than the first.

Nash slipped two fingers inside her, curling them just so, ramping Haisley up mercilessly. She cried out his name, and it sounded more like she was begging. Probably because she was.

But Nash refused her, vaulting his way up her body, claiming her mouth in a searing kiss as he lunged deep inside her again with one rough thrust. Haisley tasted herself on his lips and moaned, wrapping her legs around his waist and losing herself in this dangerous, dizzying sensation.

He stuck his hand between them, bruising fingers digging into her hip, and settled his thumb over her throbbing clit and manipulated her until she was a breathless gasp away from incinerating. "Come, baby. Let me feel you."

God, there was no holding back, especially when he nipped at the other side of her neck, marking her again and growling with possessive pride. The sound resonated through her, ramping her up even more.

As if her body was no longer her own, her back arched, her thighs trembled, and her pussy grasped him greedily, refusing to let go. The sensations converged into something powerful and breath-stealing before the sensations burst.

Ecstasy crested, crashing over her in relentless waves. Her screams echoed off the walls. Time held no meaning. Nash lavished her with pleasure, manipulating her body as only he could, drawing out her pleasure until she was trembling and oversensitive and gasping at the sheer intensity.

"Haisley... Jesus, fucking... Yes!" Nash groaned out against her lips, his voice rough.

"Do it," she answered, pulling him closer. "I'm here, Nash. Come inside me."

No way could she tell him how much she'd missed this feeling of completion. Missed him.

To her shock, he shook his head and pulled from her clasping pussy. Instantly, she felt empty, aching, almost abandoned. "What are you... Don't go!"

With a snort, Nash flipped her onto her belly and worked his arm under her. He pulled her up onto her hands and knees while he wedged his thigh between hers, spreading her legs wider. She'd barely settled onto the mattress when he aligned his cock with her opening and filled her again with one mighty thrust. Both of them groaned at the exquisite sensation of being joined once more.

"I'm nowhere near done with you," he vowed in her ear as his teeth found her neck again and marked her once more. The friction of his cock against inflamed nerve endings, coupled with the flare of pain in her shoulder from his primal bite, sparked another wave of need inside her she would have sworn was impossible a mere thirty seconds ago. But when his fingers covered her distended, so-swollen clit while he pummeled her relentlessly, another orgasm—which she'd been certain was impossible—was suddenly imminent.

"Nash!" She clawed the sheets, wishing she could reach him, touch him, share this sharp shove to ecstasy with him.

"That's fucking it. God, no one feels like you." He slammed into her again, both of them ignoring her headboard beating into the wall with his every lunge deep inside her. "Hais...baby. Fuck. Yes. Oh, god..."

"I'm here. Yes. Give me everything."

"Not until you come for me again," he growled.

Even his words had her tightening around him. Why could this man—and he alone—make her body dance to the tune of his commands? Why couldn't she stop wanting him?

Nash's pace increased, his control seemingly fraying. He buried his face in the crook of her neck, breath hot against her skin. "Now!"

His command pushed her over the edge. Haisley cried out as yet another climax crashed over her, more intense than the others combined. White-hot pleasure seized her body, suspending her. She jolted and reeled with a head-swaying, tingle-filled thrill of ecstasy. How could Nash keep undoing her over and over so perfectly?

Moments later, he followed her over the cliff, his hips jerking erratically as he found his release, filling her with a warmth that had her clenching onto him desperately again.

Their harsh breaths synched up. They clung together in the aftermath, bodies slick with sweat and trembling with aftershocks. He gripped her as if she were the most precious thing he'd ever held, tight yet gently as he peppered her shoulder and neck with soft, reverent kisses. Haisley's heart swelled, threatening to burst.

As their breathing slowly returned to normal, Nash eased free and rolled Haisley to her side, then pulled her against him. She curled into his chest, savoring the solid warmth of him. His arms tightened around her, as if he feared she might slip away.

Haisley pressed a kiss to his chest, right over his heart. The steady thump beneath her lips grounded her, a reminder that this was real. They were here, together, after so long apart.

But even in the quiet hum of her satisfaction, the weight of her secret pressed against her conscience. Haisley pushed it aside once more. The truth would only ruin them—not only this moment, but anything real that might follow. More than likely, they were doomed, but she refused to dwell on that. Just like she refused to let Nash go again until reality forced her. For now, she basked in the feeling of being loved and cherished by the man who held her heart.

As sleep threatened to claim her, Nash held her tighter and settled his finger under her chin, lifting her stare to him. "The last two years without you were some of the worst of my life. Are we finally going to stop fucking around and talk about what happened between us and why you left?"

CHAPTER SEVENTEEN

Haisley's heart stopped. She didn't want to shut Nash down. He deserved better. She didn't want to lie, either. But the truth? Catastrophic.

She settled for as much honesty as she dared. "You scared me."

His face hardened. "So your sobbing confession over the phone about me being too rough, too kinky, and too—"

"No. None of that was true. I'm sorry I lied. That wasn't fair to you, but I didn't know what to say. I had broken one of our rules. Remember, we made a pact on our very first night that we wouldn't get emotionally involved. Neither of us wanted entanglements, and I... messed up."

His breath caught. His eyes searched hers. "You cared about me?"

Haisley nodded. Maybe the adrenaline of the evening had crumbled her defenses. Maybe the power of her orgasms had wiped her out. Or maybe she should just blame Nash's closeness and her own traitorous heart. Whatever the culprit, she couldn't stop the tears stinging her eyes. "I was in love with you. And I knew if I stayed, it wouldn't last. You would only break my heart so—"

"Never," he vowed, holding her close with all his gentle might. "I would *never* have hurt you. I was in love with you, too."

Once, his confession would have sent her soaring with elation. Now it was crushingly bittersweet. If they had communicated more clearly... If she had been brave enough to tell him what was in her heart... If he had even whispered that she wasn't alone in this aching tangle of feeling and need...

But none of that had happened, and when push had come to shove, Haisley had only seen one option: to run.

Her tears fell. "I had no idea."

"I had no fucking idea how you felt, either."

They'd consigned their unspoken feelings to the dark corners of their hearts, only daring to express them wordlessly during the blissful nights of mind-blowing sex.

Why was it she'd felt little fear when she'd found herself capturing photos of protests that quickly devolved into riots or rolling video of gang violence that had long gripped LA, but the thought of bleeding out the contents of her heart and baring her soul to this man had been utterly terrifying?

"I'm sorry," she whispered, aching with how much she meant that. "I didn't handle our breakup well. I assumed that you only wanted sex and—"

"I was going to propose, Haisley. I bought you an engagement ring. I was waiting for the right moment."

Haisley's heart stopped—right before it broke. No... She couldn't have heard that right. But she replayed his gruff whisper in her head, and... yeah, he'd said those words all right. Her chest threatened to cave in.

"Oh, my god. I..." She bit her lip, staring into his eyes, feeling both a stunning spark of hope and, at the same time, deep despair. "Oh, god..."

"If I had, what would you have said?" When tears rolled down her cheeks, he wiped them away with gentle thumbs. "Baby?"

Her first impulse was a resounding yes. All her adult life, she'd ached for love, for the comfort and gentle familiarity of her person, for him to be there for her, protect her, and bolster her. To lift her up during long days of life battering away at her spirit. To light her on fire with long nights of connection and pleasure. And for a few brief, shining months, she'd had that with Nash. Being with him then… She'd feared it was too good to be true.

Finally came that terrible day she had been proven right.

After that, could they really go back? The chances of finding happily ever after now seemed so unlikely. But that didn't stop her foolish heart from yearning.

"I don't know. I would have wanted…" Haisley stopped herself. Her trembling words served no purpose except to torment them both. And what good would it do them now for her to admit how much she would have loved to be his wife? "But I don't think we would have lasted."

"Why the hell would you think that?"

She bit back the terrible truth. It would do nothing but hurt him, and after all the pain she'd heaped on him tonight, Haisley refused to add more.

She snuffed out that little spark of hope and wrenched from his embrace. "I-I don't want to talk about this. It doesn't matter anymore. It's over. It's done. It's—"

"Not. I loved you." He vaulted to his feet, his expression insistent, like he willed her to believe him. "I'm half convinced I still do."

Her heart caught and twisted. God, how happy those words made her, even as they destroyed her. She didn't deserve his love.

"You don't. You missed me. I missed you so, so much while I lived in California. I went on exactly two dates in two years, and I couldn't bring myself to let either of them touch me. I just…" Shit, she was mucking this up. "My vibrator and my memories of you got a hell of a workout. But—"

"You haven't had sex with anyone since me?" He sounded flabbergasted.

That probably made no sense to him because he'd apparently had a revolving door to his bed since she'd split, but she wanted to be as honest as she could. "No."

He closed his eyes and heaved a pained sigh. "Fuck. Baby… If I had known…"

"I'm not naive. I realize you haven't been alone. And I never expected... Why would I think that? I left you. You must have been angry."

"Furious. And confused, not to mention heartbroken as fuck. What do we do now? You still have feelings for me. I fucking know that from the way you touch me. We can't let what we have get away from us again."

Nash wanted to fight for them. Some part of her loved that. Some part of her wanted to fight along with him. But it was futile, over before it had really begun. "I think it's too late. This"—she gestured between them—"trying to revisit the past... It was a mistake. Now we have to work together, and these disappearing women—"

"Have nothing to do with us. We're giving them every bit of our effort and attention—"

"Are we? You have Benedict's burner phone in your pocket, and your brother should be examining it right now."

"Don't use that as an excuse. I'll get the device to my brother in the morning, as soon as he wakes up. He'll have it figured out in under an hour, I'll bet."

"Still, I'm sorry I derailed you. I'm sorry I messed up everything. Next time I'm overwhelmed and need comfort, and I lose my clothes and beg you, tell me no."

"That's never going to happen. I'm never going to say no to you, and I'm never going to give up on us. Why would you? Why are you so fucking eager to throw away what we could have if we just fucking tried?"

How the hell was she supposed to answer that without baring the worst horror of her life and fucking him up for good?

Suddenly, Haisley heard her phone trill downstairs and froze. Saved by the bell?

Unless... Was that Mila? Had the woman figured out that she'd been sneaking around the office earlier? Had she told Mr. Benedict? Was she going to be fired? Or worse, arrested?

"I need to get that." She darted for the door.

Nash tried to haul her back. "Don't you think our conversation is pretty fucking important?"

Yes, but she couldn't say more. Reality threatened to destroy her again, and she didn't know how she'd survive another heartbreak.

Haisley pulled from his grip and dashed down the stairs. When she reached her purse and fished out her phone, the caller ID flashed with Charli's name and photo. Haisley's gut clenched. Her friend almost never called this late unless it was important.

"Hey, Charli. You okay?" Haisley lowered herself onto the sofa in the nearby living room. When she heard Nash pad down the stairs after her, she covered her naked breasts with a nearby throw pillow self-consciously.

"No." Her friend's voice was thick and warbling, setting off alarm bells. "I'm s-sorry to bother you at this hour, but I didn't know what else to do."

"It's okay. You can always call me." Haisley glanced Nash's way, finding him staring. "What's going on? You sound upset?"

A muffled sniffle came through the line. "I d-don't know what to do, Hais. Daniel and I... I think it might be over for good."

Haisley's chest constricted at the naked anguish in her friend's voice. Charli had admitted when they'd had brunch a few days ago that she and Daniel had been having marital troubles. But divorce? After barely a year of marriage?

This was yet another reason she didn't dare succumb to her impulse to truly try a forever something with Nash.

"Oh, honey... I'm so sorry. Tell me what happened?"

"We had lunch earlier today. I wanted to surprise him, so I told him I'd made plans for us to go away for the weekend to spend time together. Rekindle our spark. I have prepaid reservations at this cute little bed-and-breakfast about two hours away, and I splurged on some new lingerie. When I told him I packed him a bag because we needed to leave right after work and that we were going to spend the weekend together in our romantic cocoon, guess what he did?"

"He refused."

"Worse than that. Not only did he say he wouldn't go because he'd volunteered for overtime this weekend and the money was too good to pass up, but when he found out I'd already put everything on our credit cards, he flipped. He was seriously pissed off that I'd spent a few hundred dollars without consulting him. I pointed out that he'd volunteered for more work without consulting me, after promising that he wouldn't."

She hurt for Charli. "Oh, sweetie…"

"I organized a surprise for him, you know? A mini vacay because we've been working so hard, and we needed some us time. But he just lost his shit even more. Then I lost mine. He's working so many hours. I only see him when he finally drags his ass home about nine each night. We barely speak before bed, and he's gone before I even get up the next morning. He swears he's just t-trying to save up enough for our dream house and eventually have kids. But at the rate we're saving, we'll never get there. I'll be in menopause before he's home enough to get me pregnant. I can't even remember the last time we had sex."

Charli dissolved into muffled sobs, and the sound tore at Haisley's heart. As cynical as Haisley had always been about love and relationships, she knew how much her friend had pinned her hopes and dreams of till death do us part on Daniel.

"Breathe. Okay? Just take some deep breaths," Haisley murmured softly. "Have you two considered marriage counseling? Maybe if a third party—"

"Counseling?!" Charli's voice hitched up an octave on a wild laugh. "Since our insurance is shit, that costs money, too, and he won't part with it. He says that in five years we might be able to swing a down payment if we're really frugal, but how can a marriage survive if I never see the man? If he invests in our bank account, but not in us? What am I going to do? I love him so much, but…but I can't keep living like this, as his perpetual last priority!"

"You're right. You should be his first priority—always. I'm so sorry…"

A soft curse made Haisley glance up. Nash regarded her with a concerned glance. She turned away for some privacy. Charli wouldn't appreciate Nash knowing all her business. And the way he stared… Haisley felt too seen.

"What do I do?" Charli sniffled.

Haisley didn't know what advice to give her friend. How could she when her own love life was spiraling out of control and falling apart? Love—the forever kind—wasn't in the cards for her. Coming to that conclusion had been bitter as hell, but facts were facts. True devotion was for the lucky few, and she wasn't one of them.

Last year, when Charli and Daniel had gotten hitched she'd hoped her friend would be different, but...sadly, they were like most everyone else.

Doomed.

"Help me," Charli sobbed in her ear.

"I wish I knew what to say. I'm probably the worst person to give romantic advice. Maybe you should pack a bag and go to the bed-and-breakfast this weekend. Use the time and distance to decide what's best for you. And if you really think it's over, then you have to do whatever serves your heart and your happiness. Don't let fear keep you trapped in a situation that's only hurting you more each day."

There was a heavy pause on the line, punctuated by Charli's occasional hiccups and sniffling wails.

When her friend finally spoke, her voice was subdued but resigned. "You're right. I need to think. I need to figure out what comes next. It's just...this wasn't how our marriage was supposed to go, you know? We were going to grow old together, gray and wrinkled like two adorable prunes spoiling all our adorable grandkids." She exhaled a shuddering sigh. "But it doesn't look like that will ever happen. Some happily ever after, huh?"

The bitter disappointment in Charli's tone lanced straight through Haisley's chest. Because she understood. Deep down, Haisley feared that shattering disillusionment—the slow, agonizing death of a dream she pinned her hopes and happiness on. If she gave into her heart's desire to try love and forever with Nash, they'd end up destroyed, too.

Shoving aside her melancholy, she mustered a gentle tone. "Oh, sweetie. I just want to reach through the phone and hug you."

"Thanks."

"Don't make any rash decisions, okay? Take the weekend. Get some space. Really think about what you want and what divorcing Daniel would mean. And I'm always here if you want to talk or vent or cry."

"Yeah. I think you might be right. I'm going to pack a bag and head out first thing in the morning, consider my options and just...try to figure everything out over the weekend." Another weighted pause. "Thanks. I love you, girl. You're the best."

"I love you, too. Chin up, okay? You'll figure it out. Ring me if you need an ear."

As the call ended, Haisley gripped her phone with a heavy heart.

God, how horrible for Charli... And how badly her friend's teary heartbreak had reinforced all her own worst fears.

Nash wandered closer, his expression carefully neutral. "Is she all right?"

"Not really. You overheard?"

He shrugged apologetically. "Hard not to. And I hate to hear she's contemplating divorce. He's not putting her first?"

Haisley shook her head. "He's too busy working and saving. I know those are supposed to be virtues, but not when you don't spend any time with your spouse. Unfortunately, they wouldn't be the first couple to split up because they both wanted different things..."

When she realized what she'd said, she squirmed in her chair. But Nash didn't notice. Or he didn't seem to care that she'd brought up the very issue that had torn them apart.

Then again, how could he understand?

Not going down that rabbit hole now...

"Anyway, this older guy I know online lost his wife or something, I think," she went on. "He told me recently that he'd sacrifice anything for just another ten minutes with her. I know Daniel means well and he's trying to do right by Charli, but she's a flesh-and-blood woman with a soft heart and needs...and he's just never there. I think about what my friend, Jasper, said, and I wonder if Daniel will wake up one day when he's older and alone and realize how badly he screwed up."

Nash didn't hesitate. "Yes."

Haisley held her breath as a weighted pause hung between them. His stare drilled into her. She swallowed.

Oh, god. It felt like he was talking about her. About them.

"You really believe that?" she breathed.

"I know it. And if he gives up, he's an idiot." Nash sat beside her, still naked as the day he was born. "And let me be clear, Haisley. I'm not stupid."

Her mouth suddenly felt like the Sahara, and her heart was beating wildly in her chest. "Nash, don't do this..."

"Why not?"

"Look around. Except for the lucky few like Matt and Madison, love doesn't usually last."

"Lucky? Maybe it lasts for the people willing to work hard for it and learn to communicate and compromise. My brother and Laila are wildly in love still. But it took a lot of shit to get there. She had to figure out how to trust him. He had to be patient. And when she ran away to solve her problems alone, he had to show her that he'd be there for her. Then he had to forgive her for nearly ripping them apart. It wasn't easy, but they both wanted their relationship to work. They were both willing to put their all into it."

Maybe that was true. Maybe she'd been too afraid to try. Hell, she still was. But if he wasn't jaded by love, if he'd grown up with a fabulously supportive family and never had his heart broken, why hadn't he put his all into their relationship two years ago?

Did it matter? He was all but declaring he would now.

God, she felt battered and confused and needed some time to think.

Haisley stood. "I'm going to shower. Unless there's some big break in the case, I'll see you Monday. Good night."

Except for the lucky few, love doesn't really last...

As Haisley made her way up the stairs, those words stabbed Nash in the chest. The sadness etched on her beautiful face twisted the blade even deeper.

That's what she truly believed? Was that her despondence over her friend's situation talking? Or had she always felt that way? Was that why she'd sworn to him the first night they'd ever spent together that she wasn't interested in any sort of commitment or future? The reason she hadn't been willing to even see what they could have together? And why she wasn't willing to try now? Nash guessed yes.

He had his work cut out for him.

"Wait." He followed her up the stairs and caught her just outside her bedroom door, clasping his fingers around her wrist and tugging her against his body before brushing a strand of fiery hair from her face. "You okay, baby?"

Haisley shrugged. "I'll be better tomorrow. Just worried about Charli and those missing women and..."

That wasn't all, but Nash didn't dare call BS. Or tell her again that he loved her. She wasn't in the frame of mind to hear either.

All he could do was show her.

"Because you're a good friend and a good person. You've had a lot going on and everything tonight has been a lot."

"Too much," she agreed.

"Let me take some of that off your shoulders."

"Oh, you don't have to—"

Nash didn't let her finish. He just lifted her into his arms and headed into her bedroom.

She gasped, surprise flickering across her face. "What are you doing?"

"You need to relax and de-stress. I'm going to give you a bath."

Haisley sputtered. "Y-you don't have to—"

"I want to." No doubt she was stunned because he'd always been sexually attentive, but never this sweet or romantic. Never reverent. He saw now that had been a big mistake—one he wouldn't make again.

"Why?"

She couldn't figure it out? Maybe she was too raw or overwhelmed. But rather than leaving her to handle all her feelings alone, he needed her to see that she could count on him.

"Do I need a reason to make you feel good? To take care of you?"

Slowly, she shook her head. "That sounds...nice, but—"

"Then it's settled."

Naked, he carried her across the room and into the attached ensuite. Gently, he set her on her feet and turned on the bath, adjusting the temperature of the water. He found her bath oil, then added a splash of the lavender scent to her tub until it was a relaxing haven.

As gestures went, it wasn't a lot. But he wanted—needed—to show Haisley that he wasn't just her booty call and that love wasn't just for the lucky few. What they had was real, precious, and worth fighting for.

He hoped like fuck he could convince her of that.

Nash turned to find her watching him prepare her bath, shoulders hunched, arms crossed over her chest. She looked small and vulnerable. Chastened and lost. Damn it, his Haisley was full of life and big personality. She should never be this withdrawn or less than ecstatically happy.

He needed to figure out exactly how he'd fucked up and fix it.

Without a word, he scooped her into his arms again and lowered her tense form into the steaming bath. As the water enveloped her, she slowly sank against the back of the tub with a sigh that told him she liked what he'd done.

Bolstered, Nash grabbed a washcloth, then knelt beside the tub and began to tenderly wash her.

Haisley's eyes fluttered closed, her tension visibly melting. "You don't have to do this."

"You already said that. I want to."

She had more objections; they were all over her face. But she didn't voice them, and he didn't say anything else. Instead, Nash massaged shampoo into her scalp, marveling at the silky strands slipping through his fingers. He loved the quiet intimacy and the way she let him cherish her. Why hadn't he treated her like a queen before?

He took his time, working the lather through her hair with gentle, circular motions. His fingers traced the curve of her neck, kneading away the tension he found there. A soft moan escaped Haisley's lips, sending a shaft of answering satisfaction through him.

"Feel good?"

She hummed, relaxing into his touch and giving herself over in a way that wasn't sexual, but still required her trust. "Heavenly."

Nash smiled as he cupped water in his hands and rinsed her hair with meticulous care. Once he'd washed away all the suds, he reached for a fluffy towel.

"Ready to get out?"

Haisley nodded, allowing him to help her stand and wrap her in the towel's warm embrace. He couldn't resist pressing a soft kiss to her forehead, his lips lingering as he breathed in the scent of her—lavender and something uniquely Haisley—committing it to memory.

Back in the bedroom, he grabbed a soft, worn nightgown from the hook on the back of her door and helped her into it. As the fabric settled around her curves, Nash's breath caught. God, she looked insanely beautiful. He felt intensely protective and possessive. And he'd never been more determined to fight for her.

Still, he knew better than to push Haisley before she was ready to be moved.

"Tea?" he asked, desperate to prolong their time together.

"If you don't mind." Haisley sounded surprised by his offer. "That would be nice."

Wanting everything to be perfect for Haisley, Nash settled her into the bed and created a cozy nest of pillows and soft blankets before he headed downstairs to turn on the kettle.

While he waited for the water to boil, he couldn't help but reflect on the past two years—the longing, the regret, the countless nights he'd lain awake missing her warmth beside him.

Now he knew why. Or at least he thought so, but he couldn't shake the notion that Haisley hadn't told him everything. If he wanted the truth—and he did—he had to proceed carefully.

Once the kettle whistled, he poured the water over the tea bags he'd scrounged from her cabinet, then returned to her bedroom with two steaming mugs. As he handed hers over, their fingers brushed in the exchange. She pulled back, pretending the contact was no big deal, like their touch didn't have the potential to start another fire between them. Like her refusing his touch now wasn't personal.

He ignored the stab of pain and settled in beside her. The herbal aroma wafted between them, comforting and homey.

As they sipped their tea in pensive silence, Nash found her free hand and intertwined their fingers. Thankfully, she didn't try to pull away. So he rubbed soothing circles on her skin with his thumb, hoping his touch conveyed everything she wasn't ready to hear.

"Thanks." Haisley turned to him, her smile soft yet strained. "This is really kind of you."

It was hardly a declaration of love, but Haisley wasn't pushing him away. She was accepting his comfort and care. It was another small crack in the walls she'd built around her heart.

He pressed a kiss to the top of her head. "You don't believe me yet, but I'm always here for you, no matter what."

She tensed, but didn't argue or push back. He wished like hell he knew what she was thinking.

"Talk to me, baby."

"Like I said, tonight was just a lot."

The break-in? The sex? Their honest, raw conversation? The news Charli had dumped on her?

Probably all of it.

"I understand. Just relax."

Together, they sat in sharp silence, broken only by the occasional clink of mugs and their steady breathing. Nash wished she'd share her thoughts and feelings, but he had to be patient. At least she hadn't shoved him out her door.

Long minutes later, she rested her head on his shoulder. He reveled in the softness of her skin, the way she fit perfectly in the crook of his arm. Being here with her almost felt like coming home after a long, arduous journey.

As Haisley finished her tea, Nash noticed her eyelids growing heavy. He took the mug from her hands and set it aside. "Tired?"

She stifled a yawn. "Exhausted."

"Lie down." He guided her deeper into the sheets and helped her settle her head on her pillow. "Get some sleep."

"You don't have to stay."

"Are you throwing me out?"

Haisley hesitated. "No."

"Then I'm not budging. I'll watch over you all night and make sure you rest," he swore. "Close your eyes and go to sleep." Maybe she'd be refreshed and ready to talk tomorrow.

With a drowsy little nod, she sighed and closed her eyes. Nash tucked the blankets around her, making sure she was cocooned in warmth.

Moments later, her breathing evened out. She might not appreciate this, but he padded to his pants and whipped out his phone, snapping a picture of her to remember this moment. Who knew if or when Haisley would ever be this soft and sweet with him again?

He brushed his lips across her temple, then straightened. "G'night."

As he turned away, Haisley stirred and reached out, her hand finding his in the dim light. "Thank you."

The vulnerability in her voice clenched his heart. "For what?"

Nash knew he shouldn't push her to explain, but his every uncertainty about Haisley sat under the surface of his skin, rubbing him raw.

"For just…being here. For taking care of me."

The moment he set his phone down and slid into bed, Haisley curled into him, her head pillowed on his chest. He melted into a fucking puddle. She might not want to admit it, but she didn't merely want him. Tonight, she'd needed him. And Nash was so damn glad he'd been here for her.

He wrapped his arms around her, pulling her closer. He stroked her back in long, soothing motions, feeling her relax further with each passing moment.

"There's no place I'd rather be and no one I'd rather be with."

As Haisley's breathing evened out, Nash lay awake, savoring every second she let him hold her. He thought about her earlier words, about love being for the lucky few. He had to prove that it wasn't about luck at all. It was about choice, commitment, and cherishing each other through the good times and bad.

He would choose her every single day until she believed that.

Nash allowed his mind to wander, imagining a future where moments like this weren't rare or tinged with uncertainty. He pictured lazy Sunday mornings, cooking breakfast together in comfortable silence. Holidays spent with their friends, Haisley's laughter ringing out as they exchanged gifts. Quiet nights curled up on the couch, her feet in his lap as they discussed their days. And children—their laughter, their tantrums, their joys and triumphs he and Haisley could share as their parents until they were grown and started families of their own. Then he wanted to share the golden, twilight years with her in quiet harmony: traveling, working crosswords, reflecting on their lives together.

He wanted the mundane and the extraordinary, the challenges and the in-betweens with her. Only her. He wanted to be the one she turned to when the world became too much, the shoulder she cried on, the arms that held her through every storm.

Nash tightened his embrace, burying his face in Haisley's damp, fragrant hair. As he breathed her in, he made a silent vow. He would prove to Haisley that love wasn't just for the lucky few. It was for them. All she needed to do was open her eyes and trust her heart.

And he'd be there, waiting patiently, for as long as it took.

CHAPTER EIGHTEEN

An insistent, annoying buzz jolted Haisley awake.

Scowling, she opened one eye. Her bedroom was as dark as the predawn morning outside. And Nash was no longer beside her. Where had he gone? The clock on her nightstand told her it wasn't even six a.m.

She touched his pillow. It was cold, suggesting that he'd left her bed a while ago. Was he downstairs making coffee? Or had something driven him away?

Memories of the night before rushed back, bringing a flush of heat to her cheeks and warmth to her heart. They'd both said some incredibly honest things and admitted their long-held feelings, baring their souls along with their bodies. No one could satisfy her like Nash, but last night had been different. Amazing. Afterward, he'd made her feel so special. So cherished. So loved. He'd been everything she'd ever wanted, and she wished it could have lasted forever.

But in the harsh gray before dawn, uncertainty crept in. Had he changed his mind? Where did they stand now?

She stretched, feeling each and every one of the sensual bites and bruises Nash had imprinted on her skin. Two years ago, the sight of his markings had always left her a little breathless and giddy. Her friends had all told her to have her head examined. But she'd reveled in his possessiveness. Last night she'd loved it even more.

The disruptive buzzing that had awakened her sounded again, breaking into her thoughts. Her phone; that's what had awakened her.

She reached for the device and found a note beneath.

Took Benedict's burner to Trees. Call me when you wake. I'll fill you in.

-N

Haisley sighed, torn between lingering in the afterglow and facing reality. Her emotions were a tangled mess—elation at finally being with Nash, fear of what their revelations meant for their future, and a gnawing worry that the secret she kept could unravel everything.

Forcing herself to push all that aside, she opened her phone to text Nash. Social media alerts tagging the Oakfield Mall exploded across her screen.

The first one read: `Land developer George Benedict and his wife, Mila, found dead in a suspected murder-suicide.`

Shock doused her veins with ice. "Oh, my god..."

Seriously? Was this news report actually real?

The next alert confirmed the first, even more brief and blunt. `Lafayette mogul George Benedict's mansion burns to ground, two bodies recovered.`

As soon as she swiped that notification away, another took its place: `Police confirm: Benedict dead from self-inflicted gunshot. Woman's remains, believed to be his wife, found in rubble.`

More headlines filled Haisley's screen. Frantically, she scrolled, trying to piece together this horrible development. Details were still sketchy, but according to police reports, the neighbors called 911 about three thirty this morning after the blaze engulfing the Benedict mansion awakened them. By the time fire trucks rolled up and put out the inferno, nothing was left of the house. The female inside, presumed to be Mila, was found in the master bedroom, burned beyond all recognition. Mr. Benedict's body was found on a chaise lounge by the pool without a single burn. He clutched a gun in one hand, dead from an apparent gunshot to the head.

Haisley gaped. What had happened to make Mr. Benedict snap?

Last night, a sobbing Mila had nearly spotted her and Nash at the office...then what? Had she gone home and confronted her husband about whatever had upset her? Haisley had sensed tension between them all week and felt sorry for the bubbly woman saddled with the curmudgeonly asswipe. Had they fought? Had it escalated into violence? Had George Benedict been so horrified by whatever he'd done to her that he'd taken his life?

Clutching her phone and trying to stop her head from spinning, Haisley leapt out of bed. What the hell should she do? What could she do?

She opened her messages to text Nash with the news, but her phone buzzed with an incoming call from a number only identified as Oakfield Mall.

"Hello?"

"Haisley Rowe?" asked a frantic female.

"Yes. Who's this?"

"My name is Julia. I was the assistant to Ben Yuslav, the former manager of Oakfield Mall."

The girl Ethan had gotten off at her desk with his hand down her panties. "Yes. Mr. Garrison mentioned that he'd...spoken to you after Mr. Yuslav abruptly quit."

"That's who gave me your number. Um...the press is beginning to swarm the mall."

"This early?"

"News is breaking. As soon as I heard, I came to work to see if there was anything I could do. Then the press showed up... They're asking if anyone representing the mall will make a statement. What's happened to Mr. Benedict and his wife... It's terrible. I don't know what to say or do."

The poor girl sounded young and panicked. Haisley wasn't sure she still had a job since her boss was now dead. And who owned the mall now that he was gone? But if the investigation into the disappearances of the five missing women was going to continue, she had to run interference and buy them some time.

But this conversation brought up a possibility Haisley hadn't considered... If Mr. Benedict was guilty of masterminding the trafficking ring, was he dead because Mila had discovered his crimes and he'd shut her up? That seemed possible. And if Haisley and Nash were ever going to find his victims, they had to pinpoint every clue possible before the police came in and took Benedict's phone, computer, and personal effects.

"I'll be there as soon as I can," Haisley told Julia. "Don't say anything to the reporters on the record. Just find a place to hold a press conference inside the mall before it opens. I'll be there no later than eight."

"Thanks. I really appreciate it. I didn't know who else to turn to and..."

"You did the right thing, calling me."

Haisley rang off. Her hands shook as she typed out a quick text to Nash.

> OMG, Benedict is dead. Murder-suicide suspected. Social media is exploding. I'm off to the mall to handle press.

His reply came moments later:

> I just read about the incident. Be careful. I have bad vibes about this. All Trees and I have managed to get from the burner phone so far is proof Benedict was having an affair. I'll update you when we know more.

As texts went, it wasn't romantic, but that was hardly the point now. He was working, just like she was. They'd talk about them later.

Haisley hurriedly dressed, covering her love bites with a high-necked blouse, then rushed to the bathroom. Her reflection startled her. Nash had sweetly washed her hair last night and tucked her in with wet tresses. Now it was a tangled mess, half sticking straight up. She quickly ran a brush through it, wincing at the knots, before twisting it up into a messy bun. Then she slapped on a light face of makeup, focusing on a hasty application of concealer, mascara, and lip gloss. It would have to do.

As she did all that, Haisley tried to think this situation through. Benedict had been having an affair? Mind-blowing. She couldn't grasp why anyone would willingly sleep with the jackass. Then again, some people would do anything for money, which he'd had in spades. Had Mila found out about his mistress last night? Was that the reason she'd been crying during her midnight visit to the office? Had it caused their following deadly altercation?

That poor woman, offed by the man who had vowed to love, honor, and cherish her forever. Love might only be for the lucky few, but Mila had been among the most unlucky of all.

Haisley sprinted around the house to find her keys. As she brewed a cup of coffee to go, she fired off a message to her fellow CSI sleuth, Jasper, informing him about the awful developments and asked if he would reach out to his Lafayette PD contacts for any additional information.

He didn't answer right away. Of course anyone who wasn't up with the sun was still cozy in their bed, catching Zs. But Jasper seemed solid. He'd get back to her. At least she hoped so. She hadn't talked to him since Tuesday night. She'd been so busy…and wrapped up with Nash. Maybe Jasper had lost interest in the case. Or moved on.

After all, he hadn't contacted her for nearly four days, either. What was up with that?

Pushing the question aside, Haisley took a deep breath, forcing herself to compartmentalize her feelings and fears so she could focus on the task at hand. She couldn't afford to be distracted right now. The women who had been abducted needed her effort and focus before bureaucracy and red tape limited her access to clues.

After finally digging up her keys, Haisley headed for the door, pausing to take one last steadying breath. As she drove to the mall, her mind kept whirling. What could she possibly tell the press about the Benedicts' untimely end and the fate of the mall when she knew so little herself?

As she pulled into the parking lot, Haisley spotted a small crowd of reporters, photographers, and independent online journalists already gathered near the door. She gripped the steering wheel, steeling herself for the morning ahead. "You can do this."

She wasn't convinced...but it was nearly showtime, so she cut the engine and plucked up her phone, cutting off her music.

Before she darkened the device, she spotted a notification about a message from someone in her CSI group.

> JasperThePrivateDick: Howdy, stranger. I hope you're okay. I've been a little under the weather. Sorry I disappeared. Feeling better today. I'll call my retired friend and see if he can get anyone who still works for the force to answer questions.

> RedHotSavvySleuth: Glad to hear you're feeling better. Thanks for any help you can give me. I'm at the mall now. I'm about to give a press conference. After that, I'll poke around and see if I can find out anything. Maybe people will be more willing to talk now that Mr. Benedict is gone.

> JasperThePrivateDick: I don't think that's a good idea. That place is dangerous.

> RedHotSavvySleuth: It's a long story, and I'll tell you later, but all signs point to my boss having been the bad guy. Now that he's gone, I'm thinking the mall is a lot less dangerous. But I promise I'll check in.

> JasperThePrivateDick: I'll be waiting. If I don't hear from you in two hours, I'll send in the cavalry.

> RedHotSavvySleuth: You don't have to, but thanks for caring enough to worry about me.

Haisley smiled as she dimmed her phone and exited her car, striding toward the mall with purpose. She ignored the cluster of press shouting questions at her.

Inside the entrance, she found Julia pacing nervously. "Ms. Rowe?"

"Just Haisley." She gave the young brunette a reassuring smile, but the girl still looked rattled.

"Thank God you're here. Everything has gotten worse." Julia wrung her hands. "The police have been calling, asking about Mr. Benedict's recent visits and personnel decisions. The press won't stop hounding us for information." She dropped her voice. "And now I hear the FBI is at his house because they suspected him of being behind all the abductions here at the mall."

Haisley tucked that nugget of information away to share with Nash and Jasper later. But if Mr. Benedict was the FBI's prime suspect, she and Nash must have pieced things together pretty well.

She placed a comforting hand on Julia's shoulder. "It's okay. I'll handle this. Where did you set up the press conference? Somewhere we can control the situation, I hope."

"The food court. It's the biggest open area. Other than employees preparing food in their units, no one will be there. Mall staff already set up a podium and arranged chairs. Should I have security escort the press in?"

A glance at the time on her phone had Haisley nodding. "I'll get started in fifteen minutes."

Julia looked as if she wanted to hug her. "Thank you."

As the woman hustled away, Haisley's phone buzzed with another text from Nash.

> More info on the affair. Benedict's something on the side is named Clarissa. No last name yet. Be careful what you say to the press. Be careful in general.

Haisley gave him a thumbs-up, but her stomach churned. She

made her way to the food court, trying to organize her thoughts into something coherent so she didn't sound like a babbling idiot...or like someone who knew next to nothing.

At the top of the hour, she took her place behind the podium as the cacophony of incoming press descended. They quickly settled into the assembled chairs, cameras at the ready.

"Ladies and gentlemen, I'm Haisley Rowe, the social media director for Benedict Land Development," she began, her voice surprisingly steady. "I know you all have questions about the tragic deaths of George and Mila Benedict. At this time, we have very little information beyond what has been reported in the news. Investigations are ongoing, and I can't comment on those."

She paused, choosing her next words carefully. "But the Oakfield Mall management and staff, along with the employees of Benedict Land Development, are shocked and saddened by this turn of events. Our thoughts are with the Benedicts' family and friends, as well as others affected. Those are all the prepared remarks I have. I'll take questions."

As Haisley fielded the reporters' queries, doing her best to deflect those she couldn't answer, a nagging feeling grew in the pit of her stomach. There was more to this story—much more—and somehow she wasn't seeing the whole picture. What had caused Mr. Benedict to go off the rails? Had he come back to the office for the loaded Glock in his humidor? Had Mila learned about Clarissa and confronted him? Or had she realized that her husband was the leader of a sex trafficking ring and freaked out?

When Haisley finally ended the press conference, promising updates as more information became available, she felt drained. She retreated to the mall's management office only to find Julia away from her desk.

Haisley collapsed into the woman's chair with a heavy sigh as her phone buzzed again—another text from Nash.

> Trees got more info off of Benedict's phone. We need to talk ASAP. I'm on my way to you. You need to see this.

Haisley's heart started racing. What had they uncovered? A breakthrough? And how deep did this rabbit hole go? She couldn't shake the feeling that something far bigger—and more sinister—was at work with the Benedicts' murder-suicide. The events of the past twenty-four hours had left her overwhelmed. Passion, love, death, and shrouded secrets. Whatever Nash had uncovered, it must be serious if he was dropping everything to show her right now.

As Haisley headed back toward the food court, her heels clicked against the generic tile floor. She passed shuttered storefronts that made the mall feel eerily quiet. Only the hum of fluorescent lights and the distant voices of early morning staff broke the silence.

Once she rounded the corner to the food court, she scanned the space. A figure caught her eye. In one hand, he clutched a yellow Caution: Wet Floor sign. With the other, he pulled an industrial cart.

Her pulse quickened. The janitor—the one Abby had described as creepy, who had been conveniently "sick" when Nash tried to interview him earlier in the week—was lingering near the women's restroom. This might be their chance to fill in some blanks. She glanced at her watch. Nash was on his way. The mall would open soon, making it far less likely the janitor would have time to speak to them later.

It was now or never.

Haisley ducked under the stanchion cordoning off the shadowy hallway and approached the man in the blue jumpsuit.

"Excuse me," she called out, her voice steady despite the nervous flutter in her stomach.

The man turned, his weathered face impassive. "Ma'am, this area is closed for cleaning."

"I know. I'm sorry to bother you." Haisley flashed what she hoped was a disarming smile. "I'm Haisley Rowe. You were scheduled to speak with my...cohort, Nash Scott, earlier this week about some recurring...incidents here at the mall."

The janitor's eyes narrowed slightly, but his expression remained neutral. "Yeah. The interview. Um..." He glanced at his watch, then back at Haisley. "I've got to get this restroom cleaned before opening. Tell you what? I can make a few minutes to sit down with you and that security guy as soon as I'm done here. Shouldn't take more than fifteen minutes."

"Perfect. I'll be waiting right there." She pointed to a cluster of tables that Julia and some of the other mall staff were hurriedly righting.

By the time she turned back, the janitor had disappeared into the women's restroom, the door swinging shut behind him with a soft thud.

Haisley blinked. That was an abrupt end to their conversation. Almost rude. Still, despite the disaster of the day and all the unanswered questions she and Nash still had to tackle, this was a step forward.

She pulled her phone from her purse and tapped out a quick message to Nash.

> Got the janitor to agree to an interview in a few.
> Meet us at the food court.

As she darkened her phone to tuck it away, Haisley glanced down the dimly lit hallway that stretched ominously into darkness. A chill ran down her spine. With a jolt, she realized she was standing in the exact spot where all five missing women had been abducted.

Her breath caught in her throat as fear pressed in on her. Mr. Benedict, the likely mastermind, was now dead. It was probably perfectly safe. But standing in this very spot, knowing what had transpired, was beyond terrifying.

Isolation pressed in on her. Usually, when she visited the food court during mall hours, it was a bustling hub of activity. Now it felt like a ghost town. It felt unsafe.

Haisley gripped her phone tighter, her thumb hovering over Nash's number. Would he think she was overreacting if she called him?

She was still trying to decide when a shuffling behind her made her blood suddenly turn to ice.

Nash gripped the steering wheel, his thoughts whirling as he sped toward the mall. The information Trees had extracted from Benedict's burner phone was explosive—details of the trafficking ring, financial records, an unusual symbol he didn't understand, and most crucially, the passcode to the Rugs Direct Unlimited website. It was the breakthrough they'd been waiting for, but it also meant the danger was far more immediate than either he or Haisley had realized.

The idea of his woman working under the same roof as a dangerous predator like Benedict fucking scared and infuriated him. He was glad Haisley never had to see or speak to the exploitive asshole again. And after last night, despite waking her up twice more in the night to make love to her, he couldn't wait to touch her again, to hold her and reassure them both.

His phone chimed, breaking into his thoughts. It was a text from Haisley.

> Got the janitor to agree to an interview in a few. Meet us at the food court.

A mixture of pride and concern surged through him. Haisley was brilliant, but the janitor had been suspiciously elusive. Nash quickly typed back.

> 3 minutes out. Be careful.

She didn't reply. Nash frowned, trying to push down his unease. She was working; she was probably busy. Hell, maybe she was already sitting down with the janitor.

Still, he pressed the accelerator a little harder.

Just over two minutes later, he pulled into the mall parking lot and jogged through the entrance mall employees used, thankfully unmanned. The cavernous mall felt eerily empty. He made a beeline for the food court, his heavy footsteps echoing against the industrial tile.

His apprehension climbed.

Finally, he reached the food court. No sign of Haisley or the janitor.

"Haisley?" Nash called out, his voice breaking the jagged hush. Silence answered him.

Heart rate climbing, Nash pulled out his phone and dialed Haisley's number. It rang once, twice… Then he heard it. The muffled sound of a ringtone, coming from the hallway near the women's room.

"No. No. No!" Nash broke into a run, skidding to a stop when he spotted Haisley's phone laying on the ground, still trilling. Her purse was strewn nearby, its contents spilled across the tile floor.

No Haisley in sight.

"Haisley!" Nash shouted, panic clawing at his throat. He spun in a circle, poked his head into the empty ladies' room, searching desperately for any clue, any sign of where she might have gone.

A distant sound caught his attention—an engine revving. Nash's blood ran cold as realization struck. Without hesitation, he sprinted down the darkened hallway and shoved his way through the double doors, into the parking lot.

In the distance, he saw an old brown conversion van speeding across the nearly empty lot—too far away to see the license plate—its tires squealing as it made a sharp turn toward the highway entrance.

Terror washed over him. His blood froze.

"No!" Nash roared, already running. But it was futile. The van was too far away, moving way too fast.

As it disappeared from view, Nash stared after it, chest heaving, fists clenched at his sides. The magnitude of what had just happened crashed over him like a tidal wave.

Haisley was gone. Taken. And he had been too late to stop it. He hadn't protected her.

Fuck.

Nash shoved down the terrible mix of fear, rage, and guilt, and leaned into his training.

He pulled out his phone, fingers flying over the keys as he sent out an alert to everyone in EM Security Management. They had mere minutes before the van hit the highway and vanished for good.

Nash hated like hell that he hadn't had time to update his bosses about this case lately. Hunter Edgington was going to be pissed that he had begun looking into George Benedict without getting the a-okay. He'd been following the leads, but...

God, had their investigation made Haisley a target? And if Benedict was dead...who was pulling the strings?

Nash sprinted back to his vehicle, jaw clenched with grim determination as he climbed in, sped out, and flew down the road to see if he could spot that brown van.

He would find Haisley. He would burn the whole damn trafficking ring to the ground—hell, the world, if he had to—in order to save her. Every second counted. Haisley's life hung in the balance, and he fucking refused to let her down again.

Nash tried not to think about the odds of finding her alive and unharmed as he jetted down the road...

Get ready for heart-pumping passion, intense drama, and unexpected twists in the unforgettable conclusion of Nash and Haisley's story.

Order your copy of their explosive, epic ending today!

WICKED AND BOUND
Nash and Hailey, Part Two
Wicked Lovers: Soldiers for Hire
By Shayla Black
(available in eBook and print)

Want the next release in this series EARLY—with digital signature and enhanced formatting not available anywhere else? Looking to binge some of your favorite spicy series—all at 40%+ off? Visit the Shayla Store at ShaylaBlack.com today for nail-biting romantic suspense, forbidden romance, steamy family drama, and more!

Dying to know what's going to happen to Haisley right NOW? Join Shayla at Ream Stories to participate, comment, and even vote on the direction of Wicked and Bound as she writes it, along with other spicy Shayla reads! Join at https://reamstories.com/shaylablack today!

Join my VIP Newsletter at ShaylaBlack.com for three FREE sizzling series starters *and* be the first to discover new releases, exclusive content, cover reveals, sales, and more. Don't miss the excitement!

Grab your signed Shayla Black print books, cool bookish merch, and her latest eBooks with early access and custom interiors you won't find anywhere else. Visit the Shayla Store.

Thank you for reading Wicked and Ruthless! If you enjoyed this book, please review and/or recommend it to your reader friends. That means the world to me!

WICKED LOVERS: SOLDIERS FOR HIRE

Thank you for joining me in the Wicked Lovers: Soldiers for Hire world. If you didn't know, this cast of characters started in my Wicked Lovers world, continued into my Devoted Lovers series, and have collided here. During Nash and Haisley's journey, you've read about some other characters, and you might be wondering if I've told their story. Or if I will tell their story in the future. Below is a guide in case you'd like to read more from this cast, listed in order of release:

WICKED LOVERS

Surrender to Me

Hunter Edgington (and Katalina Muñoz)

A secret fantasy. An uncontrollable obsession. A forever love?

Belong to Me

Logan Edgington (and Tara Jacobs)

He's got everything under control until he falls for his first love…again.

WICKED LOVERS: SOLDIERS FOR HIRE

Wicked as Sin/Wicked Ever After – Pierce "One-Mile" Walker (and Brea Bell)

She begs him to rescue his enemy from death. In exchange, he demands her body…

Wicked as Lies/Wicked and True – Chase "Zyron" Garrett (and Tessa Lawrence)

He'd protect her from the world. But who will protect her from him?

Wicked as Seduction/Wicked and Forever – Forest "Trees" Scott (and Laila Torres)

He'll protect her…even if he has to take her captive to save her.

Wicked as Secrets/Wicked and Bare - Matt Montgomery (and Madison Archer-Pershing)

He'd give his life to protect her…but he'll demand everything from her in return.

Wicked and Ruthless/Wicked and Bound – Nash Scott (and Haisley Rowe)

She knows love is a fairy tale...until her ruthless operative ex steals her heart.

Bonus Tie-in!

Forbidden Confessions: Protectors

Seduced by the Assassin – Meet younger Ethan Garrison before his EM Security days!

As the Wicked Lovers: Soldiers for Hire world continues to explode and expand, you'll see more titles with other characters you know and love, like Ethan, Kane, Trevor, Ghost, and more!

I have *so* much in store for you on this wild, **Wicked** ride!

Hugs and Happy Reading!

Shayla

Explore all the rest of the Wicked Lovers: Soldiers for Hire series and Shayla's nearly 100 titles at ShaylaBlack.com!

ABOUT SHAYLA BLACK

LET'S GET TO KNOW EACH OTHER!

With over 25 years in publishing, SHAYLA BLACK is the New York Times and USA Today bestselling author of nearly 100 novels. Known for her ability to craft rich characters and emotionally nuanced stories, she has won awards, sold millions of copies, and been published in a dozen languages. But it's her spicy, steamy romances that have readers breathless for more. After two decades with major New York publishers, she now enjoys the freedom of being independently published.

As an only child, Shayla occupied herself by daydreaming, much to the chagrin of her teachers. In college, she found her love for reading and started pursuing a publishing career. Though she graduated with a degree in Marketing/Advertising and embarked on a stint in corporate America, her heart was with her stories and characters, so she left her pantyhose and power suits behind.

Shayla currently lives in North Texas with her wonderfully supportive husband, her daughter, and two spoiled tabbies. In her "free" time, she enjoys reality TV, gaming, and listening to an eclectic blend of music.

TELL ME MORE ABOUT YOU.

Connect with me via the links below. You can also become one of my Facebook Book Beauties and enjoy LIVE, interactive #WickedWednesday video chats full of fun, book chatter, and more! See you soon!

Website: http://shaylablack.com
VIP Reader Newsletter: http://shayla.link/nwsltr
Shayla Store: https://www.shaylablack.com/bookstore/
Ream Stories: https://reamstories.com/shaylablack
Facebook Book Beauties Chat Group: http://shayla.link/FBChat

- facebook.com/ShaylaBlackAuthor
- instagram.com/shaylablack
- tiktok.com/@shayla_black
- x.com/ShaylaBlackAuth
- bookbub.com/authors/shayla-black
- pinterest.com/shaylablacksb

NEW YORK TIMES AND USA TODAY BESTSELLING AUTHOR

ShaylaBLACK

ADDICTIVE. SUSPENSEFUL. SPICY.

SHAYLA STORE (ShaylaBlack.com)
Get eBooks, audio, and signed Shayla Black print books, plus cool bookish merch! Exclusive books, special sales, and early access to Shayla's latest eBooks.

VIP READERS (eepurl.com/cD3gAH)
Be among the first to get your hands on Shayla Black news, juicy excerpts, cool VIP giveaways - and much more!

REAM STORIES (https://reamstories.com/shaylablack)
Be FIRST to read my latest works on Ream Stories BEFORE they're released. Follow or subscribe for chats, polls, videos, NSFW art, and other fun at . Free episodes available to read. Together, we'll make this the awesomest spicy romance community. Join the party today!

WICKED WEDNESDAY (youtube.com/c/ShaylaBlack)
Join me for live, interactive video chats every Wicked Wednesday. Be there for breaking Shayla news, in a fun, positive community.

Made in the USA
Columbia, SC
21 September 2024

42736445R00134